Edenbrooke

PROPER ROMANCE

JULIANNE DONALDSON

SHADOW
MOUNTAIN

Visit us at ShadowMountain.com

This is a work of fiction. Characters and events in this book are products of the author's imagination or are represented fictitiously.

Library of Congress Cataloging-in-Publication Data

Donaldson, Julianne, author.
  Edenbrooke / Julianne Donaldson.
     pages cm
  Summary: When Marianne receives an invitation to spend the summer with her twin sister in Edenbrooke, she has no idea of the romance and adventure that await her once she meets the dashing Sir Philip.
  ISBN 978-1-60908-946-7 (paperbound)
  I. Title.
  PS3604.O5345E34 2012
  813'.6—dc23   2011041093

Printed in the United States of America
Edwards Brothers Malloy, Ann Arbor, MI

33   32   31   30   29   28   27   26   25   24   23

Edenbrooke

To kindred spirits everywhere

Chapter 1

Bath, England, 1816

It was the oak tree that distracted me. I happened to glance up as I walked beneath its full, green canopy. The wind was tossing its leaves so that they twirled upon their stems, and at the sight I was struck by the realization that it had been much too long since I had twirled. I paused under the branches and tried to remember the last time I had felt the least need to twirl.

And that was when Mr. Whittles snuck up on me.

"Miss Daventry! What an unexpected pleasure!"

I started with surprise and looked around frantically for Aunt Amelia, who must have continued up the gravel path while I had stopped in the shade of the tree.

"Mr. Whittles! I—I did not hear you approach." I usually kept at least one ear tuned to the sounds of his pursuit. But the oak tree had distracted me.

He beamed at me and bowed so low that his corset creaked. His broad face was shiny with sweat, his thinning hair plastered across his head. The man was at least twice my age, and more ridiculous than I could bear. But of all his repulsive features, it was his mouth that held my horrified fascination. When he spoke, his lips flapped about so as to create a film of saliva that coated the edges of his lips and pooled in the corners of his mouth.

I tried not to stare while he said, "It is a glorious morning, is it not? In fact, I feel moved to say, 'Oh, what a glorious morning, oh, what a glorious day, oh, what a glorious lady that I met on my way!'" He bowed, as if expecting applause. "But I have something better than that ditty to share with you today. I have written a new poem, just for you."

I took a step in the direction where I suspected my aunt had gone. "My aunt would be very pleased to hear your poetry, Mr. Whittles. She is ahead of us but a few paces, I am sure."

"But, Miss Daventry, it is you I hope to please with my poetry." He moved closer to me. "It does please you, does it not?"

I hid my hands behind my back in case he attempted to grasp one. He had done that in the past, and it had been most unpleasant. "I fear I don't have the same appreciation for poetry that my aunt has . . ." I looked over my shoulder and sighed with relief. My spinster aunt was hurrying back along the path to find me. She was an excellent chaperone—a fact I had never truly appreciated until this moment.

"Marianne! There you are! Oh, Mr. Whittles. I didn't recognize you from a distance. My eyesight, you know . . ." She smiled at him with a glow of happiness. "Have you come with another poem? I do enjoy your poetry. You have such a way with words."

My aunt would be the perfect match for Mr. Whittles. Her poor eyesight softened the repulsive nature of his features. And since she had more hair than wit, she was not appalled by his absurdity, as I was. In fact, I had been trying for some time to turn Mr. Whittles's attention from me to her, but so far I had not been successful.

"I do have a new poem, as a matter of fact." He pulled a piece of paper out of his coat pocket and caressed it lovingly. He licked his lips, leaving a large drop of spittle hanging off the edge. I stared at it even though I didn't want to. It jiggled but did not fall off as he began to read.

"Miss Daventry is fair and true, with eyes of such a beautiful hue! Not quite green, never dull brown; they are the color of the sea, and they are round."

I tore my gaze away from the quivering drop of spittle. "That is such a nice idea. The color of the sea. But my eyes often look more gray than blue. I would enjoy a poem about my eyes looking gray." I smiled innocently.

"Y-yes, of course. I have thought many times myself that your eyes do look gray." He furrowed his brow for a moment. "Ah, I have it! I shall say that they are the color of a *stormy* sea, as a stormy sea often has the appearance of gray, as you know. That will be simple to change, and I will not have to rewrite the poem, as I have had to do the last five times."

"How clever of you," I muttered.

"Indeed," said Aunt Amelia.

"There is more. Miss Daventry is true and fair, I love the color of her hair! It shimmers in the candlelight, its amber hue, oh so bright."

"Well done," I said. "But I never knew my hair was an *amber* color." I looked at my aunt. "Did you ever happen to think that, Aunt Amelia?"

She tilted her head to one side. "No. I never have."

"You see? I am sorry to disagree with you, Mr. Whittles, but I do feel it is important to encourage your best work."

He nodded. "Did you prefer it when I compared your hair to the color of my horse?"

"Yes," I sighed. "That was infinitely better." I was growing tired of my game. "Perhaps you should go home immediately and rewrite it."

My aunt lifted a finger. "But I have often thought that your hair is the same color as honey."

"Honey! Yes, that is just the thing." He cleared his throat. "It shimmers in the candlelight, its *honey* hue, oh so bright." He grinned, displaying his entire wet mouth.

I swallowed convulsively. How *did* one person produce so much saliva?

3

"Now it is perfect. I shall read it for everyone at the Smiths' dinner party this Friday."

I cringed. "Oh, that would spoil it, Mr. Whittles. A poem as beautiful as this is best kept close to one's heart." I reached for the paper. "May I have it, please?" He hesitated, then put it in my hand. "Thank you," I said with real sincerity.

Aunt Amelia then asked Mr. Whittles about his mother's health. As he began to describe the festering sore on his mother's foot, my stomach churned. It was simply too revolting. To distract myself, I stepped away from them and gazed up again at the oak tree that had caught my attention earlier.

It was a grand tree, and it made me miss the country with a fresh longing. The leaves were still twirling in the breeze, and I asked myself the question that had given me pause moments before. When *was* the last time I had twirled?

Twirling had once been a habit of mine, though Grandmother would have called it a bad habit, had she known of it. It had kept company with my other habits, like sitting in my orchard for hours at a time with a book or bounding across the countryside on the back of my mare.

It must have been at least fourteen months since I had last twirled. Fourteen months since I was taken from my home, fresh from grieving, and deposited on my grandmother's doorstep in Bath while my father took himself off to France to grieve in his own way.

Fourteen months—fully two months longer than I had initially feared I would be left in this stifling town. Although I had never been given a reason to believe it, I had hoped that a year of grieving separately would be punishment enough. And so, two months ago, on the anniversary of my mother's death, I had waited all day for my father's return. I had imagined, over and over, how I would hear his knock at the door, and how my heart would leap within my chest. I had imagined how quickly I would run to throw open the door. I had imagined him smiling at me as he announced that he had come to take me home.

And yet, on that day two months ago, he had not come. I had spent the night sitting up in bed with a candle burning, waiting to hear the knock at the door that would signal my release from my gilded cage. But morning dawned, and the knock never sounded.

I sighed as I looked up at the green leaves dancing in the wind. I had not had a reason to twirl in such a long time. And nothing to twirl about at age seventeen? That was a problem indeed.

"Oozing." Mr. Whittles's voice recalled my attention. "Oozing right out."

Aunt Amelia looked a little green, and she held a gloved hand over her mouth. I decided it was time to intervene. Taking her arm, I said to Mr. Whittles, "My grandmother is expecting us. You must excuse us."

"Of course, of course," he said, bowing again so that his corset creaked loudly. "I hope to see you soon, Miss Daventry. Perhaps at the Pump Room?"

Of course he would suggest the social hub of Bath for another "chance" encounter. He knew my habits well. I smiled politely and made a mental note to avoid taking tea at the Pump Room for the next week at least. Then I pulled Aunt Amelia toward the broad green lawn that separated the gravel path from the Royal Crescent. The building curved in a graceful half-circle of butter-golden stones, like a pair of outstretched arms ready for an embrace. Grandmother's apartment within the Royal Crescent was among the finest Bath could offer. But luxury could not make up for the fact that Bath was town living at its worst. I missed my life in the country so desperately that I ached for it day and night.

I found Grandmother in her drawing room reading a letter, occupying her chair as if it were a throne. She still wore mourning black. At my entrance, she looked up and let her critical gaze sweep over me. Her eyes were sharp and gray and missed nothing.

"Where have you been all morning? Scampering around the countryside like some farmer's brat again?"

The first time I had heard this question, I had quaked in my shoes.

Now I smiled, for I knew this game we played with each other. I understood that Grandmother gloried in a good verbal sparring match at least once a day. I also understood, although I would never charge her with it, that her gruff exterior masked what she considered the greatest of all weaknesses—a soft heart.

"No, I only do that on odd days, Grandmother. I spend my even days learning how to milk cows." I bent down and placed a kiss on her forehead. She gripped my arm for a moment. It was the closest she came to affection.

"Humph. I suppose you think yourself funny," she said.

"Actually, I don't. It takes a lot of practice to learn how to milk a cow. I find myself horribly inept at this point."

I saw the quivering muscles around her mouth that meant she was trying to conceal a smile. She twitched at her lace shawl and motioned for me to sit in the chair next to hers.

I peered at the stack of mail on the side table. "Did I receive any mail today?"

"If you are asking about that care-for-nothing father of yours, then no, you did not."

I looked away to hide my disappointment. "He is probably traveling right now. Perhaps he does not have the opportunity to write."

"Or perhaps he has forgotten about his children in his self-centered grieving," she muttered. "Handing his responsibilities off to someone who never asked for them, especially in her old age."

I flinched; some of Grandmother's barbs were sharper than others. This was an especially painful topic, as I hated the thought of being a burden, and yet I had nowhere else I might go.

"Do you want me to leave?" I could not help asking.

She scowled at me. "Don't act like a ninny. I have enough of that to endure with Amelia." She folded the letter she had been reading. "I have had more bad news about that nephew of mine."

Ah, the Nefarious Nephew. I should have guessed. Nothing put

Grandmother in a sour mood as surely as hearing about the latest scandal involving her heir, Mr. Kellet. He was a rake and a scoundrel and had gambled away all of his own money while waiting to inherit Grandmother's sizeable fortune. My twin sister, Cecily, thought he was dashing and romantic; I thought him anything but. It was one of many things that she and I disagreed about.

"What has Mr. Kellet done this time?" I asked.

"Nothing fit for your innocent ears." She sighed, then spoke in a softer voice. "I believe I may have made a mistake, Marianne. He will come to ruin. The damage he has inflicted on the family name is great, and irreparable." She raised a trembling hand to her brow, looking frail and weary.

I stared at her in surprise. Grandmother had never exhibited such vulnerability before me. It was most unlike her. I leaned toward her and took her hand in mine. "Grandmother? Are you unwell? Is there something I may get for you?"

She shook off my hand. "Don't coddle me, child. You know I have no patience for such behavior. I am simply tired."

I bit back a smile. She was well enough, if she could respond like that. But her reaction was unprecedented. She could usually dismiss Mr. Kellet's bad behavior and remember why he had always been a favorite of hers. (I thought she liked him because he was not afraid of her.) But I had never seen her so worried, nor so despondent.

Grandmother gestured at the pile of letters on the table. "There is a letter for you there. From London. Read it and leave me alone for a few minutes."

I picked up the letter and walked to the window, letting the sunlight fall on the familiar handwriting. When Papa had brought me to Bath, he had found an even more suitable situation for my twin sister, Cecily. She had been staying with our cousin Edith in London for the past fourteen months and seemed to have enjoyed every moment of it.

For being twins, Cecily and I were remarkably different. She excelled me in every womanly art. She was much more beautiful and refined. She played the pianoforte and sang like an angel. She flirted easily with gentlemen. She liked town life and had dreams of marrying a man with a title. She was ambitious.

My ambitions were quite different from hers. I wanted to live in the country, to ride my horse, to sit in an orchard and paint, to take care of my father, to feel that I belonged, to do something useful and good with my time. But most of all, I wanted to be loved for who I was. My ambitions seemed quiet and dull compared to Cecily's. Sometimes I feared that *I* seemed quiet and dull next to Cecily.

Lately, all I heard from Cecily was about her dearest friend Louisa Wyndham and her handsome and titled eldest brother, whom Cecily was determined to marry. Cecily had never told me his name—he was simply "the brother" in her letters. I supposed she was afraid of her letters being seen by someone less discreet than I. Perhaps it was my maid, Betsy, that she was worried about, who was, after all, the most incurable gossip I had ever known.

I had not told Cecily this, but I had recently asked Betsy the name of the eldest Wyndham son, and she had discovered that it was Charles. Sir Charles and Lady Cecily had a nice ring to it, I thought. Of course it followed that if Cecily chose to marry him, then marry him she would. She had never failed to get something she really wanted.

Before I broke the seal on her letter, I closed my eyes and made a silent wish: *Please don't let her go on and on about dear Louisa and her handsome brother again.* I had nothing against the Wyndhams—after all, our mothers had been close friends as children, and I had just as much a claim on the acquaintance as Cecily—but I had heard of little else for the past two months, and I was beginning to wonder if I was as important to her as the Wyndhams were. I opened the letter and read.

Edenbrooke

Dearest Marianne,

I am so sorry to hear that Bath feels like a prison to you. I cannot comprehend the feeling myself, loving London as I do. Perhaps as twins I received all of the civilization in my heart while you received all of nature in yours. We are certainly not divided evenly in this instance, are we?

(Incidentally, as your sister, I can forgive you for writing things like, "I would rather have sunshine and wind and sky adorn my head than a handsome bonnet." But, please, I beg of you, do not say such things to others. I fear they would find you quite shocking.)

Knowing of your current state of misery, I shall not bother you with an account of all that I have done this past week. I will say only this: my first season in Town is as diverting as I had hoped it would be. But I will not try your patience today with saying more than that, lest you tear up this letter before reading the important news I am sending you.

My dearest friend Louisa Wyndham has invited me to stay with her at her estate in the country. I understand it is very grand. It is called Edenbrooke and is situated in Kent. We leave for the country in a fortnight. But here is the important part: you are invited as well! Lady Caroline has extended the invitation to include you, as we are both daughters of the "dearest friend" of her childhood.

Oh, say you will come, and we shall have the grandest time imaginable. I might even need your help in my quest to become "Lady Cecily" (doesn't that sound grand?), for, of course, the brother will be there, and this is my chance to secure him. Besides, it will give you an opportunity to meet my future family.

With devotion,

Cecily

Hope gripped me so hard it left me breathless. To be in the country again! To leave Bath and its horrid confines! To be with my sister after being apart for so long! It was too much to take in. I read the letter again, slowly this time, savoring each word. Of course Cecily did not really need my help to secure Sir Charles's affections. I could offer her nothing that she could not do better herself when it came to courting. But this letter was proof that I was still important to her—that she hadn't forgotten me. Oh, what a sister! This could be the solution to all of my problems. This could give me a reason to twirl again.

"Well? What does your sister say?" Grandmother asked.

I turned toward her eagerly. "She has invited me to go with her to the Wyndhams' estate in Kent. She leaves from London in a fortnight."

Grandmother pursed her wrinkled lips, gazing at me with a speculative look, but said nothing. My heart dropped. She would not refuse to let me go, would she? Not when she knew what it would mean to me?

I pressed the letter to my chest as my heart ached at the thought of being denied this unexpected blessing. "Will you give your permission?"

She looked at the letter she still held—the one bearing the bad news about Mr. Kellet. Then she tossed the letter onto the table and sat up straight in her chair.

"You may go, but only on one condition. You must alter your wild ways. No running about out of doors all day. You must learn to behave like an elegant young lady. Take lessons from your sister; she knows how to behave well in society. I cannot have my heir behaving like a wild child. I will not be embarrassed by you, as I have been by that nephew of mine."

I stared at her. Her heir? "What do you mean by that?"

"Exactly what you think I mean. I am disinheriting Mr. Kellet and bestowing the bulk of my fortune on you. At this time, your portion amounts to roughly forty thousand pounds."

Chapter 2

I knew my mouth was open, but I could not seem to find the strength to close it. Forty thousand pounds! I had no idea Grandmother was *that* wealthy.

"Of course," she continued, "there is no estate attached to it, but hopefully you will marry into one. The least you could do with my fortune is try to achieve a brilliant match." She stood and walked to her writing desk. "I know the Wyndhams. I will write to Lady Caroline myself and accept the invitation on your behalf. A fortnight will leave us just enough time to have new gowns made for you. We must begin preparations immediately."

She sat at her desk and pulled a piece of paper toward her. I could not seem to move. The course of my life had just changed, with no warning and no pause.

She glanced up. "Well? What do you have to say?"

I swallowed. "I . . . I don't know what to say."

"You might start with thank you."

I smiled weakly. "Of course I'm grateful, Grandmother. I am only . . . overwhelmed. I'm not sure I am suitable for this responsibility."

"That is the point of this visit to Edenbrooke—to make yourself suitable. The Wyndhams are a very respected family. You could learn much from being with them. In fact, that is my stipulation. I will have you become a proper young lady, Marianne. You will write to me while you are there and tell me what you are learning, or else I will call you back here and train you myself."

My thoughts were whirling, and I could hardly grasp onto one long enough to make sense of it.

"You look pale," Grandmother said. "Go upstairs and lie down. You will find your balance soon enough. But do not mention a word of this inheritance to that maid of yours! It is not the sort of information you want others to know about at this time. If you cannot discourage a simpleton like Mr. Whittles, you will be helpless against other, more cunning men who will be after your fortune. Let me decide when to make this news known. I still have to notify that nephew of mine."

I shook my head. "Of course I will not tell anyone." I chewed on my lower lip. "But what about Aunt Amelia's inheritance? And Cecily's?"

She waved a hand dismissively. "Amelia's portion is independent of yours. Don't worry about her. And Cecily does not need a fortune to make a brilliant match—you do."

This inheritance was born of pity? Because Grandmother did not think I could marry without it? I felt I should be embarrassed about this revelation, but I felt singularly unmoved, as if an important conduit between my mind and heart had been severed. I walked slowly toward the door. Perhaps I did need to lie down a while.

I opened the door and was nearly bowled over by Mr. Whittles. He must have been leaning on the door, for he stumbled, off-balance, into the room.

"Pardon me!" he exclaimed.

"Mr. Whittles!" I stepped backward quickly so as to avoid contact with him.

"I—I have returned for my poem. So that I might make the changes you suggested."

I looked beyond him to see Aunt Amelia waiting in the hall. At least that explained his presence in the house. I took his poem from my pocket and handed it to him, being careful not to touch his hand. He bowed and thanked me four times as he backed out of the room and down the hall to the front door. The man was utterly ridiculous.

But at the sight of him, a feeling of excitement rushed through me, bridging the strange gap I had felt between my mind and heart. Never mind the inheritance—I would think on that later. I would soon be able to leave Bath, and hopefully never see Mr. Whittles again. I smiled and turned to run up the stairs. I had a letter to write.

I wrote to Cecily to accept her invitation, but I did not mention the inheritance. Despite Grandmother's assurances, I could not believe that Cecily would be as indifferent about not inheriting a fortune as Grandmother felt about not leaving her one. I certainly couldn't keep forty thousand pounds to myself while my twin sister enjoyed only a small dowry. It did not sit comfortably with me to be at such an unfair advantage.

But I decided, after a few days of worrying over it, that there would be plenty of time to work it out with Cecily in the future. After all, the fortune was not even mine at this point. And Grandmother was still spry. It could be years before the money came into my possession. For my part, I would tell no one of it until it actually became a reality.

The following two weeks passed in a blur of frenzied visits to dressmakers and milliners' shops. I should have enjoyed all of the shopping, but the thought of being on display at Edenbrooke turned my pleasure into anxiety. What if I embarrassed Cecily in front of her future family? Perhaps she would regret inviting me. And could I possibly behave myself with the decorum that my grandmother expected of me? I worried over these matters until it was time to leave Bath.

On the morning of my departure, Grandmother took one look at me over breakfast and declared, "You look positively green, child. Whatever is the matter with you?"

I forced a small smile and said, "I am well. Only a little jittery, I suppose."

"You had better not eat anything. You look like the type to become sick on long carriage rides."

I remembered well the ride to Bath. I had been ill three times during the journey, once all over my boots. I definitely did not want to arrive at a strange house in that state.

"Perhaps you're right," I said, pushing away my plate. I had no appetite anyway.

"Before you leave, I have something I want to give you," Grandmother said. She reached a trembling hand under the lace shawl she wore and withdrew a locket, which she handed to me.

I carefully opened the gold locket and caught my breath at what I saw inside. Framed within the delicate oval was a miniature painting of my mother. "Oh, Grandmother," I breathed. "I've never seen this before! How old was she here?"

"Eighteen. It was done right before she married your father."

So this was what my mother looked like when she was my age. I had no trouble imagining what excitement she must have caused in London, for she was a rare beauty. It was the only picture I had of my mother, as her other portraits still hung in the silent halls of my home in Surrey. I clasped the chain around my neck, feeling the locket settle against my skin with a comforting weight. Immediately my nervousness subsided, and I breathed more easily.

A servant announced that the carriage was ready. I stood, and Grandmother looked me over critically from head to toe before finally nodding her approval.

"Now, I want you to remember what you owe to your family name. Don't do anything to disgrace me. Remember to wear your bonnet every time you go outside or you will freckle up. And one more thing—" She pointed one gnarled, heavy-knuckled finger at me and wagged it, her face set in a look of absolute seriousness. "Do not ever, ever . . . sing in front of an audience."

I pressed my lips together and glared at her. "I hardly needed that last bit of advice."

She chuckled. "No, I did not imagine you would. Who could forget the horror of the last time you performed?"

I felt myself blush in remembered embarrassment. Even though four years had passed since the evening of my first public recital, I still felt mortified every time I thought of it.

I bade good-bye to her and Aunt Amelia, eager to be on my way, but when I stepped outside, a familiar voice called my name. I cringed. Did I really have to endure Mr. Whittles one last time?

He walked toward me quickly, waving a piece of paper in the air. "I have brought you your revised poem. You are not leaving right now, are you?"

"I'm afraid I am. So this is good-bye, Mr. Whittles."

"But—but my nephew is arriving today and has expressed an interest in meeting you. In fact, he came to Bath for that very purpose."

I did not care to meet any of Mr. Whittles's relations. I wanted to leave this place and never see him again.

"I'm sorry." I gestured at the carriage, where a footman stood, holding the door open for me. "I cannot wait."

His face fell, and for a moment something like deep disappointment flashed in his eyes. Then he grabbed my hand and lifted it to his mouth. The kiss he bestowed on my hand was so wet it actually left a mark on my glove. I turned away from him to hide my shudder of revulsion. An unfamiliar coachman nodded to me as I climbed inside the carriage, where Betsy awaited me with at least an hour's worth of gossip, I was sure.

"Where is Grandmother's coachman?" I asked Betsy.

"He has been laid up this past week with the gout, so your

grandmother hired him." She gestured with her chin toward the front of the carriage. "James is his name."

I was rather relieved, actually, to see that it was not going to be a frail old man driving the carriage for twelve hours. This coachman looked much more robust, and he would probably get us there faster too. But Betsy pressed her lips together in disapproval.

"What is wrong?" I asked.

"I don't wish to speak ill of your relations, Miss Marianne, but your grandmother should not have been so tightfisted about this journey. In my opinion, she should have hired another coachman, in addition to this one."

I shrugged. There was nothing I could do about the arrangement, and as long as we reached our destination in safety, I would be content. After all, we would be traveling through the country, not on one of the main roads where we might anticipate danger.

As the carriage rolled forward through the streets, I looked out the window for a last view of the city. Now that I was leaving, I could grudgingly admit that Bath did have some beauty about it, especially with all the buildings made out of the same golden stone quarried from the nearby hills. The carriage wheels rolled over the cobblestone streets as we passed the early morning bathers who were on their way to try the waters.

Betsy suddenly leaned forward. "Is that Mr. Kellet?"

It was indeed the Nefarious Nephew, strolling past the Pump Room with his languid, devil-may-care attitude. He happened to glance our way as we passed him, and although I drew my head back quickly, he had evidently seen me, for he lifted his hat and smirked in my direction, which was his usual method of greeting me.

Thank heavens he had come today and not yesterday, when I would have had to witness his reaction to my grandmother's news that she had cut him out of her will. I had escaped just in time. I could not escape Betsy's conversation, though.

"I can't tell you how I am looking forward to visiting Edenbrooke! I have heard what a grand estate it is, and I vow I will be happy to leave Bath, for there is nobody worth talking about here, and I daresay we will have a tremendous time in Kent."

She continued talking in her nonstop fashion as we left Bath and rode through the hilly countryside. I was relieved to know that the secret of my inheritance was evidently still safe, for if Betsy had heard about it, she would have talked about nothing else.

As she chattered about the latest gossip she had acquired and her expectations for this "wonderful adventure," she occasionally looked at the squab on her right. She paused every time she did, which was such a rare thing for her to do that I idly wondered what it was about that part of the carriage that interested her. But I could not find the energy to question her, because my stomach was in a constant state of upset.

We stopped at an inn around midday, but I still thought it unwise for me to eat. The next leg of our journey took us away from the main road, and as the afternoon progressed, my stomach continued to revolt. Grandmother's carriage was old and not well-sprung, so I felt every bump and hole in the road.

That afternoon, the weather changed from sunny to overcast, the sky gray like a lid on an iron pot. My mood changed to reflect the weather, and a sense of unease settled over me. I touched my locket, reminding myself not to feel nervous. This was an exciting adventure. And no matter what the Wyndhams were like, Cecily would be there, and so there was nothing to worry about. Betsy's chatter turned to light snoring as she dozed on the seat across from me. I looked out the window and thought about seeing Cecily again.

Before the accident that had claimed my mother, my life could have been a fairy tale. This is how it would have begun: Once upon a time there were twin girls born to a man and a woman who had longed for a child for years. These girls were the sun and the moon to them.

Cecily was the sun, and I was the moon. Though twins, we only looked as much alike as sisters sometimes do. It was clear, early on, that

Cecily had received more than her fair share of beauty, and so she received more than her fair share of attention. And while I sometimes wished for my own light to shine with, I was accustomed to the way things were—to reflecting Cecily's light. I had grown up being dwarfed by her brightness. And if I did not always relish my role of being the lesser light, at least I knew how to do it well. I knew how to let Cecily shine. I knew my place in my world.

But everything I knew about myself and my place shifted and tilted in the great upheaval following my mother's death. Cecily went to London after the funeral; she had always wanted to live in Town, and Edith welcomed her with open arms. I would never have left my father. Cecily's departure felt like nothing less than desertion.

Shortly thereafter, my father had abruptly announced that I would live in Bath with my grandmother. All of my protests were to no avail. He left the country for France and had been there ever since. Our family was broken into pieces. But I hoped that this trip to Edenbrooke might be an opportunity to set everything right. I would be with my sister again, and perhaps between the two of us we could persuade Papa to come home.

I pressed the locket close to my heart and felt a greater surge of hope. Surely my mother's portrait had magical powers over my heart. Perhaps over my stomach as well, for I soon felt it calm and settle. Soon after, I dozed off myself while the carriage rocked and swayed.

I don't know how long I slept, but I awoke with a jolt, disoriented for a moment in the dim light. I looked around, trying to discern what had awakened me. Betsy was snoring loudly, but she had been snoring before I fell asleep, so that could not have been what had awakened me. Then I realized the carriage had stopped. I peered out the window, wondering if we had arrived at Edenbrooke. I saw no lights, no grand house, not even an inn. I did notice, however, that the sky had cleared, and a bright full moon illuminated the scene.

A loud shot erupted in the silence. I jumped, startled. A man cried out, and the carriage jerked forward, then stopped again.

Betsy stirred. "What was that?" she mumbled.

I pressed my face to the window. Two eyes stared back at me from behind the glass. I screamed. The carriage door was wrenched open and a large, dark shadow filled the doorway.

"Stand and deliver!" The voice was deep and muffled.

I had heard of highwaymen and knew what I should do. I was supposed to alight from the carriage and hand over all my jewels and money. Yet at the sound of the threatening voice, some instinct warned me that it would be foolish to leave the protection of the carriage.

I fumbled for my reticule and threw it out the open doorway. "There. There is my money. Take it and leave."

But the masked man ignored the money, grabbing instead at my neck.

I shrieked, pulled away, and heard a snap. I saw a glint of metal chain dangling from the robber's fingers before he clenched his hand tightly into a fist. My necklace. My locket. My only picture of my mother. I lunged for it, but he held it out of reach, laughing lightly.

And then I saw what he held in his other hand. A pistol.

"Now, step out of the carriage."

He spoke in a voice so soft it chilled me to the bone. Cold sweat seeped between my shoulder blades. I scrambled backward into the far corner of the carriage. If he wanted me out of the carriage, he would have to drag me out.

He evidently had the same thought. He gripped my ankle, then twisted hard. A pain shot up my leg. I fell on the floor of the carriage, face down, and was pulled backward. I scrabbled at the floor, my fingers grasping for anything to hold onto, and screamed. The scream went on and on—horrible, terrifying. I finally realized it was not me screaming. It was Betsy.

I had forgotten about her, but now her scream filled the night air with a horrific, chilling sound that made my heart race. She sounded like a madwoman. In a flash, I realized that she did not know about the

19

highwayman's pistol. I opened my mouth to warn her when above my head cracked a sharp, deafening sound.

The screaming changed to gasping, the sound joined by a loud cursing and the neighing of panicked horses. Smoke filled the air. The carriage swayed, and the door swung shut on my ankle. I yelped at the sharp pain and pulled myself up to my knees.

"Betsy! Are you hurt?"

I scrambled to my feet and grabbed her shoulders, struggling to see her clearly. She shook her head, still gasping as she held something toward me. Moonlight shone off the silver pistol clutched in her trembling hand. I gaped at her, then grabbed the pistol and set it down carefully on the seat.

The sound of hoofbeats caught my attention, and I looked out the window to see a man galloping away on a horse. It appeared our highwayman had escaped.

Betsy collapsed on the seat, and I sank down beside her, leaning forward with my head in my hands.

Her gasps turned into hiccups. "Oh, no! I ju-just shot a man. What if I k-killed him? W-what will happen to me?"

My head was spinning. I tried to take a deep breath but choked on the lingering smoke. "No, I am sure you did not kill him. I saw him ride away. But how on earth did you get his pistol from him?"

"I d-did not," she said, still hiccupping. "I u-used the one h-hidden in the squab."

I lifted my head at that. "There was a pistol in there? All along? How did you know?"

"I d-discovered it while you were s-speaking with Mr. Whit-Whittles."

I nearly laughed with relief. Betsy had saved us! I hugged her until her hiccups made our heads hit together. As I pulled away, a thought occurred to me.

"Wait. Where is James? Why did he not come to our rescue?"

I suddenly recalled the sound of the first gunshot right after the carriage had stopped. A man had cried out. My heart filled with dread. I turned, and through the broken window I saw a figure lying on the ground. It was our coachman, James.

Chapter 3

I jumped from the carriage and ran to him. I called his name and shook his shoulder, but there was no response. I threw off my bonnet to lean my face against his. A faint breath brushed my cheek, and I sagged with relief. He was alive. My hands fluttered over him as I searched for a wound. I froze when I felt a sticky wetness on his shoulder. He *had* been shot.

"Betsy! I need your help! Quickly!"

I had a vague memory of my father's dog getting shot in a hunting accident. My father had pulled off his cravat and pressed it onto the bleeding wound; to staunch the flow of blood, he had told me. If it worked for a dog, surely it would work for a man.

I shrugged out of my short jacket and folded it into a large pad. It was all I had on hand that I could access easily. I was certainly not going to try to get out of my petticoats at this dire moment. I felt for the wettest spot on James's coat and put the folded jacket there, telling Betsy to push on it.

Then I stood and turned to the carriage. In the commotion, the horses had spooked and dragged it several meters from where James had fallen. I debated quickly. Should we carry him to the carriage, or bring the carriage to him? I looked doubtfully at James. I was sure I could not lift even half of his weight, and Betsy was nearly as small as I was in stature. The carriage would have to come to him, then.

The horses were still spooked and threatened to rear up when I grabbed the reins. It was not easy to convince them to move, especially to move backwards, and at one point I was afraid we were going to run right over James and Betsy. As it was, it took much too long to position the carriage.

I was sweating, my hands shaking. I tried to hurry and tripped on something. I sprawled hard in the dirt, scraping my hands on the little rocks in the road and hitting my cheek on the ground. I struggled to stand, my skirts getting in the way, and found my reticule at my feet. The highwayman had not wanted my money? I stuffed my reticule into my gown and turned back to the task at hand. Now came the difficult part—moving James up to the door of the carriage and lifting him inside.

I took him by the shoulders, Betsy by his feet, and we dragged him, in an agonizingly slow fashion, inch by inch, pausing frequently to set him down and catch our breath. When we finally had him at the door to the carriage, I looked at the height of the step from the ground and nearly cried. My arms shook with fatigue, and we still had to find a way to lift him up.

I put his shoulders back on the ground and looked grimly at Betsy. She slumped against the carriage.

"We must do it, Betsy. I don't know how, but we must."

She nodded, and we each took a boot, pushing his feet into the carriage. Then we climbed over him and into the carriage. We pulled and tugged on his legs until we had his hips through the door. I climbed back out and jumped down, sure that if he was still alive, he must be bleeding profusely with all of the pushing and dragging we were doing. I lifted his shoulders and shoved against him while Betsy pulled on his arms. We finally managed to fold him into the space. I shut the door quickly before he could unfold and drop back to the ground.

"Keep pushing on his wound!" I called through the broken window.

"How can I? He's all folded over."

"Just try!" I climbed up on the driver's box, teetering as I realized how high up I was, and grasped the reins. At least I knew how to drive a carriage, thanks to my father's training. The horses moved restlessly under my unfamiliar touch. "I wish James was driving as much as you do," I muttered, slapping the reins across their backs.

We seemed to be in the middle of nowhere. I drove on and on, until my arms and shoulders burned with fatigue. It was not easy to keep four spooked horses under control.

When I finally saw a light in the distance, it was the loveliest sight I had ever seen. As we drew nearer, I was even more relieved to find the unmistakable marks of an inn. "The Rose and Crown" hung on a rough-hewn wooden sign above the door. I pulled into the yard and climbed down from the carriage, my legs shaking beneath me.

I hurried to the door, but in my urgency, I opened it with more force than was necessary. It banged loudly against the opposite wall. A tall gentleman standing by the bar looked my way, his attention captured, no doubt, by the noise of my entrance.

I walked to him as quickly as my weak legs could carry me.

"I need help in the yard. At once." I sounded authoritative to the point of rudeness, but I was so anxious about James's state that I did not care.

The gentleman raised one eyebrow as his gaze swept over me, from my disheveled hair (where had I left my bonnet?) to my muddy boots. "I am afraid you have mistaken my identity." His words were clipped, his tone cool. "I believe you will find the innkeeper in the kitchen."

I blushed at his disdainful look, and then my nerves, strung so taut with everything that had happened, suddenly snapped. How dare he speak to me like that? Anger flared hard in my chest and pride reared its head. In that moment I felt as strong and haughty as Grandmother.

I lifted my chin and said, "Pardon me. I was under the impression that I was addressing a gentleman. I can see that I was, as you said, mistaken."

I registered briefly the look of shock on his face before turning toward the open doorway behind the bar. "Hello! Innkeeper!" A stout, balding man appeared, wiping his hands on his shirt. "I need help in the yard at once!"

"Yes, of course," he said, following me out the door.

I opened the door to the carriage and there was no need to explain. It was a horrible scene: James bent over on the floor, Betsy looking up, her face chalky pale, the dark stain of blood on both of them. I was appalled, even prepared as I was for the sight.

I was immediately thankful that this innkeeper was a man of action, as well as large in stature. He reached in, lifted James in his arms, and carried him into the inn. I nearly cried as I watched him do easily what had taken Betsy and me such a long, torturous effort to accomplish.

Betsy stepped down from the carriage and wobbled a bit. I wrapped my arm around her waist, steadying her as we walked inside and followed the innkeeper up the stairs. Out of the corner of my eye, I saw that arrogant gentleman standing nearby, but I ignored him.

The stairs seemed almost too much to ask of my tired, trembling body. The innkeeper reached the landing ahead of us and turned to a room on the left. I just wanted to find a bed for Betsy and then see to James. But a robust woman planted herself in front of us as soon as we reached the landing.

"What is all the to-do about?" she asked, hands on her ample hips. "This is a respectable inn, it is, and I'm not one to put up with any strange goings-on."

I lifted my chin. "My coachman was injured and my maid is on the verge of collapse. Please be so good as to show us to a room."

She snapped her mouth shut with a startled look, bobbed a curtsy, and said, "Pardon me, miss. I was not aware . . . yes, of course." Then she waved me to a room on the right of the landing. I gathered from her reaction that she had not recognized me as a lady until I spoke. The thought rankled.

It was only after I helped Betsy sit on the bed that I noticed how stricken she looked. She had suffered quite a shock, what with firing a pistol and then holding a bleeding man while I drove.

"Lie down," I said. I was relieved that she felt no need to talk about it, but merely collapsed across the bed, one arm thrown across her face. I watched her with some concern until the innkeeper's wife (for so I assumed she was) bustled in with a basin, a piece of soap, and a towel.

"In case you want to wash up," she said with a pointed look at my hands. I glanced down at them. Yes, they looked nearly as ghastly as Betsy's. She hesitated at the door and said, "You look like you could do with a nice hot meal. Come down to the parlor, and I'll have something prepared for you. It's mighty hard to withstand such things on an empty stomach."

I nodded and thanked her quietly, relieved to find that she was helpful after all.

When I submerged my palms in the basin of water, I felt every red welt and raw scrape. I hissed at the sting as I soaped my hands, washing all the way up to my elbows. The water in the bowl turned red, and my empty stomach heaved at the sight. I closed my eyes and breathed deeply, fighting off the wave of nausea that washed over me.

I left Betsy snoring on the bed, her mouth hanging open like a hinged gate, and crossed the hall to the room I had seen the innkeeper enter with James.

James lay on the bed, eyes closed, while the innkeeper cut away his shirt. He moved deftly as he cleaned the wound, his face quiet and composed, his hands roughened by work but clean. I felt infinitely better knowing that James was in this man's large, capable hands.

"Doctor will be here shortly, miss," he said. "I've seen worse wounds than this—looks like he might have been clipped—can't even see a bullet lodged in there."

At the sound of his kind, gruff voice, relief flooded through me with such force that my knees went weak. "Thank you," I said, my words choked by emotion.

The innkeeper looked sharply at me. "You'd best sit down, miss. You look none too good."

"No, no, I'm fine," I said, but I did notice that the ground seemed unsteady and my knees were shaking.

"Go warm yourself by the fire. There's nothing for you to do in here."

I nodded, feeling my head float in a strange, detached way. A chair by the fire sounded heavenly. I turned from the room and started down the stairs just fine. But somewhere halfway down, my legs trembled and my knees buckled underneath me. I sat down hard on a step, willing myself not to tumble down the staircase. The walls started to waver, the floor heaving up. I covered my eyes with one hand, my other hand braced against the wall, and struggled to keep my sense of balance.

A strong hand suddenly grasped my arm above the elbow. My eyes flew open in surprise. It was that hateful, arrogant man from earlier, standing a few steps below me. He looked at me with a strange expression on his face. It almost looked like . . . concern. What did he want? I tried to ask him, but the walls were falling in on me again. I closed my eyes tightly.

"I think you're about to faint," a low voice said.

Whose voice was it? It was too nice to belong to that man. I shook my head and said weakly, "I don't faint." And then darkness rushed up while I swooped down. We met in the middle and it swallowed me whole. I was relieved that it didn't hurt.

Chapter 4

I awoke slowly, aware first of something soft beneath me, then a low murmur of voices nearby. I could not make sense of where I was. It was not home; it didn't smell like home. I knew I should open my eyes, but somehow I could not. So I lay still and listened to the murmur. It was very pleasant. It reminded me of something from my childhood—when I fell asleep in the carriage at night and heard my parents talking softly around me.

The carriage.

My memory came flooding back to me all at once, so vivid that I gasped out loud. The murmuring stopped, and I felt someone bend over me.

"Well? Are you finally coming to?"

The abrasive voice sounded vaguely familiar. I wrenched my eyelids open and looked into the no-nonsense face of the innkeeper's wife. Close as she was, I could smell the garlic on her breath and count four long hairs growing from the mole on her cheek. Both served to waken my senses immediately.

"I thought you were going to faint," she said, "and sure enough, you did."

As I sat up, I felt an excruciating headache swell behind my eyes. I put my hand on my forehead and looked around carefully, trying not to move my head too much. I could see now that I was in some sort of parlor. A table in the middle of the room was set with food. There was a fireplace at one end and curtained windows along the long wall.

The woman's beefy hands encircled my arms, and she pulled me to my feet. She led me to the table. "Sit down and eat," she commanded. I obeyed her first order, grateful to be off my wobbly legs. She glanced behind me and asked, "Is there anything else, sir?"

I looked quickly over my shoulder and immediately regretted the action, as it made my head swim and the pounding intensify. I pressed both hands to my forehead as that hateful man said something to the woman— I hardly heard what—and she walked out of the room without a backward glance, closing the door firmly behind her.

The gentleman—no, he was not a gentleman; there was nothing gentle about him, he was just a plain man—did not leave with her, but he did approach the table so that I needn't turn my head to look at him. I glanced at him out of the corner of my eye. He was watching me. It was very unnerving. I could only imagine how I must look after traveling all day, falling out of a carriage, lifting a bleeding man, and then fainting. I grimaced at the thought.

He stepped forward and asked, "Are you hurt?"

I looked at him appraisingly. He looked genuinely concerned, which surprised me.

"No," I answered, but my voice sounded rough, my throat as dry as stale bread. I reached for the glass at my elbow and drank, hoping to clear my head a little. I decided some food was a good idea and that I would just ignore the odious man until he left.

My plan did not work.

He was so obtuse he actually walked to the chair opposite mine and asked, "Do you mind if I join you?"

I wished I could think clearly. Where was my quick wit when I needed it? There was no civil way to refuse him, and I was too tired to think of a witty retort. I shook my head and watched him walk to the door. He opened it before sitting across from me. I felt instantly more comfortable, not even aware that I had been tense about being alone with a strange man behind a closed door. As I ate, the pounding in my head turned into a slight tapping, then the low hum of a dull headache.

The man did not eat at all. He only sat there and drank a little, all the while watching me as if I might fall off my chair at any moment. I was still intending to ignore him, but I found myself studying his face in quick glances. In the tumult of the earlier commotion, I had not noticed his features before. Now that I was at liberty to see him clearly, I was dismayed by how handsome he was. He had chestnut-brown, wavy hair and a solid jaw. I wondered what color his eyes were. He obliged me by looking up suddenly.

Oh. Blue. Yes, an extraordinarily handsome face, I thought, and then I realized that I had been caught staring at him. I quickly lowered my gaze, feeling my face burn. He was handsome. That made everything worse. The food had enlivened my senses, and I soon felt with full force the awkwardness of my situation.

Resentment flared within me as I remembered his snub and the way he had looked at me when I first entered the inn. He had undoubtedly thought I was some sort of common person beneath his notice. The fact that I had looked like an unkempt milkmaid did nothing to lessen the sting. It also did not help that he was not talking to me at all. Well, he thought he was dining with some vulgar person. Of course he would not make conversation. Arrogant, hateful man! Resentment and embarrassment burned into hot anger within me.

I glanced up at him from under my lashes. If a commoner is what he expected, then a commoner is what I would give him. He probably had no wit, like most handsome people. This would be easy.

"Thank you for the meal, sir," I said demurely, imitating Betsy's accent. I caught a brief look of surprise on his face.

"You're welcome." His expression was guarded, his eyes slightly confused. "I hope it is to your satisfaction."

"Oh, yes. Upon my word, I never had such a fine meal at home."

He leaned back in his chair. "And where is home?" he asked. His voice was low and rich and very pleasant. I tried not to think about that.

"Oh, it's just a little farm in the north part of Wiltshire County. But now I'm off to my aunt's house, where she's going to teach me to be a lady's maid, which I think will be much better than milking cows."

I looked at him over the rim of my glass as I took another drink. I thought I saw his lips twitch, but I was not sure.

"So you are . . . a dairymaid?"

"Yes, sir."

"How many cows do you have?" he asked, a sly look flashing in his eyes.

I watched him carefully. "Four." I wondered about that look.

"What are their names?"

"Who?" I asked, momentarily taken off guard.

"The cows." He looked at me blandly. "Surely they have names."

Did people name their cows? I had no idea. "Of course they have names."

"And they are . . . ?"

I saw an unmistakable twinkle in his blue eyes, and in that instant I realized with a start of surprise that he was playing with me. When he looked at me again, his face was carefully smooth, but his eyes looked too innocent. He was definitely playing with me. Well, he did not know how good I was at this game.

"Bessie, Daisy, Ginger, and Annabelle," I answered coolly, challenging him with a look.

A look of pleasure passed over his face. "And when you milk them, you sing to them, do you not?"

"Naturally."

Leaning toward me across the table, he gazed into my eyes and said, "I would *love* to hear what you sing to them."

I gasped. Wicked, wicked man! I hesitated, not sure if I could carry this off. But then I saw a look of smugness in his expression. He thought he had already won! That settled it.

Hardly knowing what I was doing, I began to hit the table with one hand as I sang in a low voice, "Big cows"—*thump*—"lumps of meat"—*thump*. His eyes widened. "Give me milk"—*thump*—"warm and sweet"—*thump*.

I stopped abruptly, pressing my lips together as I realized what I had just sung. The ridiculousness of it struck me forcibly, and I knew I could not go on without laughing. We stared at each other, locked in a stalemate, his eyes brimming with laughter, his lips trembling. My chin quivered. Against my will, a sound burst from me. It was a very unladylike snort.

He threw his head back and broke into a roar of laughter. It was the most infectious laugh I had ever heard. I joined him spontaneously, laughing until my throat ached and tears streamed down my cheeks. When I finally stopped, I felt a tremendous sense of release. I mopped at my face with a napkin.

"'Lumps of meat'?" he chuckled.

"I was improvising," I said.

He shook his head and looked at me with admiration. "That was . . . amazing."

"Thank you," I conceded with a smile.

He returned my smile for a moment, then suddenly leaned toward me across the table. "Shall we be friends now?"

I caught my breath. Did I want to be his friend? His eyes were lit up and warm and smiling into mine. "Yes."

"Then, as friends, I must apologize for my behavior to you earlier. It was beyond rude—it was unpardonable—and I am thoroughly ashamed of myself for it. I beg you to forgive me."

His sincerity cried out in every line of his face, every accent of his words. I had never expected my insult to be taken so much to heart. I was instantly contrite.

"Of course I will forgive you, if you will also forgive me for my rudeness. I should never have implied that you were . . ." I hated repeating the words, as I now realized how shockingly insulting I had been. I cleared my throat, looking down at my plate. "Not a gentleman," I finished faintly.

"That was an implication?"

I glanced up at him.

He looked faintly amused, one eyebrow raised. "I feel sorry for the person you decide to insult."

I grimaced, looking away with embarrassment. I was too much like Grandmother.

"But I deserved the rebuke, and you were right to deliver it. As a gentleman, I should have come to your aid no matter what your need. If I may offer a defense, though, I must clarify that my rudeness had nothing to do with you, and was simply a result of . . . trying circumstances earlier this evening. Your request, unfortunately, happened to be the straw that broke the camel's back. But that is no excuse, and I am sorry that I added to your distress this evening."

There was no smugness about him now. It took a strong man to say such things. I felt the honor of his humility, and I was strangely touched by it.

"Thank you," I murmured. I did not know what else to say. I was completely disarmed.

"And you should know," he said, leaning back in his chair, "as entertaining as that charade was, nobody would have believed you were a dairymaid."

"Are my acting skills so poor?" I asked defensively.

"I was not referring to your acting skills." A small smile played around his mouth.

I tried to puzzle out his meaning, but without success. Curiosity tugged at me, leading me on when I should have shrugged off his comment.

"Then to what were you referring?" I asked.

"You must know."

"No, I don't." I was frankly bothered by his refusal to explain himself.

"Very well." In a voice as cool and detached as if he were critiquing a work of art, he said, "Starting at the top: your brow is marked with intelligence, your gaze is direct, your features are delicate, your skin is fair, your voice is refined, your speech reflects education . . ." He paused. "Even the way you hold your head is elegant."

I was suddenly, excruciatingly self-conscious. I dropped my gaze, my face on fire.

"Ah, yes," he said softly. "And then there is your modesty. No milkmaid could have blushed like that."

To my mortification, I felt my blush deepen until the tips of my ears were tingling with the heat.

"Shall I continue?" he asked with a hint of a laugh in his voice.

"No, that is quite enough, thank you." My grandmother would be having fits if she saw me right now. Inept did not begin to describe how I felt.

"Then may I ask you some questions?" He asked so politely that all I could do was nod.

He stood and walked around the table, stopping behind my chair to pull it out for me as I stood. Motioning toward two chairs angled in front of the fireplace, he said, "I believe you will be more comfortable by the fire."

Hmm. He was thoughtful.

The fire crackled in welcome as we sat before it. I was pleasantly surprised to find the chair soft and comfortable, and I sank into it, suddenly aware of feeling sore and tired. He looked at the fire, and, now that I was at closer range, I took advantage of the opportunity to study him in more detail. In profile, as he was now, he looked youthful, with the firelight highlighting his fine features, his straight nose, the smoothness of his cheek, the soft curl falling over his brow. But that impression was dispelled when looking at him directly. There was a firmness around his mouth and a confidence in his eyes that defined him as a man who knew his place in the world: a man of authority.

The gentleman (I supposed I could grant him that title, if he continued to behave himself) asked, "Now that we have agreed you are not a milkmaid, would you mind telling me who you are?" He smiled so kindly, so worthy of my trust, that I felt no hesitation in confiding in him.

"Miss Marianne Daventry."

His expression froze, his eyes narrowing as he looked hard at me.

I grew self-conscious under his scrutiny. "What is it? Do I look worse by firelight?"

A little smile touched his lips. "No, quite the contrary. It is a pleasure to meet you, Miss Daventry." He turned his gaze back to the fire and said nothing more. I waited for a moment for him to finish the introduction.

"Do you intend to tell me your name?"

He hesitated, then said, very politely, "No, I would rather not."

Chapter 5

I was taken aback. "Oh. Well . . ." I did not know how to respond.

"Now tell me what brings you to this area."

I was irked by the feeling that this man once again had the upper hand. "I don't believe I should confide in you."

He sighed. "I thought we had agreed to be friends."

"Yes, but that was before I knew you would refuse to tell me your name. I can hardly be friends with someone who has no name."

He looked as if he found everything I said to be very entertaining. "Very well. As my friend, you may call me Philip."

"I can't call you by your Christian name." Consternation colored my voice.

"Would you feel more comfortable if I were to call you Marianne?"

"You would not."

"Yes, I would, Marianne." He had a teasing glint in his eye.

I felt myself blushing. "You are very improper."

He chuckled. "Not normally. Just tonight."

I realized that I was still looking into his eyes, which were a darker blue than I had first thought them to be, and that he actually looked more handsome when he was smiling, as he was now. It was a very disconcerting realization, for I could not forget how tragically unbecoming my own appearance was. I broke my gaze away, embarrassed at the thought of what I must look like.

"If you must know," I said with a show of dignity I did not feel, "I was invited to visit a friend of my mother's."

"Why did she invite you to visit?"

His voice sounded casual, but his look betrayed interest. I wondered why he would want to know that. It seemed a harmless question, though.

"My sister was first invited to visit, and Lady Caroline was very gracious to extend the invitation to include me." Lady Caroline's letter had arrived just a few days after Cecily's, confirming the invitation.

After a moment of silence, he asked, "And what happened to your coachman?"

All at once I remembered James, lying wounded upstairs, maybe even dying, and here I had been playing a silly game, laughing myself to stitches, and thinking about this man's eyes. What was wrong with me? Did I have no sensibility?

"He was shot when we were held up by a highwayman," I said, trying not to remember the terrifying details of the encounter.

His eyebrows drew together. "A highwayman? On this road? Are you quite sure?"

"If a highwayman wears a stocking mask and demands that you 'stand and deliver' and then forcibly takes your necklace, then yes, I am quite sure."

The horror of the event was catching up with me. I suddenly felt too emotional to speak.

"Did he hurt you?"

The emotion I was trying to suppress clawed at my throat, unleashed by the gentleness in Philip's voice. Without warning, a tear slipped down my cheek. I swiped it away.

"No. He tried to drag me from the carriage, but my maid shot at him with a pistol. He rode away, but by then he had already shot my coachman." I put a hand to my forehead. I could remember the feel of the highwayman's hand around my ankle, the sharp sting as he pulled my mother's locket from around my neck. "I feel horrid. I was not even thinking about James. He could be dying up there, and it would be all my fault." A tear slipped out, then two, and I dashed them away.

"It would not be your fault, and I don't believe your coachman will die from his wound. I saw it myself. It was high on his shoulder and did not hit any organs, and the doctor is very capable."

I nodded, relieved to hear his words, and tried to stop crying. If my grandmother had witnessed this behavior she would probably disown me. But I felt just as out of control with my tears as I had earlier with my laughter. Philip handed me a clean white handkerchief, which I took without meeting his gaze. This was so unlike me. And so embarrassing.

"Forgive me." I wiped a stream of tears from my cheek. "I am not normally such a watering pot, I assure you." He was bound to think I was one of those fragile creatures who fainted at the sight of blood and cried for sympathy.

"I am sure you are not." He was so very polite that I felt increasingly worse about my first assessment of his character.

When I finally felt myself in control of my emotions again, I turned to him. "Do you think that you could forget that any of this happened?"

"Why do you ask that?" A small smile lurked around his lips.

"I am quite embarrassed by my behavior tonight," I confessed.

His eyes lit up with amusement. "Which behavior?"

"Yes, there is so much to choose from. I insulted you, fainted, pretended to be a milkmaid, sang a ridiculous song, cried, and on top of it all, I am relatively sure . . ." I glanced down, seeing red streaks of dried blood on my sleeves and the front of my gown. "No, I am *certain* I look completely unpresentable."

Philip chuckled. I thought he was laughing at me, but then he turned and leaned over his armrest so that he was looking right into my eyes. "I don't think I have ever met a lady like you, Miss Marianne Daventry, and I would feel very sorry to forget anything about this evening."

I suddenly could not breathe. My blush spread to my ears, and I knew, deep in my bones, that I was no match for this man, not with my games or my confidence or my wit. I leaned back, away from those smoldering eyes and smiling lips. I wanted to run from the room and hopefully never see him again.

Before I could carry out my plan, though, he asked, "What are you going to do now?"

The weight of my predicament settled on me suddenly. "I suppose I will need to arrange for someone to care for James, then find someone to drive me to Edenbrooke. Oh, and I should notify Lady Caroline that my arrival will be delayed." I sighed. "But all I really want to do is to go to sleep and try to forget this day ever happened."

"Why don't you let me take care of everything?"

I glanced at him sharply. "I can't let you do that, sir."

"Why not?"

"It is too much. I barely know you. I could not impose on you."

"It's not too much, and you would not be imposing. How would you go about it on your own? You probably don't even know where you are, do you?"

I shook my head.

"Let me help," he said persuasively.

"I can manage on my own," I insisted. I did not want him to think me weak and helpless. I was my grandmother's heir, after all, and I was more like her than I cared to admit.

"I have no doubt you would be able to manage, Marianne, considering what I have seen of you tonight. But I would like to be of service to you."

"Why?" I asked, genuinely puzzled.

"Isn't that what a gentleman does? Rescues a damsel in distress?" His tone was light, but his eyes were solemn.

"I am not a damsel in distress," I said with a laugh.

"But I *am* trying to prove that I am a gentleman."

Now I understood his persistence. It came back to the insult I had thrown at him. He should not have taken it so much to heart. "You don't have to prove anything to me."

He looked heavenward with a sigh. "Are you always this stubborn?"

I thought about it for a moment. "Yes, I think I am."

Philip's expression wavered between exasperation and amusement. Amusement won with a reluctant laugh. "I relent. You will never say something predictable. But I do agree with your plan. You should get some sleep and worry about all of this in the morning. It will all wait."

He sounded very reasonable, and it was a relief to think that I could put it off until I was better rested.

"You're probably right," I said. "I think I will take your advice."

"Good." He smiled at me. "Can you make it up the stairs on your own?"

"Of course." That reminded me of something. "I fainted on the stairs earlier, didn't I?"

He nodded.

"And then what happened?"

"I caught you and carried you here." Amusement lit up his eyes.

"Oh." I was not sure what to think. I felt embarrassed and strangely pleased at the same time. I looked at him from under my lashes, noting the strain of coat against the muscles in his shoulders and arms. Yes, he certainly looked strong enough to carry me . . . probably quite easily, I imagined. My face grew warm at the thought. "Well, thank you."

"My pleasure," he murmured, a smile teasing his mouth again.

I decided to pretend I hadn't heard that. "I believe I can make it up-stairs by myself. I'll not be needing any more of your services tonight."

He looked unconvinced. "Stand up then."

I tried and found I was grafted to the chair with exhaustion.

"Just as I suspected." He stood and took my hand, pulling on it to help me up.

I sucked in my breath with the sudden sting of his hand on mine and flinched. Philip's look sharpened with concern, and he quickly turned my palm over. The wounds looked worse in the firelight than they had upstairs. Red scrapes and welts covered most of my palms. They throbbed, and there were a few places where several layers of skin had been scraped off.

"I thought you said he didn't hurt you." His voice was harsh. When he looked into my eyes, my heart turned over. He looked angry and rather dangerous, and all the more handsome for it.

"He didn't. It was the reins, mostly. The horses were spooked, and I'm not accustomed to driving four of them. And then I fell when I was trying to hurry and James was so heavy . . ." I stopped as I noticed the look of amazement on Philip's face.

"You lifted your coachman?"

"Well, my maid helped."

He looked at me as if he couldn't believe what he was seeing. "I saw him. He is more than twice your size. And I also saw your maid. I wouldn't think it possible."

I shrugged. "It had to be done. I couldn't leave him there."

He held my gaze for a long moment. I realized that the fire was very warm, and that I was standing very close to a very handsome gentleman who held my hand in his. Philip looked down.

"You brave girl," he murmured, running a light finger along my palm. It was so soft a touch that it did not hurt at all. But it did send a wave of feeling through my hand, up my arm, all the way to my heart. I had never experienced such a sensation before, and I found it completely unnerving.

I pulled my hand out of his grip and tried to comprehend what had just happened. But my exhaustion was beginning to feel like a fog in my head, and I could make no sense of my reaction to him. Perhaps I was becoming feverish. Even delirious.

"You must be exhausted," Philip said, as if he could read my mind. "Come." He took my elbow and steered me toward the open door.

I wanted to insist that I could walk up the stairs just fine on my own, but I was no longer certain that I could. Not tonight. Philip only let go of me when we reached the landing.

He bowed. "Good night, Marianne." I smiled at the sound of my name on his lips. It had somehow become not shocking at all.

"Good night," I said. "And thank you. For everything."

I felt like there was something else I should say to him, but I couldn't think what it was. All I could think about was falling into bed. I walked to the door of the bedchamber where Betsy was still snoring.

With my hand on the door handle, I heard Philip quietly say, "Lock your door before you go to bed."

A chill of alarm spread through me, reminding me that I had been in very real danger not so long ago. It sharpened my thoughts, and I realized what I should say. I turned around to ask Philip if I would ever see him again.

But he was already gone.

Chapter 6

I awoke feeling far from rested. Betsy had been all legs and arms in the night, and I was sure she had caused at least a few of the bruises I felt. She must have awakened before me, for she was not in the room, and I was tempted to fall back onto my pillow and sleep some more. But there were things that only I could take care of, and I couldn't put them off any longer.

So I blinked against the bright morning sunlight, stretched, and sat up, groaning as I did. My body hurt everywhere. The door opened quietly and Betsy tiptoed in. When she saw me awake, though, she shut the door and hurried to plop down onto the bed beside me.

"Miss Marianne," she cried, bumping into my sore shoulder. I winced. "I am so sorry I fell asleep before you last night, but there was nothing so shocking as shooting at that man, and I declare I do believe I hit him, although I am not entirely sure as it was so dark last night." She paused to draw in a breath, and I quickly interrupted before she could start up again.

"No, Betsy, please don't apologize for anything. Now, if you will please help me dress, I must see to James."

"Oh, of course, miss, but you needn't worry about James because a woman came here early this morning saying she was sent to offer her nursing services and she has taken over the sickroom as if she owned it."

"A nurse?" I pulled my gown over my head. "But . . . who is she? I have not had a chance to speak to anyone about it. Did the doctor send for her?"

"Oh, no. He was here when she arrived and seemed quite as surprised as the rest of us."

I dressed quickly, ignoring my protesting muscles, and walked across the hall to the room James had been in. The door stood open and a small, plump woman bent over the bed. She turned at the sound of my footsteps and hurried to the door.

"Ah, you must be the young lady he spoke of," she said in a soft voice. "Much too young to be taking care of such things. I can see he was right, yes, he certainly was. Now, don't worry about a thing, I have everything under control."

I blinked in surprise. "Thank you, I am very grateful you have come . . ." I paused, waiting for her name.

"Oh, pardon me, I've forgotten my manners. I'm Mrs. Nutley." She bobbed a curtsy, holding out her skirt with clean, small hands. Her round, rosy cheeks jiggled a little with the movement. Her brown hair was pulled into a neat bun. I liked her immensely.

"I am so happy to meet you," I said, "and so grateful to have your help. But if I may ask—who engaged your services?"

She pursed her heart-shaped mouth and clasped her hands together. "No, no, I cannot tell, I promised I would not. And you mustn't question me any further, my dear, for I do hate to be impolite, but I must keep my promise."

I rocked back in surprise. "Well, then . . ." I was at a loss for words. I looked over her shoulder and saw James in bed, looking pale, his eyes closed. "How is the patient?"

She put her arm around me and nudged me out the door. "He is well, but resting right now. Go on downstairs, and please don't worry about a thing. I have it all under control, and you will be able to say good-bye to him later." She smiled, her red cheeks like apples beneath her merry eyes.

I felt no qualms about leaving James in her care. But as I went down-stairs, the mystery of who had arranged for her service bothered me. It was like when Philip had refused to tell me his full name last night. That still bothered me as well, now that I thought about it.

I found the innkeeper in the taproom and asked if I might have my breakfast served to me in the parlor. I tried to sound nonchalant as I asked, "Do you know the name of the gentleman who dined with me last night?"

His expression was instantly guarded. "I don't know who you mean, miss."

Before I could respond, he made a hasty retreat into the kitchen. I looked after him, puzzled by his reaction. It appeared the mystery would continue a bit longer.

I made my way to the parlor, finding the room bright and sunny. In the center of the table stood a vase of fresh wildflowers, and propped up next to the vase was a letter with "Miss Marianne Daventry" written in a strong, elegant hand across the front. I picked it up and turned it over, examining the seal in the red wax on the back. It was a crest, but one I did not recognize. I broke the seal and opened the letter.

Dear Marianne,

I have engaged the services of a respectable nurse to care for your coachman during his recovery. A carriage will arrive at noon to convey you and your maid to your destination. The carriage you arrived in will be transported back to Bath. I have also taken the liberty of send-ing a message to Edenbrooke to inform them of your impending arrival. I trust I have left nothing undone.

Your obedient servant,

Philip

I stared at the letter in surprise. This was impossible! I had refused his assistance, and still he had persisted in giving it. I wasn't sure how I felt about it. To go to so much trouble to help me was very kind, I had to admit. But then there was his closing—*your obedient servant.* I could easily imagine him laughing as he wrote the words.

I was still flustered when the innkeeper's wife entered with my breakfast. I looked up from the letter. "Do you know the name of the gentleman who stayed here last night?"

She shot me a strange look. "No gentleman stayed here last night."

What was this? I held up the letter as proof that I had not imagined him. "There was a gentleman who dined with me. He caught me when I fainted?"

"He did not stay the night, miss." She set the dishes on the table with a rough clatter. "He left close to midnight."

That seemed strange. Why would he travel so late? Why not sleep here and start his journey in the morning?

The innkeeper's wife turned to the door, and I called out.

"Wait. Do you know his name?"

"I'm not at liberty to say, miss, and I'll not take any badgering, not after the night I had and the morning too." She glared at me, as if daring me to argue with her, and then quickly left the room. I stared after her with wide eyes. This was the strangest inn I had ever known.

I reread the letter as I ate breakfast, feeling more irritated with Philip with every passing moment. I convinced Betsy to take a walk with me to pass the time, and, later, I sat for a while at James's bedside, until Mrs. Nutley shooed me away. Finally a knock sounded at the parlor door. It was the innkeeper, coming to tell me that a coach was here to collect me.

The coachman stood in the taproom. He doffed his hat when he saw me. "Pleased to be of service, miss."

"Thank you. But before we go anywhere, I must ask you who engaged your services." I was determined to discover Philip's identity from someone. This was my last hope.

He shook his head. "I'm sorry, miss."

I glared at him. "Do you mean to tell me that you are not at liberty to disclose the person's identity?"

"Yes, miss."

I huffed. "Very well. If you refuse to tell me, then I refuse to go with you." I heard how childish I sounded, but I did not care. That Philip was too much, making everyone play along with his little mystery and making me the object of his game. I could imagine everyone here laughing at me behind my back.

The coachman cleared his throat. "I was warned that I might encounter such a response, in which case I am to forcibly put you in the carriage myself."

I gasped. "He did not."

"He did." He allowed himself a very small smile.

My frustration turned to anger. Philip was a heavy-handed, impertinent, odious man! What right had he to meddle so much in my affairs? I turned on my heel and tried not to stomp my feet as I climbed the stairs. Betsy was just finishing packing our things. I said good-bye to James, who assured me he was perfectly content to stay right where he was for the time being.

The last thing I had to do was to settle our bill with the innkeeper. When I approached him with my reticule, however, he said, "No, miss, I'm not to take it. I've already been paid handsomely for your stay as well as for anything your coachman might need."

I seethed. "I see the gentleman who was here last night thought of everything."

The innkeeper hefted my trunk and gave me a big smile. "Aye, that's right."

I muttered insults about Philip under my breath as I climbed into the carriage with Betsy. As we drove away, I was glad to leave behind the strange inn and everyone I had met. In fact, I hoped I would never have to see these people again. Especially Philip. Though if I did, he would surely get an earful from me.

After stewing for a few miles, I decided that I would not let that man ruin the rest of my journey. My twin sister and a marvelous time were awaiting me, and I wanted to forget about everything that had happened yesterday. So I took a deep breath, pushed aside my frustration, and watched the countryside roll by.

This carriage was much more comfortable than Grandmother's, and I did not feel half as ill as I had yesterday. Betsy spent a good part of the ride guessing what Edenbrooke would look like and what the Wyndhams would be like. I smiled indulgently, listening with half an ear to her prattle. Her conversation rarely required a response.

I sometimes wondered what it would be like to have a quiet maid who knew her place and who did not bother me with her constant chatter. But I could not imagine dismissing Betsy. When my father had arranged for me to go to Bath, Grandmother had insisted I come with a maid. Betsy, the daughter of one of my father's tenant farmers, was chosen. It had been a great comfort to me to have somebody from home, even if she was often aggravating.

We traveled through the afternoon, until Betsy ran out of conversation and my sore body protested against the bumps in the road. When we finally pulled off the road onto a long drive leading through woods, I sat forward, eager to see our final destination. But the trees kept us from seeing much of anything until we crested a small hill.

"Oh, stop, please!" I called to the coachman. I climbed out of the carriage and stood looking down on what I was sure was Edenbrooke.

The house was impressively large, stately, and perfectly symmetrical, built out of cream-colored stone and surrounded by beautifully manicured gardens. Giant trees dotted the expanse of grass, the green so brilliant in the sunlight that I had to squint to look at it. A river ran through the estate, behind the house, and I saw a beautifully arched stone bridge spanning the water. Farmland spread out beyond it like a peacock's tail, with neat fences and hedges and productive fields stretching as far as the eye could see.

"Oh," I heard Betsy sigh with pleasure, and then she was silent. For Betsy to be silenced by beauty meant a great deal, and I smiled in agreement. Edenbrooke appeared to be everything one would want in an estate.

"It is a beauty, to be sure," the coachman said. "Best farmland in the county."

I thought of my own home in Surrey. It was very modest by comparison, with only two floors and eighteen rooms. My father owned a few hundred acres of land, which was worked by tenant farmers, but his holding looked like child's play in comparison to the grand estate of Edenbrooke. It surely took a competent hand to manage all of this. My estimation of my host rose considerably. Cecily had certainly chosen well for herself. What a privilege to be able to stay here for any length of time.

I climbed back inside the carriage, even more eager to arrive. As we rode down the hill and approached the house, I experienced a sense of coming home after being gone for a long time. It was a nonsensical feeling, for this elegant place bore no resemblance to my home. But still, I felt as if I already loved every blade of grass, every tree, every neat hedge and wild rose.

I shook my head in an effort to clear it. I was, no doubt, still suffering from shock due to the horrific events of last night. My mind was coming unhinged because of fatigue. I was only imagining this sense of homecoming—this urgency to be here at last.

The large front door opened as the coach pulled through the curving drive and came to a halt. A footman emerged from the house and opened the carriage door, offering a gloved hand to help me descend. I had no sooner touched ground than I heard a feminine voice greet me. I looked up, expecting to see Cecily's golden hair and bright blue eyes. But the lady approaching me with outstretched hands could be no one but Lady Caroline. She was tall and slim. Her brown hair was lightly shadowed with gray, and her eyes crinkled at the corners as she smiled at me.

"I should have invited you long ago," she said. "I can't tell you how happy I am that you've come. May I call you Marianne?"

"Y-yes, of course you may," I stammered, surprised by her familiar air. But then, she and my mother had been close friends for much of their lives—almost like sisters. I felt, in her request, that she was inviting me not just into her home, but into her family. I found that I liked the idea very well.

"I have been so anxious about your safety since learning of your mishap last night. I could hardly believe it!" She put an arm around my shoulders and walked me toward the door. "A highwayman, in this area? I've never heard of such a thing."

So Philip had evidently written more in his letter than simply my expected time of arrival. This seemed the perfect opportunity to ask his identity, but it struck me that it would seem very strange to admit that I had dined alone with a man last night without even knowing who he was. I hesitated, afraid Lady Caroline might think less of me if she found out, and then I lost my opportunity, for we entered the house.

As soon as I stepped inside, I had to stop and stare. The entryway was three stories high, light and airy, with windows letting in slants of sunlight that fell on white marble floors. I tipped my head back to take in the paintings that stretched up to the high ceiling. A butler and a housekeeper stood at attention, and several footmen lined up before the grand staircase.

I gulped, feeling quite small and inexperienced in the midst of all this stately grandeur.

Lady Caroline led me upstairs to a bedchamber on the second floor. The room was decorated in blue, with a large bed, a writing desk by the window, and an overstuffed chair by the fireplace. Through the window I could see a beautiful view of the river and the bridge that I had seen from the coach. The room was both elegant and comfortable, and I felt an immediate desire to call this place home.

I suddenly remembered who *did* plan on calling this place home. "I should have asked earlier," I said, "but where might I find Cecily?"

"Oh, Cecily?" She moved to the window and rearranged the fold of the drapes before answering. "She is in London." She turned to me with a smile. "I hope you will not mind being here without her for a week."

"A week?" I hoped I did not sound rude, but I was surprised by the turn of events. "I am sorry. Perhaps I misunderstood the invitation. I thought she would have come with you from London."

"Well, yes. That was the plan. But I decided to come ahead, to make things ready for your visit, and left Cecily and Louisa with my son William and his wife, Rachel, who live in London. You see, there is a masquerade ball the girls were very keen on attending there, and I couldn't bear the thought of denying them their entertainment. It is only an extra week, and it will give us time to become better acquainted before everyone else arrives."

"Oh." How awkward to be here a week before Cecily. "I hope I'm not imposing."

"Of course not. We are happy to have you." She seemed sincere, but I still felt embarrassed by the circumstances. It would be so much more comfortable to have Cecily here with me. Then Lady Caroline added, "My sister and her husband are also staying here while they have some work done on their house. So you will not be the only guest."

I relaxed a little at the news. After making sure the room was just as it should be, Lady Caroline suggested I rest from my journey and then invited me to join them in the drawing room before dinner, which would be in one hour.

Lady Caroline left the room, but I did not think I could rest if I wanted to. Betsy was unpacking my clothing and prattling on about how beautiful and grand everything was. I only gave her half my attention, the other half intent on seeing as much from my bedroom window as I could. The grounds looked so inviting, and I really only needed a half hour to change for dinner.

I quickly made up my mind. "I'm going to explore the gardens. I'll return shortly," I told Betsy as I rushed from the room. I heard her call after me, but I ignored her and hurried down the stairs. I did not have time to search for a door leading into the back of the estate, so I slipped quietly out the front door and walked around the side of the house. I was determined to see the river and that lovely bridge.

It was farther from the house than I had expected, but it was well worth the effort. The water ran clear over a rocky bed, and I saw a few fish swim by. I turned to the bridge, which was made of old stone with tall Grecian arches supporting the roof overhead. I sighed as I ran my hand over the stones. Even the bridges here were beautiful.

I looked back at the house, trying to gauge how long I had been gone. Probably ten minutes. Which meant I had another few minutes to explore. I crossed the bridge, my footsteps ringing on the stones. The land on the other side of the bridge was wilder, not as smooth or neatly manicured, which suited my tastes just fine.

Oh, how I had missed living in the country! I walked along the riverbank a short ways, but knew I had to turn back soon. I told myself I would have plenty of time—an entire summer—to explore and enjoy this paradise. For that was exactly what it seemed to me. After more than a year in a cobblestoned city, I felt like a bird that had just been released from a cage. To finally be free and in the country again!

In my rapture, I closed my eyes, tipped my head back, and twirled with my arms outstretched, wanting to take in everything, with every sense. It was so glorious! It was so divine! It was so . . . muddy!

My eyes flew open as my feet slipped out from beneath me. I cried out as I hit the ground, my momentum sending me rolling down the embankment. I landed with a splash in the cold water.

Chapter 7

When my head broke free of the water, I shrieked and coughed in a most inelegant fashion. I noticed with alarm that I was moving rapidly away from the house. Even though the water was not very deep, I struggled to find my footing on the rocky bed. Between the slick stones and the current, I failed at my attempt to stand up.

Seeing a large weeping willow up ahead with its branches trailing into the water, I locked my gaze on one branch that looked like it might be sturdier than the rest. When the current swept me within reach, I grabbed the branch and clung to it, kicking frantically until I could reach the bank.

I scrambled up the bank, rolled over, and sprawled on the grass for a moment as I caught my breath. When I stood up, I noticed that among the wet folds of my gown were patches of mud, blades of grass, and soggy leaves. I reached up and felt my hair, which seemed to be hanging in strange configurations, and picked a leaf out of it.

Oh, bother. Now I would have to find a way to look presentable before dinner, and I had probably already spent too much time away. I would have to hurry to make it back in time for dinner. And what if somebody saw me?

I pushed my hair out of my face and walked toward the bridge as quickly as my damp skirts and squelching boots would allow. Why, oh why, did I have to go exploring? And why did I twirl? This was precisely the sort of behavior my grandmother disapproved of. This was why she wanted me to change my ways. After all, what sort of heiress goes falling into rivers?

I had just reached the bridge when I heard the sound of a trotting horse coming from behind me. I whipped around and saw a man on horseback approaching. Not wanting my first impression here to be marred by someone seeing me all wet and muddy, I quickly slipped around the side of the bridge and crouched down, hiding myself in the tall grasses by the river.

I waited tensely as the hoofbeats sounded nearer. Whistling accompanied the sound. Curious, I looked up just as the horse reached the bridge. I was so shocked by what I saw that I reared back and promptly lost my balance. I waved my arms wildly as I tried to resist tipping backward. But my flailing did nothing to save me, and I shrieked as I fell, once again, into the river.

I resurfaced quickly and saw the horse splashing into the water and a hand reaching down toward me.

"Take my hand," came the voice I least wanted to hear.

I refused to look up. "No, thank you." I frantically tried to stand up.

"No, thank you?" the voice repeated, sounding surprised and amused.

I made my way to the other side of the bank, half-walking, half-swimming. I was much more successful at getting myself out of the water this time. No doubt the incentive was much greater. Scrambling up the bank, I said, "I am quite able—" I grunted as I tripped on my wet skirt and sprawled stomach-first in the mud. I got to my feet quickly. "Quite able, I assure you, sir, of walking on my own."

I proved it by walking away from the river as quickly as I could. I heard the sound of the horse coming out of the water and following me. I kept my face turned away, intent on ignoring the man behind me and praying that he had not gotten a good look at my face.

There was the sound of moving leather as he dismounted, and then I felt him walking beside me.

"May I ask what you were doing hiding by the river, Marianne?"

Oh, bother. He *had* recognized me! I glanced up at him. Philip—if that was even his real name—looked even more handsome than he had last night. The sun glinted on his hair, and his eyes sparkled with amusement. And here I was, muddy, with leaves in my hair, and dripping wet. It was too much. No young woman should ever have to be subjected to this much embarrassment.

I lifted my chin, feigning dignity. "I was hiding so that I would not be seen wet and muddy."

He raised an eyebrow. "You were wet and muddy? Before you fell in the river?"

I cleared my throat. "I fell in twice."

He pressed his lips together and looked off in the distance, as if trying to regain his composure. When he looked at me again, his eyes were brimming with laughter. "And may I ask how you came to fall in the river the first time?"

My face burned as I realized how silly I had been, how childish and inelegant. Of course, he already knew those things about me from my actions at the inn last night. Singing that song! Laughing, and then crying! And now falling into a river! I had never been more aware of my faults than I was at that moment.

"I was, er, twirling," I said.

His lips twitched. "I cannot imagine it. You must demonstrate for me."

I glared at him. "I certainly will not. It was not meant for an audience. It was just something I did because . . ." I waved my hand around, at a complete loss for words.

Philip stopped, pulling his horse to a halt beside him, and I turned to face him. He was waiting for a real explanation, I could tell, and I sighed with defeat.

"I just thought it was so lovely," I confessed in a quiet voice. "Everything." I gestured to the view before us. "Rapturous, even. And I was so caught up in it, in how happy I was to be here, to have all of this beauty to look forward to, and so I . . . twirled. And lost my balance." I held my head high and dared him with a look to laugh at me. "I suppose you think that's humorous."

To my surprise, he did not look inclined to laugh. The amusement in his eyes had softened to something nicer. He shook his head and said, "Not at all. In fact, I was just thinking how well I understand the sentiment."

My cheeks grew warm at his soft look, and I had to turn away. I shivered in the light breeze, and Philip quickly shrugged out of his coat and wrapped it around my shoulders. I grasped the lapels and tried not to imagine how I must look, all muddy and wet with my gown clinging to me. Thankfully, Philip's eyes had never strayed below my face. He was obviously more of a gentleman than I had first assumed.

A discreet cough sounded behind me. I turned. It was the coachman who had driven me here. He gestured toward Philip's horse and asked, "Shall I take him for you, sir?"

"Yes, thank you."

Philip handed him the reins, and the man led the horse off toward some buildings on the north side of the house. Those must be the stables, I thought. Then I realized, belatedly, that Philip was *here*, at Edenbrooke. And that the coachman seemed to know him. Suddenly everything became clear to me, like pieces of a puzzle snapping into place. With the puzzle complete, all of the frustration and anger I had felt that morning at the inn resurfaced.

"You live here," I said. It sounded like an accusation.

"Don't be angry with me." Philip's eyes were warm, his smile cajoling.

I smiled sweetly. "Why should I be angry?"

He looked surprised. "That was easier than I had anticipated."

"No, I am asking you a question. Which action are you specifically asking me to not be angry about? Concealing your identity?" I glared at him. "Deceiving me so that I would confide in you? Or could it be your heavy-handed methods of getting me here? Sending your servants to manipulate me into coming on your terms?"

Philip leaned toward me and spoke quietly in my ear. "Your anger might be more impressive if you were to stomp your foot. Perhaps you should try that next time."

I gasped in outrage and pulled away from him. He smiled wickedly.

I took off his coat and shoved it at him, then turned on my heel and strode toward the house, intent on leaving behind that man and the amusement on his face as quickly as I could. Venting my anger had done nothing to diffuse it—it still coursed through me, pounding against my mind with every beat of my quickened pulse. Arrogant, presumptuous, deceitful man!

Betsy shrieked when I walked through the door of my bedchamber.

"What happened to you?"

"I fell into the river."

Her mouth dropped open.

"Please. Don't say a word." I did not want to explain to her my latest embarrassment.

Betsy started pulling leaves and sticks out of my hair while I tried to unfasten my gown, which was that much more difficult for being wet.

"Oh, it will not do!" she said. "There is too much mud. I shall have to wash it."

I groaned in frustration. "Perhaps you can send word that I will be late for dinner."

Betsy ran out of the room, and I continued to try to unfasten my gown. I wished I could blame all of my bad mood on Philip, but the truth was I was equally frustrated and angry with myself. If I had not been so impulsive and childish this would never have happened.

Betsy returned with the news that the cook had already been told to hold dinner half an hour. No doubt that was Philip's doing. Now I would have to think he was thoughtful, and I did not want to think anything nice about him.

My thoughts turned to Philip's little mystery at the inn as Betsy washed and arranged my hair. I wondered why he had worked so hard to conceal his identity. He must have known I would discover it soon enough.

"Betsy, do you know the names of Lady Caroline's children?" She was so good at collecting information.

"Charles, Philip, William, and Louisa," she rattled off.

"In that order?"

She nodded.

It was as I had suspected, then. Philip was the younger brother to Sir Charles, whom Cecily planned to marry. But why did he bother keeping his identity a secret from me? I could think of no good answer.

When I entered the drawing room with damp but tidy hair, Lady Caroline introduced me to her sister, Mrs. Clumpett. She had a genteel air about her and a pleasant face with a mouth that tended to curve upward, so that she looked as if she was always smiling.

Mr. Clumpett stood tall and lean by the fireplace, one finger keeping his place in the book he held. He bowed and said he was pleased to meet me, but his eyes strayed to his book as he spoke.

"Wild animals of India," he said, catching me looking at his book. "Do you know much about them?"

I shook my head.

"You may borrow this when I'm through. It's simply fascinating."

The door opened behind me, and without looking, I knew who it was by the sudden tension in the air.

"Finally," Lady Caroline said.

I turned around and there was Philip, with a little glint of amusement in his eye.

"I believe you two have already met," his mother said.

Philip bowed to me. "Miss Daventry. I trust you had a pleasant journey."

Was he referring to my journey down the river? Probably, if his smile was any indication. I noticed he wore a different coat, which reminded me that I was angry with him, but I also wanted to make a good impression, so I curtsied and said, "Yes, thank you."

Before I had to think of anything more to say, the butler announced dinner. Philip held out his arm to me. I had to take it, but that did not mean I had to enjoy the experience. I found it impossible to enjoy, actually, because his closeness mixed with my anger made me feel awkward and stiff.

As we walked down the hall to the dining room, with his mother behind us, he said in a low voice, "Try taking a deep breath."

I looked up in surprise.

"It might help you relax." He smiled as if he could read every thought in my mind and considered them all highly amusing.

What an obnoxious man! He knew I was uncomfortable and yet he chose to tease me about it! I glared at him before turning my gaze away. I pulled as far away as I could while still touching his arm as he led me to the chair placed at the right hand of the head of the table—the place of honor. Of course, he sat at the head of the table, because he was determined to make me miserable. Well, just because I was sitting next to him didn't mean I had to talk to him.

As we ate dinner, Lady Caroline led the conversation with questions put to me about how I had liked Bath and how my father was faring. I did my best to ignore Philip and gradually found myself relaxing amid the graceful politeness of Lady Caroline and the friendly smiles of Mrs. Clumpett, who was sitting across from me. Actually, she may not have been smiling at all, but merely watching me with her curved mouth. The effect was the same, however.

Mr. Clumpett asked me if I knew about the bird life in Bath, and then he began a very long, one-sided conversation about his favorite birds and their habitats. His wife said something about the birds in India (evidently she had already read the book), and before I knew it they were involved in a happy argument about the Jungle Bush-Quail. I was so entertained by it all that I accidentally glanced at Philip while I was smiling.

It was as if he had been waiting that whole time for my gaze to turn to him. He leaned toward me and, under the noise of the footmen changing courses, he quietly asked, "Won't you forgive me?"

I knew he was asking forgiveness for withholding his identity from me at the inn. By now, most of my anger had been replaced with growing curiosity. After debating within myself for a moment, I finally said, "It would be easier to forgive you if I knew why you did it."

He shook his head. "I can't tell you that."

I narrowed my eyes. "Can't or won't?"

"Both," he said with a little smile.

I found myself wanting to relent, especially when Philip smiled like that. But my pride demanded *something*, however small.

"Then answer me this: Were you making a game of me for your own amusement?"

"No, I was not making a game of you, and no, it was not for my amusement." But as if to belie his words, there was a familiar spark of light in his eyes.

I lifted an eyebrow in disbelief.

His lips twitched as if he was trying to hold back a smile. "That's not to say that I haven't been entertained. But that was not my motive."

I thought of how I had sung that ridiculous song for him and fallen into the river—twice—and how I must have looked earlier, sprawled in the mud while refusing his help. My cheeks burned with renewed embarrassment. No wonder he looked as if he was trying not to laugh. Oh, how my pride stung.

"I'm gratified to know that I provide you with so much entertainment," I said, my voice sharp with sarcasm.

His eyes lit up, just as they had at the inn when I had started my game. "Are you really?" he asked. He leaned closer. "In that case, I will tell my mother that you plan to entertain us all with a song later."

I gasped. "You'd never."

He smiled broadly, then turned to his mother and said, "Mother, I have discovered that Miss Daventry is an accomplished singer. You must persuade her to perform for us later."

She smiled at me. "Oh, yes, we would love to hear you sing."

I clutched my fork in one hand as terror flew through me. "I . . . I am not an accomplished singer. In fact, I rarely sing for other people."

"Let this be an exception, then," Philip said.

Mrs. Clumpett spoke up. "I would dearly love to hear you sing, Miss Daventry. And I will accompany you, if you wish."

I was trapped. In my nervousness, my clear thinking deserted me. "Very well."

Lady Caroline turned to say something to Mrs. Clumpett. I set my fork down and plotted revenge on Philip. The first thing I would do was tell him exactly what I thought of him. But when I looked at him, ready to deliver a scathing diatribe on his horrible manners, he winked at me. The action surprised the words from my lips. The audacity of this man was beyond anything I had known before. I was at a complete and total loss. The only thing I could do was accept my defeat as graciously as possible.

"A hit, sir," I murmured.

"Thank you," he answered with a self-satisfied smile.

I had lost my appetite. The thought of singing in front of everyone had frightened it away. Staring at my plate, I tried to settle the butterflies that were suddenly migrating in my stomach. Singing a little made-up song for Philip, when he knew it was a joke, was one thing. This was completely different. This was not a joke, and I was going to humiliate myself in front of all of these nice people. It was inevitable. There was a reason Grandmother had warned me not to sing.

My heart raced in nervous anticipation, panic streaming through my veins. I picked up my glass but found my hand was shaking too much to carry it safely to my lips. I set it back down. The last thing I needed was to spill my drink down the front of my gown.

"What is wrong?" Philip's voice was low, and his brow knit with concern.

"Nothing," I lied. I stared at my plate, trying to breathe slowly, or at least normally. It wasn't working.

Philip was still watching me. Luckily, no one else seemed to be paying attention. "You're a terrible liar. What is it?"

My face was burning, my stomach in knots. This was only getting worse. I had to tell him. "I can't sing," I whispered.

He looked surprised. "Yes, you can."

I shook my head.

Lady Caroline turned to me. "Marianne, I am so pleased to hear that you are musical. You know, Philip and Louisa are both very musical. I think we shall have many enjoyable evenings here now that you have joined us. Why, perhaps you and Philip could sing a duet!"

Terror seized me. I looked at Philip in mute appeal. His lips twitched, then quivered, then his shoulders shook. I glared at him as he gave up the fight, leaned back in his chair, and laughed out loud. Odious man!

Mrs. Clumpett asked, "Oh, what joke have I missed?"

Philip said in a shaky voice, "I'm afraid we have effectively terrified Miss Daventry. She may run away tonight and never come back."

Lady Caroline's brow wrinkled in consternation. "Philip, please explain yourself."

I was surprised at how stern her voice could sound.

"She doesn't want to sing for us, Mother. I volunteered her without her permission." He chuckled.

Mrs. Clumpett gasped. Mr. Clumpett rubbed a hand over his mouth, as if to remove a smile, and looked at his plate. Lady Caroline looked horrified.

"Philip. It sounds to me as if you've been a terrible host! You have forced our guest into an uncomfortable situation, manipulated us into playing along with your game, and then laughed at her discomfort! And on her first night here!" She glared at him. "I am very disappointed in you."

All my terror changed to gratification upon hearing him rebuked so thoroughly. Philip at least had the decency to look chagrined, his cheeks faintly flushed as he received his scolding.

Lady Caroline turned her attention to me. "You might suppose, based on my son's behavior, that we have no sense of how to honor a guest in our home. Please believe me when I say that Philip's actions do not reflect the values of our family."

I glanced at Philip and noticed his jaw was clenched and his cheeks ruddy. How humiliating to be so scolded in front of a guest. A small bloom of compassion unfolded within me.

"Lady Caroline, I'm afraid you misunderstood. I knew that he was playing a game the whole time. In fact, I am probably responsible for what happened just now." I glanced at him. He was watching me with an arrested expression. "I started this game at the inn last night and this is simply a continuation of it. So if you are angry with your son's behavior as a host then you should also be angry with mine as a guest. I am sorry to have been the cause of such discord."

Lady Caroline listened to my speech with surprise. "Well. If you are not offended, then I will not be angry." Her voice had softened to its normal mildness. She looked from me to Philip in obvious curiosity. "It seems you two understand each other and would get along better without my interference. I apologize for scolding you, Philip."

He smiled affectionately. "Mother, you should never apologize for scolding me. I am sure I would miss it if you ever stopped."

She laughed and I sighed with relief. I did not have to sing, Lady Caroline was not angry, and Philip was not humiliated. Everything was comfortable again. Dessert was brought in, and during the momentary distraction, Philip turned to me with a warm look of gratitude.

"I deserved that rebuke, and you knew it. You should have enjoyed it instead of stepping in to save me." His eyes narrowed as he contemplated me, as if I were a puzzle he could not quite put together. "Why did you do it?"

I shrugged, unable to explain even to myself why I had done it. "Deserved or not, I hated to see you embarrassed."

He looked into my eyes for a quiet moment before leaning closer and saying, "I can see that you are just as powerful an ally as an opponent."

Something passed between us then, in the quiet and the smiles that no one else appeared to notice. An agreement, it seemed. Perhaps even a truce.

Chapter 8

After dinner, we retired to the drawing room. Nobody had to sing, although Mrs. Clumpett did play the pianoforte for a while. While she played, Philip joined me as I stood admiring a landscape hanging on the wall.

It was a view of Edenbrooke from a distant perspective. The artist had captured the grandeur of the building and the vastness of the land surrounding it. Gazing at the scene, I was overcome with a desire to use my own paints. I had not painted in so long—not since my mother died. I would love to paint this place, I thought, where there was so much inherent beauty.

When I looked up at Philip, I discovered he was studying me as intently as I had been studying the painting.

"It's beautiful," I said, nodding toward the painting.

He turned to face me and leaned one shoulder against the wall. "That was precisely what I was thinking."

Did he mean me? I felt myself blush and saw a look of pleasure cross his expression. I wondered if he had only said that to see me blush and, if so, why he would want to do that. I also wondered why I seemed to blush so easily in this particular man's presence. I felt like a schoolgirl again, and it bothered me. I was frowning at the thought when I saw Lady Caroline glance our way, her look sharp with worry.

"Watch out," I said in a quiet voice. "Your mother thinks you're being rude again."

"That's because you're blushing and looking grave. Smile, Marianne, or I'll receive another scolding."

I discovered it was nearly impossible *not* to smile, especially when he looked so highly amused, and leaned toward me when he spoke as if we shared a delightful secret. But I tried to resist.

"You will receive another scolding if your mother hears you calling me Marianne. You know you should not, sir."

"Yes, but my mother's not listening to our conversation right now." He grinned. "So call me Philip."

I glared at him, trying to hide how much I liked his wicked smile. "You only got away with that behavior last night because of your little mystery. I'm sure you normally have better manners than this."

"You're right. I normally do." He took a breath. "But this is not normal, is it?" He looked intently into my eyes, as if searching for something important.

My heart stuttered at his warm look and his quiet voice and his nearness. Once again it struck me that I had never met a gentleman in quite the same league as Philip. I felt stupid with discomfort, and I did not know what to do. I wracked my brain for options.

My first instinct, which was to run away, wouldn't do. I could pretend I hadn't heard him and say something unrelated to his question. But that could leave me looking foolish. I wished Cecily was here to advise me. She had always been better at flirting. Wait—was that what Philip was doing? Flirting? But why would he want to flirt with *me*?

I realized I had taken so long with my own internal discussion that awkwardness now filled in the space where my answer should have been. Why could I not think of a response? Why didn't Philip say something else? I looked toward the pianoforte, wishing for an escape to open before me.

As if he could read my thoughts, Philip leaned away from me and said in a casual tone, "I'm sorry for putting you in such an awkward situation earlier. I had no idea the thought of singing would discomfit you, especially considering your song last night." His eyes held a look of teasing.

I breathed a sigh of relief. This was the sort of conversation I knew how to respond to. Lighthearted I could do. "Last night was different. It was a challenge I couldn't refuse. Besides, you knew it was a joke."

"I wish you could have seen your face when my mother suggested we sing together. I have never seen a look of such pure and absolute terror on anyone." He chuckled. "Tell me something—which were you more afraid of? Being attacked by a highwayman or singing for us?"

"The latter," I said, laughing at myself. "Without a doubt."

"I thought as much. I feel certain there's a very entertaining story behind this fear of singing for people."

I felt my face warm.

"Ah, the telltale blush. Now I'm very curious. Won't you tell me?"

"No, I would rather keep some embarrassing stories to myself."

He laughed again, then gestured toward the pianoforte, and we joined the others, which was a relief to me.

When the evening ended and I lay awake in bed, my thoughts went of their own accord to that intent look in Philip's eyes and his unanswerable question about whether or not this was normal.

It was a very long time before I was able to fall asleep.

Despite my inability to fall asleep quickly, I awoke before the sun the next morning. I wasted no time, but jumped out of bed, threw on a gown, and hurried outside. The morning was glorious, with the sky fading from night to dawn, and a light mist rising off the grass. I ignored the orchard, the bridge, and the rose garden that I had planned on exploring. Instead I walked to the north side of the house, to the buildings I had noticed after I had fallen into the river.

The new morning sunlight streamed through the windows, showing a neat and orderly stable absolutely empty of people. Perfect. I passed several stalls occupied by horses sleeping or quietly munching on oats.

I stopped in front of a stall where a tall black horse looked expectantly over the door, as if waiting for me to come and greet it. I thought it might have been the horse Philip had been riding when I fell into the river, but I wasn't positive because I had tried so hard to avoid looking at him. As I approached the stall, the horse reached out its nose and nuzzled my hand. I smiled in delight.

"What a beauty you are. What's your name?" Affixed to the stall door was a brass plate. "Rowton," I read. "Is that it?" He threw his head up and whinnied as if in acknowledgement. I laughed. "A very well-trained horse, I see. Do you know any other tricks? I wonder what you would do for a little sugar. I wish I had some with me."

"You might try singing to him," Philip said from directly behind me. I jumped a little, then spun around. "I see it's not just cows you have a rapport with."

I wondered how long he had been standing there. "I did not think anyone else would be here," I explained sheepishly.

"Neither did I." He came to stand next to me and looked directly into my eyes. His smile felt like a gift meant just for me. "Good morning," he said in a voice that matched the quiet of the stable and the warm friendliness in his eyes.

I did not know how to respond to that warmth and quiet. I was clearly just as hopeless as I had been last night. The only thing I could think to do was to retreat into formality.

"Good morning, sir," I said, dropping a curtsy. "I hope you don't mind my visiting your horses."

He lifted an eyebrow. "I don't mind at all. But I will throw you out immediately if you call me 'sir' one more time."

I laughed a little and relaxed into the informality he seemed to insist on and prefer.

Philip reached into his pocket and handed me a sugar cube. Rowton lipped it from my hand. I rubbed the horse's muzzle, and the soft skin with short whiskers tickled my palm. A small sigh escaped me. It had been too long since I had last been in a stable.

I felt Philip's gaze on my face and looked up at him. He was studying me, just as he had the night before, when I had been looking at the painting. It made me aware of the fact that I had spent less than three minutes attending to my appearance this morning. Philip, on the other hand, had a freshly shaven jaw, and his wavy hair was slightly damp. I also noticed he was carrying a riding crop.

"Are you going for a ride?" I asked.

"I am. Would you like to join me?"

I took a deep breath and nodded before I could lose my courage. "I would. If you don't mind."

"Not at all. I keep a couple of gentle mares for my mother and sister. I am sure they wouldn't mind if you rode one."

I smiled to myself. If I was going to do this, I would do it properly. "What would I do with a gentle mare? Invite her to tea?"

Philip's head reared back a little with surprise. Then he chuckled. "What was I thinking? Of course you wouldn't want a gentle mare. In that case, I think I may have the perfect horse for you."

He led me down the aisle to another stall and introduced me to Meg. She was a light chestnut-colored filly with a delicate face and nice proportions.

"What is she? Fifteen hands?" I asked.

Philip nodded.

She was the same size as my horse. I quickly banished the thought from my mind. It had been a very long time since I had allowed myself to

L

JULIANNE DONALDSON

think about my horse. It seemed disrespectful, in a way, to miss her when I missed my mother so much more. Turning my thoughts away from what once was, I studied Meg closely. She looked absolutely perfect.

I nodded, hiding my delight behind a straight face. "I suppose she'll do."

Philip said he would have the horses readied while I changed. I ran back to my room and, with Betsy's help, changed into my dark blue riding habit.

"Lucky for you it still fits," she said. "Don't understand why you refused to try it on before you left Bath."

I smoothed the skirt as I looked in the mirror, taking a deep breath. Trying on the riding habit had seemed too monumental before. My hand moved to my neck before I remembered that the locket was gone. I dropped my hand to my side, wishing for something to hold onto, but all I had was what I saw in the mirror. I squared my shoulders. It would have to be sufficient, then.

When I returned to the stable, Meg was saddled and waiting for me at the mounting block. A groom stood at her head next to Philip.

"That was quick," Philip said approvingly, then nodded at Meg. "Up you go."

Meg shifted impatiently as I settled into the saddle. Perhaps my nervousness was apparent to her. It was nothing more than a fluttering in my chest, but the fact that it existed at all seemed both strange and justifiable to me.

For most of my life I had preferred the back of a horse to any other seat. But I had not ridden since the accident. I held the reins in one gloved hand, leaned forward and spoke quietly to Meg while stroking her neck. Her ears turned back as she listened to me, and after a moment, the fluttering in my chest and Meg's restless shifting had both subsided. I could tell that we were going to be fast friends.

The sun broke over the treetops as we set off toward the south end of the estate. Philip held his horse to a trot and rode next to me. The groom rode several paces behind us, at the discreet distance of a chaperone.

When we reached a wide stretch of open field, I asked Philip, "Is there any reason we're going so slowly?"

70

His bright, easy smile flashed. "None at all."

I let Meg have her head, and she sprang into a gallop. It was exhilarating to feel the crisp morning air rushing past me. I knew I had missed this, but I did not know how much until now. I felt like something of myself flew back into me with the wind and the horses and the bright morning sky. Eventually the open ground ended at the woods, and we reined in our horses.

"How do you like her?" Philip asked, nodding toward Meg.

"She's perfect." And she really was. "Just spirited enough to keep it interesting without being difficult to manage. And so beautiful." I patted her neck and flashed him a smile. "A gentle mare would have never been able to keep up with you."

He smiled too, but as if at a private thought. "You are absolutely right."

I wondered what secret lurked beneath his smile.

The morning sun had cleared off the mist from the land, and I was eager to see everything I could.

"Will you show me the estate?" I asked. "It looks magnificent from what I've seen of it."

"With pleasure." He turned his horse and I followed him to a knoll with a lone tree atop it. We could see almost all of the estate from here.

"What a fine prospect," I remarked. We were on the wilder side of the estate, looking down at the house. The tailored lawns and gardens were backed by the river and the wooden bridge spanned it gracefully. Something about this view rang with familiarity. After a moment of thought, I placed it. This was the same perspective as that depicted in the painting in the drawing room.

Admiration turned again to my desire to paint this scene myself, and I vowed to find some painting supplies and come back here on my own.

Philip began to point out the boundaries of Edenbrooke. From our vantage point, we could see for miles in all directions. It appeared to be a prosperous estate, without any sign of neglect. My estimation of Sir Charles grew. He must be a skilled landlord to manage everything so well.

Of course, Cecily would only set her sights on the best of the best. I was more than a little curious to meet him. Lady Caroline had not mentioned his plans, but I assumed he would arrive in a week with Cecily and Louisa.

When we turned to head back, Philip said, "Shall we see how these two match up? I'll race you back to the stables."

Meg gave it her all, but Philip's horse looked like a blackbird, his hooves barely skimming the ground as he flew over it.

"That wasn't even close," I complained when we reached the stables.

He grinned. "I know. I had an unfair advantage." He patted his horse's neck. "He was bred to be a racehorse—he has the blood of the Godolphin stallion in him."

"He is magnificent." I looked admiringly at the pair of them. There was something about a handsome man astride a powerful horse that made my heart skip.

"Do you ride every morning?" I asked after we had left the horses with the groom and were walking back to the house.

"Yes, nearly. And you?"

"No. My grandmother doesn't keep horses in Bath. I had to settle for a brisk walk—with a chaperone, of course." I grimaced at the thought of returning to that life.

"I'll have to amend that practice while you're here. Consider Meg yours any time you want her."

"Do you mean it?" I tried not to sound as eager as I felt.

"I do. You're well-suited to each other: spirited enough to make it interesting without being difficult to manage." He winked as I narrowed my eyes at him. Comparing me to a horse! What nerve!

We reached the house and he stopped to open the door for me.

"And so beautiful," Philip said as I passed him.

I cast him a disparaging glance, and he laughed, as if he had said that only to see my reaction. Philip Wyndham was an incorrigible flirt, and I did not like that about him. Not one bit.

Chapter 9

At breakfast, Lady Caroline announced that she would be busy all morning. Having just returned from a month in London, she expected to be called on by all of her neighbors, and she was sure I would not want to spend my morning sitting in the drawing room. She was right, but I still felt obligated to insist.

"I wouldn't mind meeting your neighbors," I said.

She waved a hand, shooing away my good intention. "Some other time, my dear. But I wouldn't dream of leaving you alone on your first day here. Philip, do you mind changing your plans? You can make up for your bad behavior last night by giving our guest a tour of the house."

Philip cast an amused look at his mother, who smiled back at him with an air of innocence. "I would be happy to," he said.

"Oh, may I join you?" Mrs. Clumpett asked, looking up from her plate with a smear of eggs across her upper lip. "I missed my morning walk with my husband, and I do feel it is important to have some form of exercise every day."

I smiled at her. "Please do." Now it seemed less of an imposition and more of a joint adventure.

I had seen most of the first floor, so we started on the second floor, which consisted mostly of bedchambers, similar in elegance and comfort to mine. Philip was behaving himself so well—being nice and friendly without flirting at all—that by the time we reached the third floor, I felt almost completely comfortable in his company.

Mrs. Clumpett exclaimed in soft tones of amazement over every room we stopped at as if viewing it for the first time. I found it impossible not to smile in her company, and credited her presence for Philip's proper behavior. He even referred to me as "Miss Daventry."

On the third floor, we came to a long gallery bearing paintings on each wall. I followed Philip's lead and stopped in front of the family portraits. The landscapes I would come and look at later on my own, when I would have time to really enjoy them.

I looked at one portrait after another as Philip identified his various ancestors. I learned that his great-great-great-grandmother had insisted on calling the place "Edenbrooke" because she thought it was as beautiful as the Garden of Eden. After viewing a long line of distant relatives, we stopped at the portraits of his immediate family. There was Lady Caroline, years younger, and quite a striking beauty. Next to her hung a painting of a distinguished-looking man with the same wavy brown hair as Philip.

"My father," Philip said, his voice hushed.

Philip's father was not a particularly handsome man, but there was a quiet, serious expression in his eyes that made me pause and look at him again. "He looks kind," I remarked, finally identifying the look of his countenance.

Philip nodded. "He was."

I looked at the rest of the group, recognizing a younger Philip. The girl in the painting next to his must be his sister Louisa, who had become such good friends with Cecily. Philip pointed to a portrait of a young man with light hair and a bright, carefree smile. "My younger brother, William. He is coming with his wife, Rachel, in just a few days."

They were the ones that Cecily and Louisa were staying with in London.

There was one portrait left. "And who is he?" I asked, noting he had the same jawline as Philip, but there was a languid expression about his blue eyes, as though he was bored with life.

"My eldest brother, Charles," he answered curtly. Philip turned his gaze from the painting to me. In his eyes was a look so grave, and so regretful, that I had the distinct impression he had lost something he valued very much. The impression was fleeting, though, and by the time I recognized it, it was gone, and Philip had turned back to the painting. I was almost convinced I had imagined it entirely.

I stole a quick glance at Philip to compare him to his brother. Even though they were both handsome men, Sir Charles had a look about him that made him seem unapproachable. In contrast, there was something so very likeable about Philip's countenance. He was both handsome and friendly, and, in comparing the two, I had no trouble deciding which one I would prefer to spend my time with.

Pausing before the painting, a thought flitted through my mind. This man—this Sir Charles—who was completely unknown to me at this moment, was the man my twin sister would marry. It was as good as done in my mind, for Cecily had never failed to achieve something once she set her mind to it. And she was not one to easily change her mind.

That would make Sir Charles like a brother to me, and Philip . . . well, Philip would be like a brother to me as well. We would be family, connected by Cecily and Charles's marriage. I found myself smiling at the thought. I had never had a brother, but I thought I could imagine Philip excelling in that role.

Mrs. Clumpett was still examining the landscapes when Philip turned from the portraits and motioned for me to follow him down the hall. He stopped in front of a door on my left, which led into a large room with wooden floors.

"It's a fencing room," I said, noting the epees lined up inside the case on the opposite wall. I liked the echoing sound of our footsteps in the empty room and its lofty ceiling, lit from above by high windows. I sighed with pleasure and a touch of envy. "I have always wanted to fence."

I immediately regretted my words. That was precisely the sort of thing that an elegant young lady would not say; Grandmother would be appalled.

But Philip did not look appalled—only curious. "Why this unholy interest in a man's activity?" he asked with a smile.

"It seems like men are permitted to do so many fun activities—like fencing and hunting—while ladies are supposed to sit quietly in the house and practice their embroidery all day." I cast him a pained look. "Do you have any idea how boring it is to *embroider*?"

"Actually, I don't," he said, with an amused smile. "But then again, I've never given it much thought."

"Well, let me assure you that there is nothing exciting about embroidery. But fencing, on the other hand . . ." I looked at him appraisingly, wondering how bold I dared be with him.

He raised an eyebrow. "What scheme are you plotting?"

I considered the odds and decided it was worth a try. "I was wondering, since my father will not teach me, and I don't have any real brothers, if you might . . . perchance . . . teach me how to fence?"

"Any *real* brothers?" Philip stared at me with a look that was part frustration and part amusement. "Am I correct in assuming you've chosen me to play the role of a *pretend* brother?"

I bit my lip. It was clear I had offended him. Of course it would seem very presumptuous of me, especially considering our short acquaintance, to think of him as family. But I could not explain my thoughts to him—I did not dare reveal Cecily's plan to snare his older brother.

I tried to cover my embarrassment by smiling innocently. "Would you mind?"

His smile twisted, taking on an edge of mocking. "I already have a sister, Marianne."

I cringed inwardly. It was just as bad as I had feared. My offense was obvious, and I felt stupid—so *stupid*—to have said what I did. Asking him to teach me how to fence? What young lady did that? And to assume a familiarity that he did not return? I burned with humiliation.

"Pardon me," I said. "I should not have presumed . . ." I cleared my throat. "Please excuse me. I am sure you have better things to do today than entertain me."

Turning on my heel, I hurried to the door, wishing the floor would open up and swallow me whole. I had made it across the wide room and had my hand on the door handle when he spoke.

"I'm disappointed in you, Marianne."

I froze with my hand on the door.

"I never thought you would give up so easily. Especially after just one paltry set-down."

I turned around, my pride responding to the challenge in his voice. I was not one to scamper away with fright. Especially not when handed a challenge. Lifting my chin, I said, "I am not giving up. I am going to ask Mr. Clumpett to teach me how to fence."

It was a lie, and I was sure Philip knew it, but he smiled as he moved toward me. "Ah, but do you really dare face him with a weapon in his hand? Wasn't dining with him dangerous enough?"

I bit back a laugh as I recalled the moment of alarm when Mr. Clumpett had launched his fork into the air while demonstrating the flight pattern of a certain species of bird.

"You may be right," I said in an unsteady voice, my lips twitching.

Philip grinned. "I have a better idea," he said, reaching behind me for the door handle.

I did not move, trapped as I was between Philip and the door. Tipping my head back, I looked into his friendly eyes, my pride draining from me along with my embarrassment. I had a feeling that no matter what his idea was, I would want to say yes to it.

"What?" I asked, smiling without reservation.

"Why don't you join me for a game of chess? It's not as exciting as fencing, but it can't possibly be as boring as embroidery."

I had been right. I did want to say yes to him. I was surprised at myself, for holding a grudge was one of my greatest strengths, or weaknesses, depending on how one looked at it. But a game of chess with Philip sounded like the most pleasant way to pass the afternoon.

"I would like that," I said. "Where are we to play?" I asked as we left the fencing room.

"You will see," he said, smiling at his aunt as she joined us at the top of the stairs. "I have saved the best of the tour for last."

⚜

The library was tucked away on the main floor, down a short hall across from the drawing room. We had to turn a corner from the hall to find the door to the library, and when Philip opened it for me, I felt as if I had been granted entry into a hidden sanctuary.

It was definitely a man's room—the furniture was rich brown leather in straight lines, and a stone fireplace dominated one wall. Bookshelves embraced the room on every side. At the end of the room, farthest from the door, was an alcove with two leather chairs and a small table between them, which faced a large window that stretched from the floor to the high ceiling. The window filled the room with light and framed a view of the southeast side of the estate.

I walked slowly into the serene, sunlit space, hardly noticing that Mrs. Clumpett had excused herself and barely registering the maid who stood in a far corner, removing books, dusting covers and spines, and then quietly returning them to their places. I stroked the back of a chair, gazed out the window, and turned in a slow circle, trying to take it all in. I was so captivated I did not even feel the least desire to twirl. To do so would have been irreverent, somehow.

"You like it," Philip said, smiling.

I shook my head. "No, I love it." I gestured to the bookshelves. "Do you mind?"

"Help yourself," he said, settling gracefully into one of the chairs by the window. He looked pleased.

I looked at the titles on the nearest bookshelf and found a book on Greek mythology next to a book of poetry, which was flanked by a book on German philosophy. "How are these organized?"

"They're not."

I turned to him. "How do you find anything? There must be thousands of books here."

"I like the search. It's like visiting old friends."

I studied him for a moment, intrigued by what he had just revealed about himself. Philip fit in this room as if it were a set of well-worn, comfortable clothes. I noticed with a twinge of admiration that he looked elegant even lounging in his chair, with his long legs stretched out before him. Catching a look of amusement on his face, I realized that I had been staring at him—again.

"You look surprised, Marianne."

"I am," I said frankly.

He smiled as if he liked my answer.

I returned to my perusal of his books and lost myself in the task. Unorganized like this, every step led to a surprise. I saw several books I wanted to look at more closely later, including a history of French politics and a book on gothic architecture. I was so absorbed in my reverie that I jumped a little when Philip spoke again. I had almost forgotten he was there.

"I'm curious about something," he said. "What were you doing in Bath?"

I walked to the chair across from his and sat down. "My father sent me to live with my grandmother after my mother died."

"And how did you feel about that arrangement?"

It surprised me that he would ask such a personal question after our morning of impersonal conversation. I sighed. My feelings were too complex to delve into, so I picked the simplest one as an answer. "I missed my home."

"What did you miss about it?" His tone was quiet and the room was hushed, the sky outside growing overcast.

I picked at a thread on my skirt. The maid was still dusting books in the far corner of the room; she would probably be at it all day and for many more days to come, considering the number of books on the shelves. She was too far away to hear us clearly, but that was not what made me hesitate to confide in Philip. Trust did not come easily to me, and I was not sure I was ready to confide in this man who was unlike anyone I had ever known before.

I had worked so hard these past fourteen months to build up layers around my heart, to shield myself from the wounds it bore, that I wasn't sure I knew how to open it anymore. I didn't know if I even wanted to open it. The very thought frightened me, and I had to seriously consider whether this was worth the risk of making myself vulnerable.

Philip waited patiently for my answer, as if he would give me all the time I needed. He could be a friend to me until Cecily arrived. I enjoyed his company, and, I admitted to myself, I needed a friend. Perhaps a friend would be worth the risk.

Taking a deep breath, I finally said, "I missed everything. My family, of course, but also my home, my land, my neighbors and friends. Everything." I gestured out the window. "I was thinking about how I even missed our orchard. I used to go there a lot, to paint, or to read, or just to be by myself."

"Why the orchard?" Philip asked. It was another question that required a personal and honest answer. He seemed intent on uncovering as much of my heart as he could.

"I haven't exactly thought about it before now—at least, not enough to put words to it." I studied the orchard. The sky was gray, and the colors of the trees were muted. Under the vastness of the sky, the group of small trees was like an embrace, a protective space.

"There's something solid and constant about trees." I said quietly. "They may change through the seasons, but they're always there. They're dependable. And the orchard is not so vast as the woods. It's just big enough to hold me when I . . ." I stopped, unsure of how to complete the thought.

"When you what?"

"When I need to be held, I suppose." I laughed self-consciously, embarrassed a little by what I had admitted. "That sounds odd. But sometimes I want to be away from other people, and I feel safe there." I looked quickly at him, anxious for his reaction. For once, there was no hint of teasing in his expression as he studied me.

"It's your sanctuary," he said simply. "That doesn't sound odd at all."

I hadn't realized I was tense until I felt my shoulders relax in relief. I nodded. It was a rare thing to be understood so quickly—and not merely understood, but accepted. I sensed that in his response. It made me want to tell him more.

"Our orchard at home is not as big as the one here at Edenbrooke," I continued. "But the trees are just as thick and old. I used to hide there when I was in trouble as a child. I would climb right up, as high as I could, and my governess would stand below and yell at me to come down."

Philip looked amused. "And did you?"

"Come down? Not as long as she was standing there. One day she brought a chair from the house and sat down in it with a book as if she would spend all day there waiting for me if she had to. I was too stubborn to give in—"

Philip raised an eyebrow.

I laughed. "Yes, it's one of my faults of which I have never been cured. Well, I refused to come down, and she refused to leave, so I sat up in that tree for most of the day. I finally had to come down because I had eaten so many apples that I had a horrible stomachache and couldn't hold myself up any longer.

"My governess thought she had won our little contest of wills, and had a terribly smug look on her face as she marched me into the house. But my mother took one look at me doubled over in pain and gave her such a severe scolding that she packed her bags and left the next day. I felt terrible about that, and apologized to my mother for my stubbornness. Of course, I still received a scolding for my actions, but only once we were alone. That was one thing I always liked about my mother. She never scolded me when other people were there to witness my shame."

"You're like her in that way. I can understand why you would appreciate that quality so much."

I was puzzled for a moment.

"You rescued me last night from a scolding as well, remember?"

"Oh, that was nothing," I said.

He shook his head. "Not to me."

I looked away from the sincerity in his eyes, not knowing what to say in response.

"I'm sorry I never met your mother," he said. "What was she like?"

I wished for my locket, so that I might show him her picture, so he would not think I exaggerated. But words would have to suffice. "She was exquisitely beautiful, with striking blue eyes and skin like porcelain. Her hair was so light it was almost white. When I was a little girl, and she came into my room at night to tuck me in, I thought her hair looked just like moonlight." I paused, remembering her beauty. "My sister Cecily looks very much like her. I . . . do not." I smiled in a gesture for pardon. "I'm afraid I'm quite plain in comparison."

Philip shook his head. "I think you are taking modesty too far. I couldn't disagree with you more."

I immediately regretted that I had brought up the subject of beauty with Philip, who had already proven himself to be an incorrigible flirt. He was undoubtedly only saying what he thought I wanted to hear.

"I am not too modest," I said, hot with embarrassment. "And I didn't say that in the hope that you would contradict me. I simply stated a fact in response to your question."

Philip's lips twitched. "Forgive me," he said. "I didn't realize a compliment would offend you so. I will try not to do it again."

I struggled to press my own lips into a firm line. The amusement in Philip's eyes was too infectious to resist, though, and I laughed reluctantly. "I'm sorry I reacted that way."

"Don't apologize," he said, stretching his arms and folding them behind his head. "It is so refreshing to be treated with contempt."

I laughed again. "It is not."

"Yes, it is," he insisted. "I can't tell you how much I enjoy it." He grinned as if he really did enjoy it.

"Now you're being absurd."

"Actually, I am quite serious. But knowing your stubborn streak . . ." I cast him a dark look and he chuckled. "I'll let it drop for now. Tell me— besides your beauty, what else have you inherited from your mother?"

I chose to ignore the first part. "She taught me how to paint. She was a talented artist, much more talented than I am. And she loved to ride. She took me riding nearly every day, early in the morning, and she was such a bounding rider that she would take any jump fearlessly, no matter how high it looked—" I flinched at the words I had spoken, surprised that they had escaped me.

"Is that how she died?" Philip asked, his tone respectful.

I looked out the window. I nodded, keeping my gaze on the orchard, imagining I was safely encircled there right now.

"Were you with her?"

I cleared my throat to speak past the lump that was suddenly there. "No. I didn't ride with her that morning. My father found her. I am sure you can imagine the rest easily enough."

After a long pause, Philip said, "Actually, I cannot."

I looked at him in surprise.

He studied me for a moment, as if choosing his words. "I cannot imagine why your father would take everything from you right after you lost your mother—your home, your family, your friends, his protection and care."

Philip's words pierced me so sharply, so suddenly, that I felt almost breathless from the pain. He had found so easily what I had been hiding at the very core of my heart. This was why I did not open my heart. This was why I kept it bandaged so tightly. It had been foolish of me to think I could safely unbind it.

My eyes pricked with sudden tears. I stood and walked to the window, keeping my back to Philip. The sky was turning dark gray, clouds rolling together. It would rain soon. I pressed my hand against the glass. It felt cool and soothed the aching wounds on my palm. I wished I could as easily find a balm for the ache in my heart.

I saw Philip's reflection in the window as he came to stand behind me. I felt his warmth at my back, and I was hot and cold in the same moment. Part of me wanted to lean into the cool glass of the window, away from him, and the rest of me wanted to lean against him, into his warmth.

Chapter 10

"I'm sorry," Philip said in a hushed voice as he stood behind me.

I didn't know if he felt sorry for what had happened or for asking me about it, but it didn't matter. My defenses were already up. It had been a mistake to make myself vulnerable. Now I wanted to run from this room and go somewhere far away from this man who made me say things I didn't want to say and feel things I didn't want to feel. I stepped aside so I was no longer trapped between him and the window and turned around.

"Are you ready to play chess?" I asked in a brisk voice. "Or should we save it for another day?" I did not meet his gaze, and I was already turned toward the door. My emotions were too close to the surface, and I needed to be alone to put them back in their proper places. I was ready to run away.

But then Philip touched my arm. "Wait," he said.

I turned back to him reluctantly.

"Are you hungry?" he asked.

"Actually, yes, I am." I hadn't even realized it.

"Will you excuse me for a few minutes? Please, make yourself comfortable."

I watched him walk away with mixed emotions. I was still balanced between hot and cold. I had not decided which way I would fall—away from Philip or toward him. But now that he had left, I did not feel the desire to run away, and so I stayed and waited for his return.

Choosing a book of poetry from the bookshelf, I sat in a chair by the window and tried to shake off my unsettled mood. I lost myself in the poetry, and when the door opened again, I was surprised to see by the clock on the mantel that half an hour had passed.

Philip brought in a tray loaded with food, which he set on the small table between our chairs.

"I hope you appreciate what I went through," he said. "You should have heard the scolding I received from the cook for raiding her pantry. I was terrified."

I laughed, relieved that he had returned in a less serious mood. "You were not."

"I was," he said with a grin. "There's something about servants who have watched you grow up—they never hesitate to treat you like a child, no matter how old you are." He picked up a plate. "What would you like?"

"Oh, I can do that." I set down the book and reached for the plate, but he held it back.

"Nonsense. Allow me to serve you. A little of everything?" His eyes twinkled as he smiled at me, and I was surprised by both his gesture and his look.

"Yes, thank you," I said, watching him as he filled the plate with fresh fruits, bread, cold ham, and cheese. I took the food from him with a teasing smile. "You're not going to insist on feeding me as well, I trust."

"I would if I thought you would let me," he murmured.

My face grew hot at the look he cast me from under his lashes.

"Ah, there it is," he said. "I've missed your blush this past half hour."

I glared at him. "I think you do that on purpose."

He chuckled. "What?"

"Make me blush."

"It's the easiest work I've ever done," he said shamelessly. "And the most enjoyable."

I sat there feeling hot and irritated while he poured lemonade into a glass and held it out toward me.

"Thank you," I muttered, reaching for it.

Philip held onto the glass after I had wrapped my hand around it, and I looked up. I was surprised to see his expression completely serious.

"Don't think because I like to tease you that I don't take you seriously," he said in a quiet voice. "It is an honor to know what's in your heart, Marianne."

I was so taken aback that I would have dropped the glass if he hadn't still been holding on to it. He set it down on the table and began to dish food onto his plate without looking at me. Would he ever do something predictable? I doubted it. I felt off-balance, yet at the same time flattered for a reason I couldn't name. I was at a loss as to what to say or do.

I stared at my plate until Philip said, "It's food, Marianne. You're supposed to eat it."

My eyes flew to his face. The amusement I saw there was irresistible. I laughed and started to eat, feeling comfortable once again—extremely comfortable, in fact. I curled my legs beneath me and looked out the window, content to eat in silence and watch the steady fall of rain. It surrounded the room with a hushing sound and blocked out the rest of the world, hiding the land and orchard from view.

"What a wonderful room," I said. "How long did it take to build up this collection?"

"Only a few generations, actually. My grandfather had a passion for books. Probably half of what you see came from him. My father added to it every time he traveled to the Continent. He was always on the lookout for unique books. When he came home, he would invite me in here to look at the new titles. It felt almost as if I had been on his travels with him."

I caught a little nostalgic smile in Philip's eyes.

"And then, when I was on Tour, I found myself drawn to little book-stores everywhere I went. I came home a year later with dozens of boxes of books. We arrived just in time, the books and I." His voice grew quiet. "I was able to show them to my father before he died. It was like one last travel for him."

I was intrigued by the reverence in Philip's voice. "What was your father like?"

Philip leaned back in his chair. "He was generous and quick to for-give. He was a man of principle, of high moral character. He was respected by all who knew him." He glanced at me. "He was a gentleman, in every sense of the word."

"And you want to be just like him." I could see it in his countenance.

"Of course," he said.

I suddenly realized that my insult when I met him at the inn must have been especially cutting. "I didn't know—when I said what I did at the inn—I didn't know what it would mean to you. I must have offended you deeply. I am sorry."

He smiled ruefully. "I have never needed an insult more than I did that night. Please don't apologize for it."

I watched Philip intently, drawn to his easy smile and the way his eyes softened when he spoke of his father. All I knew about him were the few little crumbs he had cast my way. I was hungry for more.

"What books did you bring back from your Tour?" I asked.

"Anything that caught my eye. I wasn't as selective as my father. He read mostly philosophy and religion. I picked up histories and mythol-ogy and poetry." He gestured to the book I had been looking at earlier. "I found that one in a tiny bookstore in Paris that my father had told me about. The owner knew my father from his numerous trips there. He had a shelf of philosophy books that he pointed me to, and I think he was quite surprised when I bought the poetry instead."

I smiled at the picture he had painted. "What else did you do on your Tour?"

Philip spread his hands. "A year of traveling around Europe is difficult to sum up."

"Then don't sum it up. Tell me everything." I blushed at how eager and demanding I sounded. "I didn't mean to say it like that. It's just . . ." I shook my head and didn't know if I should even go on.

But Philip asked, "What is it?" and he looked so curious that I tried to finish my thought.

"It's different in Bath. I have only my grandmother and aunt for companions. My grandmother talks only if she has a criticism to make, and my aunt has more hair than wit. We never go out much in society because my grandmother doesn't like people. So I've been rather starved for good conversation."

"I imagine it's more than conversation you've been missing. Haven't you also been starved for friendship?" He said it with a soft look around his eyes, and my pride flared suddenly.

"I didn't say that to make you feel sorry for me. And I don't want friendship if it's based on pity." My voice sounded sharper than I had intended.

Philip studied me for a minute. I held his gaze with defiance.

"I understand that better than you may believe," he finally said. His words effectively disarmed me.

"Do you?" I asked, surprised.

He looked pensively out the window. "You don't want to be loved for your misfortune; I don't want to be loved for my possessions. Are we not similar in that way?"

When he turned his gaze to me, his expression reminded me of how he had looked when showing me the portrait of his elder brother, Charles. The look of loss in his eyes tugged at my heart, daring me to ask a question.

"Did somebody love you for your possessions?"

Philip should have looked offended by my personal question, but instead he smiled a little and asked, "Did somebody love you for your misfortunes?"

"No."

"But you're afraid someone might."

I nodded, thinking of how I hated imposing on others simply because I depended on them.

"Then we're similar in that way too." His gaze held mine and understanding passed between us in a look.

"Well, then," I said. I watched Philip's lips curl into a smile at the same time that mine did.

He leaned toward me and said in a low voice, "I promise not to love you for your misfortunes."

I blushed at the idea of saying the words "promise" and "love you" in the same sentence . . . to Philip. But I had to return the vow. Anything else would be rude.

"And I promise not to love you for your possessions."

There. I had said it. I felt daring and bold. Maybe that was why I had the strange urge to grin. My cheeks ached with the effort of forcing my mouth into a moderate smile. I picked up the book as a distraction.

"I would still like to hear more about your Tour. Unless I'm keeping you from something?"

"I am wholly at your disposal, Marianne, but I wouldn't want to bore you with stories of my travels."

"Bore me?" I stared at him. "Philip. I have never been outside of England. I've never even been to London. Do you know what I would give for your experiences? How could you possibly think you would bore me?"

He didn't answer, but there was such a look of delight in his eyes that I had to ask, "Why are you looking at me like that?"

"You called me Philip. For the first time."

I blushed. It was true; I had called him by his Christian name. But surely it wasn't my fault. He was the one who insisted on calling me Marianne and told me to stop calling him *sir*.

"It's only because your horrible manners are rubbing off on me," I muttered.

He laughed. "I am glad to hear it."

I didn't know how to answer, but thankfully I didn't have to because Philip asked, "Where shall I begin?"

"Paris."

Philip told me more about the little bookstore where he had found the book of poetry, then about the palace at Versailles and the balls and assemblies he had attended. He told me about the Notre Dame Cathedral, and then he walked to the bookshelf, looking around vaguely for a minute.

I went to the spot where I had been browsing before and pulled out the book on gothic architecture. "Was this what you were looking for?"

He flashed a smile at me as he took the book and set it on the table in front of us. He pointed out the various features he had seen on the Cathedral, turning pages rapidly, his voice growing rich with interest.

From Paris, he moved to Italy—Venice and Rome and Florence. He stood again and this time searched for a few minutes before coming back with a book of sketches. He handed it to me and let me look through them at my leisure, pointing to statues he had seen, talking about the artists and the preservation of the work. He told me about Italian operas, and the time he had stayed in a villa on the coast where the water was so clear that he could see to the bottom of the ocean.

After Italy came Austria and Switzerland—the Alps, the songs, the beautiful countryside. And more books. He brought me a book on Bavaria and a book of traditional Austrian folksongs. I asked him to sing one for me. His voice was low and rich and easy to listen to, not forced or unnatural. It was a very pleasant sound.

As Philip talked, his eyes lit up. He gestured with his hands as he spoke, and when he smiled, his whole face was bright and captivating. After a while I didn't have to ask questions. He just talked, and I could sit there with my chin on my hand, feasting on stories and images and ideas foreign to my own. Philip opened up worlds to me with his words. I had no sense of time, and the overcast sky hid the passage of the sun from view, entrapping us in one endless, enchanted moment.

I only noticed the outside world when Philip paused at the end of a story and I heard voices outside the library. They pierced the bubble I had been suspended in, and I felt the world and time rush back at me. I did not want it to come back. I wanted to pull myself back into the hours that had just passed. I wanted to shut the door and let the rain go on and keep myself right here for forever. But Philip paused, and his silence marked the end of our time together.

"I love this room," I said with a sigh, reluctant to leave.

"You're welcome here any time."

"This is your sanctuary." I knew as soon as I had seen Philip in here that this was his orchard. "I wouldn't want to intrude."

"Not even if I asked you to?" he asked with a smile.

"Oh. Well . . ." I didn't know how to respond. I blushed at my own awkwardness. "You're too kind."

"I'm not too kind. The library is for everyone, and you should consider yourself free to come here whenever you like."

"Thank you. And thank you for spending the day with me. I can't remember when I've enjoyed a day more . . . not in a long time."

He reached a hand across the small space between our chairs. I put mine in it naturally, instinctively. He leaned toward me, his blue eyes twinkling, his smile as warm as a patch of sunlight. "The pleasure was all mine, Marianne."

I felt trapped in his gaze. I was suddenly overcome with the sensation that if I looked deeply enough into Philip's eyes I would find a beautiful, important secret. I drew in a breath, and as I did, I leaned closer. The sensation grew stronger, convincing me that it was only the distance between us that was keeping me from uncovering the truth. If I leaned toward him, something would happen. I was sure of it. But if I leaned away, nothing would happen. So I stayed perfectly still, balanced between something and nothing, not knowing which way I wanted to fall.

Philip stayed perfectly still, too, as though waiting for me to decide. His eyes, though, were not standing by like impartial witnesses to my decision. His eyes were persuading me that I wanted that *something*. They were inviting me closer, drawing me closer, convincing me to lean, to fall, to dive into their blue depths and never resurface.

"Oh, pardon me." Mr. Clumpett's voice suddenly broke over me.

I startled, as if awakened from a dream, and pulled my hand out of Philip's grip. The sensation I had experienced vanished like smoke from a snuffed candle, leaving behind wisps of nameless longing.

Of course Philip had left the door to the library open. He was such a gentleman that way. But I wondered what his uncle had seen. Had he seen me gazing into Philip's eyes for that long moment? My cheeks burned at the thought.

Philip stood and turned toward Mr. Clumpett, who had halted a few steps inside the room.

Mr. Clumpett cleared his throat. "Didn't realize you two were having a *tête-à-tête* in here. The door was open, you know." His eyes flicked to the maid in the corner, who had been diligently dusting all afternoon.

"Yes, I know," Philip said with a smile in his voice. "Did you need something?"

Mr. Clumpett held up a book. "This doesn't mention anything about the Indian rhinoceros. I was looking for a companion to this volume." He tilted his head back, letting his gaze traverse the high bookshelves with a hopeless expression. "You wouldn't happen to know, would you, if such a thing can be found . . . in here?"

"I'm not entirely sure," Philip said, with a look that was part amusement and part pity.

Mr. Clumpett heaved a sigh and approached a bookshelf. He shook his head and muttered something that sounded like *disorganized*.

Glancing at the clock on the mantel, I was shocked to see that it was nearly six o'clock and time to change for dinner. Had I really spent the entire day here?

"We never did play chess, you know," I said to Philip. "I'm sorry."

"Don't apologize," Philip said. "Our conversation was much more enjoyable than a game of chess. And now I have a reason to claim your time another day. Do you have plans tomorrow afternoon?"

The only plans I had made were to immerse myself in the loveliness of the estate. I told him so, and he smiled and said, "Meet me here after lunch, then."

I left the library feeling a decided urge to do something close to twirling. As I walked to my bedchamber to change for dinner, I wondered what had happened to me today. Something *had* happened—of that I was certain. Where before I had been partially empty, now I felt somehow full inside—complete. It was a feeling as buoyant as sunlight. Examining my heart, I found that there were pieces of me that had gone missing in Bath that I had found again, today, with Philip. And they were pieces of happiness.

I entered my room with a smile on my face, knowing who was responsible for the happiness I had found. Philip had become a friend today, and I had not known until that moment how much I had missed the company of a friend. Perhaps I had never known before today the value of such a friend—a person to whom one could talk for hours without noticing the passage of time. Although I had had many friends in my life, I had never known how it felt to be accepted and esteemed so completely, and so immediately.

A letter rested on my writing desk, catching my attention while Betsy brought out a gown for me to change into for dinner. My initial excitement at seeing the envelope changed to disappointment when I realized it was merely Mr. Whittles's poem, which he had given to me before I left Bath. Betsy must have removed it before taking my gown to be laundered.

While I dressed, I thought of Mr. Whittles and how relieved I was to be done with him. I had been very fortunate to come here and find such a warm welcome among the Wyndhams.

But to simply enjoy my current state of happiness with no thought of others seemed very self-centered. Perhaps I could do something to help Aunt Amelia win her heart's desire. Mr. Whittles needed only a nudge in the right direction, and I felt sure he would be very happy with my aunt. Her sincere admiration would stroke his ego quite nicely, and she was not an unattractive woman.

I slipped the poem into the drawer of my writing desk, determined to come up with a way to bring those two together.

Chapter 11

When I met Philip in the library the next afternoon for our game of chess, he said, "I know it's not as exciting as fencing, but I wondered if you would be interested in archery."

I was interested in almost anything that took me away from the quiet pastimes of the drawing room. We went outside to the southwest lawn, where a target had been set up for us. A couple of servants stood nearby, and Philip motioned for me to go first. We practiced until my arms were too tired to shoot one more arrow. As we walked back to the house, Philip said lightly, "I suppose the chess will have to wait until tomorrow."

But the next afternoon, when I met him in the library, he asked if I had seen the gardens yet. I hadn't, so he took me on a tour of the grounds and showed me the water garden and the Oriental garden and the rose garden. We talked and strolled around the grounds until a sudden rain shower drove us inside.

I was surprised once again to discover that hours had passed while I was in Philip's company, though it had felt like mere minutes. And when I tried to account for the passage of time by recalling exactly what we had talked about, I could only remember bits and pieces—a story here, a memory there—and the fact that I had never had to search for something to say to him.

Days blended together, and between our morning rides, our afternoon activities, dinner, and time spent with the family in the evening, there was hardly a moment when I was out of Philip's presence. I felt as if I were enjoying a guilty pleasure and that I should turn my mind to something more productive than enjoying my new friendship with Philip. But I felt as wild and free as a bird suddenly released from its cage. I grew unguarded, and blissfully happy, and content to the very core of my soul. And although only a handful of days passed in this manner, I felt as if I had known Philip all my life.

Philip and I had taken five rides together, and he had beaten me five times, when a letter arrived for me one morning. I was frustrated, because I knew that Meg had untapped potential within her, and I was determined to prove it.

"One of these days, you will be seeing the backside of Meg," I told Philip as I sat down to breakfast.

He laughed with the familiar glint in his eyes that made me think he was enjoying a secret. He had too many secrets. I narrowed my eyes at him, but by now I knew him too well to hope that he would reveal any of his mysteries to me.

The butler cleared his throat as he held a silver salver toward me. On it rested a letter. The envelope bore Grandmother's familiar, shaky handwriting. She must have mailed this immediately after I left Bath for it to have arrived so soon. I set it beside my plate and looked at it with misgiving. Seeing it made me anxious, as if I had been living in a dream. I feared whatever the letter contained would cause me to wake. I decided to read it later, in private.

Lady Caroline spoke up. "I think we ought to host a ball for our guests while they're here. What do you all think?"

Mrs. Clumpett looked up with her ready smile. "Oh, I love a ball. And so does Mr. Clumpett. Don't you, my dear?"

I couldn't imagine that he actually loved a ball, but he grunted in response.

"Philip?" Lady Caroline said. "Do you have any objections?"

"You know you have free rein here, Mother."

That seemed odd. Why should she have to ask his permission to hold a ball? If she needed to ask anyone, it should have been Sir Charles.

"I think a ball will be delightful," she said. "We'll introduce Marianne to all the eligible gentlemen in the area and watch them fight over her. What fun it will be!"

I looked at her in surprise and blushed. "I am sure you're mistaken about the level of interest I will inspire," I murmured.

"I am never mistaken about such things," she said, smiling like a cat before a dish of cream. "What do you think, Philip? Won't she be all the rage?"

I couldn't look at Philip. He would undoubtedly say something polite, which everyone would know was a lie. But then, when he didn't immediately answer, I *had* to look at him. I was so surprised by what I saw that I looked twice.

Philip held his mother's gaze with a hard look in his eyes. A muscle jumped in his jaw. He almost looked angry, but I couldn't fathom why her words would spark such a reaction in him.

Lady Caroline's smile turned hard—almost mocking—from across the table.

After a tense silence, he finally said, "Undoubtedly."

I took a quick breath. Something was amiss here, and it made me uncomfortable to be the cause of it. "A ball sounds wonderful," I said, wanting to clear the tension, "but I have no desire to be fought over. I would rather just enjoy the dancing."

Mr. Clumpett suddenly looked up from his book. "This sounds very much like something I just read." He flipped through some pages while I looked at him in surprise. I didn't think he had been listening to us at all. "Ah, here it is." He cleared his throat before reading: "'The male rhinoceros will not tolerate any other male entering his territory during mating season. If such a thing occurs, dangerous fights are bound to ensue.'"

He looked up with bright eyes. "That would be a sight to see, wouldn't it? A dangerous rhinoceros fight?"

"Fascinating," his wife said with feeling.

I stared. Had he really just read something over breakfast about animals *mating*? I didn't know where to look in my embarrassment. Philip cleared his throat, but it sounded to me as if he was trying not to laugh.

"Very *apropos*," Lady Caroline said with a smile. "Well, then, it is settled. I will organize the guest list and start writing the invitations this afternoon."

I took that as permission to excuse myself; I was eager to escape the charged emotions of the room. I picked up my letter and walked to the door. But I felt a gaze on my back as I did so, and I glanced over my shoulder. Philip was watching me with a very solemn expression. I gave him a questioning look in return. Abruptly he smiled, and all traces of that foreign look were erased. It lingered in my mind, though, as I left the dining room. In that moment, Philip had reminded me very much of someone else, but I couldn't think of whom.

I sat at the writing desk in my room and stared at Grandmother's letter for several minutes before daring to open it. Finally, I succumbed to the inevitable and broke the seal. The morning sunlight slanted through the window and warmed my back as I read.

Dear Marianne,

I imagine you have already started scampering around the countryside like some farmer's brat, so I am writing to remind you of the conditions of your visit. You are to learn all you can from the Wyndhams about how to behave like an elegant young lady. Write to me and tell me what you are learning. Consider this an assignment. If I do not recognize some signs of improvement in you I will not hesitate to call you home. If you cannot change your ways, I will not hesitate to cut you off without a penny, just as I did to my nephew. I am committed to this plan, and I will see you become all that you can be, both for

*your own future happiness as well as for what you owe to the family
name. Do not disappoint me.*

Sincerely,

Grandmother

I gazed out the window while considering the ramifications of
Grandmother's message. The fact that she had mailed it before I had been
absent one week illustrated her lack of faith in me. I had to smile as I
admitted to myself that her lack of faith in me was partly justified, for I
had not given one moment's thought to her assignment since I had fallen
into the river.

In fact, that event—falling in the river—highlighted the problem perfectly. I did not have the instincts of an elegant lady. But, according to my
grandmother, I would have to become an elegant lady in order to win an
inheritance.

As I considered this quandary, I did not attempt to deceive myself.
Young ladies of elegant birth with no fortune had little hope for comfort in
the world. Work was not an option. And marriage without a sizeable dowry
. . . well, only the very blessed achieved that. I did not need a mirror before
me to know that I was not among the very blessed. My figure was too petite
for the current trend in beauty, and my looks, while passable, did not have
the striking quality needed to attract a gentleman's attention.

Besides that, the fact remained that I had no desire to be married
simply for the achievement of it. That was Cecily's ambition, and I had
learned at a young age that if I ever wanted the same thing Cecily wanted,
I would inevitably lose to her.

It was the doll that had made that point clear to me. When we were
six, our great-aunt had sent us a doll she had bought in Paris. She wrote
in the letter accompanying the package that it was unique in the whole
world. It was finely made, with hazel eyes and real, curled auburn hair.

Having no children of her own, it did not occur to my great-aunt
what problems one doll between two girls would present. Cecily and I

fought over it the moment it arrived. Of course, we were meant to share it, and sharing may have come later, but we fought over the right to be the first to hold that doll. Since Cecily was the eldest, she claimed that right. It didn't matter that it was only by seven minutes. Those seven minutes were a lifetime between us and could never be made up.

So she held the doll first. Something fierce and unyielding grew within my young heart as I watched my sister stroke the doll's pretty auburn hair and hug it to her chest. I despised the feeling of losing to her, and I decided in a moment of jealousy and resentment that I would do anything rather than lose to her again.

So when it was my turn to hold the doll, I claimed that I didn't want to touch the ugly thing. No matter how much Cecily held and caressed the doll and talked about how pretty it was, I remained stoically insistent that I did not want to touch it. And I never did. Eleven years passed and I never once touched that doll, not even to feel her hair. A maid once put it on my bed by mistake, but even then I did not touch it. I put a handkerchief over my hand and picked up the doll by the foot and flung it onto Cecily's bed.

At first it was only possessions we fought over. But as we grew older, the list lengthened—talents, beauty, attention from boys. I applied the lesson of the doll and decided it was better to want something different from Cecily instead of lose to her. I learned to hide my desires, or to change them as soon as learning hers.

There was nothing I could do to become more beautiful than she was. But when she excelled at singing, rather than trying to match her, I refused my lessons and turned my focus instead to painting. When she proved herself a devoted flirt, I scorned such artifice and either avoided talking to eligible gentlemen or deliberately spoke my mind to them, which I discovered they did not like.

I had to be different from Cecily so I would not be inferior. We could not occupy the same space together. Like horses in a race, I was tired of jostling for position and losing. I chose a different course so that losing would not be an option.

And so while she planned her season and dreamed of the achievements she would make with her marriage, I did the opposite. She planned to marry someone wealthy, titled, and with a good parcel of land. I dreamed quietly of marrying someone whom I loved deeply, and who loved me madly in return. If such a man could not be found, then I would not marry at all.

Such was my attitude when Cecily and I came of age to be presented to society and enter the marriage mart in London. Cecily dreamed of nothing but town life; I dreamed of nothing but living comfortably in the country. I did not envy Cecily her season, because I had no such ambition. I did not aspire to a brilliant match, because it would be a contest with Cecily and she would win. I never wanted to be an elegant lady, because that was Cecily's role.

But now, faced with this challenge from Grandmother, I realized I would be foolish to throw away a fortune simply because I had never been ambitious in the same way Cecily was. I might not have planned to be a wealthy heiress, but only a simpleton would turn down an opportunity to live very comfortably for the rest of her life.

In fact, this inheritance was exactly what would give me the freedom to choose whether or not I married for love. And all I had to do to earn it was to prove myself an elegant young lady. I was certainly not entirely hopeless in that regard, or else my grandmother would not have given me a chance to try. I would try, and I would earn the inheritance that would give me unparalleled freedom.

But there was another hope that lived in my heart—the hope that if I proved myself, my father might come home. If he could be proud of me, he might return. I might be able to go home. I might be able to convince him to stay and let me take care of him. With my inheritance from grandmother, we would live comfortably. He would want to keep me there, and he would want to stay with me, and I would never have to wonder again if I was wanted.

At the thought of my father, I remembered where I had seen the look that Philip had given me as I walked out of the dining room. I propped my chin on my hand and remembered the day shortly after my mother's funeral when I had passed by my father's study. He had held a framed portrait of my mother in one hand, and his eyes were cast downward as he gazed on her image. He did not see me, and so I caught him in a private moment, where concern for me did not guard his expression. His expression was exactly what I had seen in Philip's countenance. At the time I had thought it was only a look of grief, but recollecting it now, after seeing it so clearly on Philip's face, I thought—perhaps—it wasn't grief I had seen, but longing.

But no. I must have been mistaken, or else he had been thinking of someone else. There was no earthly reason for Philip Wyndham to ever look at me with . . . *longing.* My cheeks suddenly warm, I banished the thought from my mind and turned my attention to responding to Grandmother's letter.

> *Dear Grandmother,*
>
> *I am happy to report that I am getting along very well here. There are plenty of cows, and the farmers have been quite eager to teach me the secrets of milking. With any luck, I shall be proficient at it before I leave so that I may have a trade to fall back on should I fail to meet your expectations.*
>
> *In the meantime, here is what I have learned so far about being an elegant young lady: An elegant young lady should never insult a gentleman she might have to dine with later. If she feels inclined to twirl, she should watch out for patches of mud. And she should learn how to sing at least one song so that she won't die of fright if she is called upon to perform.*
>
> *Give my love to Aunt Amelia.*
>
> *Yours,*
>
> *Marianne*

I smiled as I imagined what she might make of this letter. It would surely frustrate her, but it would probably also make her laugh. She had a throaty laugh, which was always given up reluctantly—when it was given up at all—and that made it so much more worth the earning. It was something I was proud of—being able to make her laugh, or smile, when she normally repressed such instincts.

In this, Cecily did not share the same talent as I. My twin might outshine me in other accomplishments, but she had never made Grandmother's gray eyes twinkle with suppressed amusement, and she had certainly never earned a laugh from her. It was not a charitable thought, but one which made my heart swell with pleasure nonetheless.

Despite my flippant response to Grandmother, I did feel the need to focus some of my attention on her assignment. And so, after I sealed the letter to her, I took another piece of paper and made a list. If I were going to improve myself, I needed to be honest about my failings.

> *Marianne's List of Improvements*
> - *Stop twirling.*
> - *Wear a bonnet outside.*
> - *Learn to sing at least one song for company.*
> - *Learn to flirt with gentlemen.*

That seemed like enough to work on for now, and I did not want to overwhelm myself. Heaven knew the last one on the list might be impossible. But I knew there was one more item I should add, although it was more general than specific in nature.

> - *Follow the example of other elegant young ladies.*

I knew this would mean having to sit at tea with them and talk about the things they were interested in, like bonnets and lace and such. But if doing so meant bringing my father home, I would try. If it meant avoiding my return to Bath, then I would try.

After finishing my list, I took my letter downstairs and found Mrs. Clumpett, who had mentioned wanting to walk to Lamdon, the nearest village. She agreed to accompany me to mail my letter. I felt proud of myself that I remembered to wear a bonnet.

"This is fortuitous timing," she said. "Mr. Clumpett has just asked me to join him in a search for a certain species of beetle. And although I enjoy exploring the woods, I do not like insects."

I welcomed her company. There was something odd but at the same time pleasant about her. She did not prattle on about inconsequential things like bonnets and fashion. She knew about things I had never considered, and she seemed to be an equal to her husband in terms of her quest for knowledge. I liked how she had been able to hold her own in their debate over dinner about the Jungle Bush-Quail. But I doubted she was what my grandmother had in mind when she told me to make myself into an elegant young lady.

As we walked into town together, it occurred to me that she looked nothing like her sister, Lady Caroline. Mrs. Clumpett stood no taller than I, and although there was no real fault to find in her nose, or her chin, or her eyes, there was also no real asset to any of those features. Except for her upturned lips, it was a forgettable face.

Lady Caroline, though, was a true beauty, from her rich brown hair to her dark blue eyes, from her statuesque figure to her high cheekbones and aquiline nose. Noticing the differences between them made me like Mrs. Clumpett even more. We had something in common, the two of us; we had both been cursed with beautiful sisters.

After mailing my letter, I found a shop where I bought a sketchbook, pencils, paper, and paint supplies, along with a satchel to carry everything. The idea of painting had taken such a hold of me that I felt the need to do something about it. Besides, I would like something of Edenbrooke to take away with me when I left. It was the closest thing to paradise I had ever known, and I wanted to remember it always.

"Are you an artist?" Mrs. Clumpett asked as she helped me carry my purchases.

"No, not at all," I said with a laugh. "But I do enjoy it, and I hope to improve myself. It is one of the socially acceptable talents for a young lady to possess, you know."

"Hmm." She slanted a glance at me. "I hope you are not offended by my saying this, Miss Marianne, but I think there are more important things to consider than what talents are *socially acceptable.*"

I smiled to myself. It was all very well for Mrs. Clumpett to be a little odd and something of a Bluestocking—she was married and appeared to be well-matched. I, on the other hand, still had to secure my future happiness, and I knew that my future depended entirely on my becoming socially acceptable.

"I'm not sure my grandmother would agree," I murmured.

Mrs. Clumpett laughed. "Neither would mine. But I hope you do not let anyone else's expectations direct the course of your life." She gently touched my arm, stopping me in the path. I turned toward her. "I have discovered happiness in being true to who I am. I hope you will give that idea some consideration."

I nodded, touched that she seemed to care enough about me to offer such heartfelt advice. "I will consider it. Thank you."

A cart coming down the path called me to attention, and I stepped aside to let it pass.

Riding in the cart was a plump woman. She was holding onto her hat with one hand and gripping the side of the cart with the other as she was jostled about on her seat. She looked up just as the cart was passing us and suddenly grabbed the arm of the driver.

"Please, stop here!"

"Why, it's Mrs. Nutley!" I said, hurrying toward her. I had not heard anything from her about James, so I had assumed everything was going well with his recovery.

Mrs. Nutley clambered down gingerly from the cart and walked to us with small, quick steps. "I was just on my way to Edenbrooke to see you."

She grasped my hand and I noticed a wrinkled handkerchief clutched in her other hand. I wondered why she was not at the inn taking care of James.

"I do not know what to think," Mrs. Nutley said, dabbing at her eyes. "I only meant to stretch my legs—I walked down the path only a little way—but when I returned to the inn, James was gone!"

Chapter 12

I sat on the edge of my chair and watched Mrs. Nutley sip her tea. She seemed calmer now that we had her settled in the comfortable drawing room at Edenbrooke. But I felt sorry that she had spent so much time worrying about James and whether it was her fault he had disappeared. Lady Caroline joined us in the drawing room and gently posed questions to Mrs. Nutley.

"He was returning to good health?"

"Yes, I was taking excellent care of him. In fact, the doctor had visited early yesterday and said James looked healed enough to go home in the next few days."

"Has anything unusual happened that may explain his disappearance?" Lady Caroline asked.

"No, not today." She set down her teacup. "But now that I think of it, something unusual did happen yesterday. I came downstairs while James was resting and saw a gentleman speaking with the innkeeper. The gentleman asked if a young lady had recently stayed the night. The innkeeper told him that, yes, there had been. Then the gentleman asked if she had had a companion with her. The innkeeper told him, yes, her maid. I thought, of course, of you, Miss Daventry."

"What did this gentleman look like?" I asked.

"Rather dashing, I thought. I noticed he carried a walking cane."

Mrs. Nutley could have been describing any number of young gentlemen in the area. And a walking cane was certainly not an unusual accessory.

"What else did the innkeeper tell him?" Lady Caroline asked.

"Why, he told him that you had left the inn and were on your way to Edenbrooke." She turned worried brown eyes to me.

I chewed on my lip as I wondered who might be looking for me, and why. A run-of-the-mill highwayman wouldn't come looking for his latest victim. But who else would guess that I had stayed at that inn? And who would care?

That afternoon I met Philip in the library with the intention of finally playing that game of chess. But it was a beautiful day, and when he suggested an excursion instead, I could not resist the temptation. He had the horses saddled while I fetched my sketchbook, and then we rode to the top of the knoll. It was the same spot he had led me to the first morning we rode together.

The same groom accompanied us, and when we reached the top of the knoll, he led the horses to graze nearby while Philip and I chose a shady spot beneath the large tree. From where I sat, I could look around and see almost all of Edenbrooke below me. We talked while I sketched, and sometimes Philip just watched me in silence. It was a comfortable stretch of moments together.

We had been silent for some time when Philip suddenly asked, "Where is your father?"

"A little village in France." I felt sad saying the words.

"Have you any idea if he is coming home soon?"

I studied him before answering, surprised by his question. But he didn't look at me, and I could read nothing from his profile. "No, I have no idea what his plans are."

And then Philip did turn to me, in time to see the flare of sadness I felt at the thought of my father's absence. His eyebrows contracted in an expression of concern. "Do you want him to come home?"

I sighed and plucked a blade of grass. "Of course I do."

I hoped that would be the end of his line of questioning, but Philip said, "Does he know how you feel?"

I shrugged. "I've never told him, in so many words. I haven't wanted to. If he is happier there, then that is where he should be."

"You spend so much time thinking about other people's feelings," he said quietly. "I wonder how much thought you give to your own. Is your father more deserving of happiness than you are?"

I took a deep breath, struggling to push my emotions back down to their normal level. Philip, somehow, in the hours I had spent with him, had developed a special ability to unravel my defenses and access secrets that I didn't share with anyone. Today his words plucked at the sore parts of my heart, tearing off raw bits of sadness.

Philip was waiting for a response, his serious blue eyes on me.

"Perhaps," I said, striving to sound light, when inside I felt like weeping.

He shook his head. "I disagree."

I didn't want to discuss this anymore. "Let's not talk about that. Not when the day has been so pleasant." I forced a smile and waved the piece of grass at the view before us. "Look at all of this beauty before you. Wouldn't you rather just enjoy it?"

"I am looking at it," he said, never taking his eyes off of me. "And I am enjoying it," he added with a smile and a wink.

My face grew hot even as his smile grew. He had only said that about my supposed beauty to make me blush. I hated that he could affect me with just a look or some pretty words. And I hated that he wanted to affect me, as if I were a plaything to him.

I frowned and threw the piece of grass at him. "Can you never be serious for more than two minutes?"

"What makes you think I'm not serious?" he asked, looking up at me through his lashes.

I shook my head, utterly exasperated. I had done everything in my power to discourage Philip from flirting with me, from scowling at him to ignoring him to scolding him. But nothing worked. He still insisted on trying to flirt with me every time we were together.

Didn't he know that if I ever attempted to flirt back with him, it would change everything? Ruin everything? Because then we would not simply be friends. We would be friends who flirted, and I would be a dismal failure at it.

I felt he should not treat our friendship with so little care. But perhaps it didn't mean to him what it meant to me. Perhaps he could afford to lose me as a friend. I stood up, suddenly very upset, and took a step away from him.

Philip grabbed the hem of my gown. "Wait," he said, laughing.

I looked down at him, my hands clenched into fists.

"Please don't leave," he said, a cajoling smile turning his lips up charmingly. "I won't do it again."

Well, at least he knew why I was upset. But the idea of him not doing it again? Hah! I raised an eyebrow in deep skepticism.

"In the next five minutes," he added with a chuckle.

I tried to stay angry with him, but he looked so endearing, smiling up at me, holding onto the hem of my gown as a child might cling to his mother. Right then I could imagine him as a little boy, with his soulful blue eyes and chestnut curls. He must have been adorable. My heart thawed. It would have to be made out of stone not to.

I felt a smile twitch at my lips, and at that instant I knew that Philip would always be able to charm me out of a bad mood.

I sat down again and looked at the view, fighting against a smile. I finally said, "You're very good at that, you know."

"At what?" I could hear the smile in his voice.

"Charming me into a good humor."

"Just like you're good at making me laugh?"

"Am I?" I turned to him in real curiosity. I hadn't realized that I had sat down closer to him than I had been before, so when I turned to him, suddenly, leaning toward him in my curiosity, I discovered Philip's face just inches from my own. He grew absolutely still—I could have sworn he was holding his breath—and I was reminded of that day in the library. How still he had been then, too, as if he was waiting for me to discover something within him.

Philip drew in his breath as if he were going to say something. But he paused, and for the first time since I had met him, I saw uncertainty in his expression, like a wash over a painting, clouding his clear, confident look. It surprised me. I thought Philip was unfailingly confident.

He looked away and said quietly, "Yes, you are."

I sat back, feeling something new and intense buzzing inside of me. I didn't have a name to put to it. I just knew that it was unsettling.

The silence between us stretched longer and longer, until it lost its tension and became a part of the scene we were enjoying together. I felt no desire to break it. I set my sketchbook aside and leaned back on my hands. The afternoon heat settled over me like a blanket, and I felt drowsy and content sitting in the shade of the tree.

Philip stretched out on the ground, his arm folded under his head. I felt jealous. I wished I wasn't a lady in a gown, or I could have done the same. Instead I had to sit modestly, trying to make sure my ankles were covered. The heat was making me sleepier than I realized, and my eyelids became heavy.

Philip glanced at me. "You look like you're about to fall asleep."

"I am," I yawned.

He stood up and shrugged out of his jacket, then folded it into a square and set it on the grass. "If you're going to have a nap outside you may as well lie down and enjoy it."

"I shouldn't," I said, looking at the tempting pillow he had made out of his jacket. "I'm sure it's breaking one of the rules of being ladylike."

"I won't tell anyone," he said with a perfectly polite smile, not teasing or mischievous.

I glanced over my shoulder. The groom was resting in the shade of another tree, on the other side of the knoll, with his back to us.

It was too tempting to resist. I managed to keep my skirt tucked modestly in place while lying down. Philip's jacket smelled like the woods on a summer day mixed with some other pleasant masculine scent and made a very nice pillow. I curled onto my side and Philip stretched out next to me, at what I thought was a proper distance, his arm under his head, looking out at the view. The warm silence settled into me, soothing me to my bones. I think I was smiling when I fell asleep.

I couldn't have slept very long. I awoke to a soft breeze across my skin and the tickle of grass along my arm. I opened my eyes and looked straight into Philip's. He was facing me, reclined on his elbow, and watching me with a thoughtful expression. I wondered how long he had been watching me like that. A drowsy thought flitted through my mind that I liked seeing him in his shirt and waistcoat. He seemed more casual, more familiar, more like how I thought of him—comfortable.

"How was your nap?" he asked.

"Very nice, thank you." I smiled contentedly.

A breeze blew under the tree, teasing a lock of my hair loose so that it escaped its twist and flew across my face. Before I could move, Philip caught the lock of hair and tucked it behind my ear, his fingers brushing my cheek and neck in a surprisingly intimate gesture. My heart skittered at his touch, a blush rising to my cheeks. His gaze grew into something I had never seen before. More than warm, different than serious—it was intimate, gentle, and significant. Nobody had ever looked at me like that before.

I felt completely unnerved and deeply confused, both by Philip's actions and by my reaction to him. I was also keenly aware of the very inappropriate position I was in, lying down less than an arm's length away from a man. What had seemed harmless and innocent a moment before now felt almost scandalous.

I sat up and frowned at the grass, growing more self-conscious by the second. I could feel Philip's gaze on my face as he sat up next to me, and I blushed hotter with the awkwardness of the moment. I didn't know what to say or do. I was beyond inept. This was excruciating.

Suddenly Philip said in a light tone, "You snore, you know."

I looked up sharply and gasped. "I do not!"

"You do." He had that familiar teasing glint in his eyes.

"I have never been told that I snore. I am sure you're mistaken."

He grinned. "You snore like a big, fat man."

A laugh burst from me. I was sure he was lying. "Stop it," I said, swatting at his shoulder. "You are so inappropriate. What gentleman tells a lady that she snores?"

"What lady falls asleep in a gentleman's presence?" He lifted an eyebrow and looked at me as if I had done something scandalous.

I felt my blush flare up again. "You said it was alright," I said defensively.

He chuckled. "No, I didn't. I said I wouldn't tell anyone."

I pressed my lips together to keep myself from smiling and shot him a dark look. He grinned wickedly. To my astonishment, I suddenly had the strongest urge to kiss those grinning lips, wicked or not.

I looked down, flustered, and so surprised with myself that I couldn't gather my wits. I had never wanted to kiss a man before—at least, not a specific man. I picked up Philip's jacket, stood, and brushed the grass off of it.

"Thank you for the pillow," I said politely, handing it to him as he stood.

"You are welcome to borrow my pillow any time," he said with such a rakish glint in his eyes that I thought I should slap him for it.

Instead I glared at him, hands on hips. "Philip Wyndham! That is the most inappropriate thing I have ever heard, and if your mother were here she would give you the scolding of your life! In fact, I have half a mind to go tell her what an atrocious, incorrigible, scandalous tease she has raised."

He didn't look the least bit chagrined. He just smiled and said, "If my mother were here I wouldn't have said it. That was for your ears only." And then he winked.

I stared at him in disbelief. There was no stopping him. He had no limits to how far he would go with his outrageous flirting.

"Ugh!" I clenched my fists and stomped my foot in frustration.

His head tilted to one side; his lips twitched. "Did you just *stomp your foot?*"

I pressed my lips together tightly, but the amusement in his eyes was too much. A little laugh escaped me, and then his shoulders were shaking, and suddenly we were both laughing like we had that first night at the inn. I laughed until my throat ached.

"Well, I'm glad to see you took my advice about the stomping." He chuckled. "Although it really didn't help."

"You are the most infuriating man I have ever known," I told him, and I meant it.

But he just smiled. Of course. Nothing penetrated him when he was in this mood. "You are so enchanting when you insult me," he said.

I abruptly turned and walked to the horses.

What a scandalous, inappropriate, odious flirt! He would never leave me alone. He would never just be my friend. He always had to make me feel childish and awkward with his outrageous flirting! I felt churned up inside and embarrassed for a lot of reasons, not the least of which was the fact that I had thought about kissing that scandalous, inappropriate, odious flirt.

Well, I would just ride off and show him what a good seat I had and that I didn't need his company *or* his flirting *or* his horrid teasing. I waved off the groom as he hurried toward me. I did not need any man's assistance. I untied Meg and then looked at the stirrups. I had never mounted her without a mounting block, and I could see immediately that I wouldn't be able to. The lowest stirrup hung level with my shoulders.

I heard Philip approach and turned reluctantly to him, although I didn't look at his face. His cravat was closer to my eye level and was a good substitute when I didn't want to meet his eyes.

"It looks like I'll need a leg up," I muttered, mad that I couldn't ride off dramatically on my own like I had planned.

He stepped right up to me, but instead of cupping his hands into a step for me, he wrapped his hands around my waist. I caught my breath and looked up at him, surprised by how my heart thumped around in my chest and how my skin tingled under his strong hands. His eyes were such a deep blue—almost navy. He looked at me as softly as a caress.

"I'll help you up if you'll forgive me for my *horrid teasing*." He spoke in a soft voice, a regretful twist to his smile. "It's no excuse, but I have always found it extremely difficult to behave as I ought to when I'm with you, Marianne."

I felt oddly breathless, and suddenly all of my anger drained from me, leaving me lightheaded. "Are you saying I bring out the worst in you?" I asked, smiling, ready to be charmed.

He took a breath, held it, and I could almost see the words hanging off the edge of his lips. But then, for the second time today, I saw a flash of uncertainty in his eyes. When he released his breath, it sounded like a sigh.

"Something like that," he murmured. I wondered what he had really wanted to say.

Then he lifted me as easily as if I were a small child and set me gently on my saddle. I was so unnerved by the interaction that I sat in a daze for a minute before realizing that he had mounted his horse and was waiting for me.

When I caught up with him, he said, "Don't worry—I won't tell anyone that you snore." Then he grinned at me and I couldn't help myself. I laughed. I knew I shouldn't. I knew it would just encourage him to behave in his atrocious way in the future, but the laugh bubbled out of me before I could stop myself. He looked very satisfied and challenged me to a race.

He won, of course. He always won.

Chapter 13

To make good on my resolution to learn from other elegant ladies, I joined Lady Caroline in the drawing room the next morning, even though it went against my natural inclinations. I longed for a brisk walk through the woods. Or a ride. Anything but being confined to this chair and this room and the polite conversation of polite women. But this sacrifice was one of the changes I was making in order to improve myself. Lady Caroline looked pleased when I joined her.

The third visitors of the day were Mrs. Fairhurst and her daughter, Miss Grace, who lived just three miles away. Mrs. Fairhurst entered the room grandly, seeming to dominate the elegant apartment with her bold, sweeping gaze and the lofty tilt of her head. I recognized her sort from other ladies I had met in Bath. She was well dressed but looked as if she were trying too hard to appear elegant. Her lace was a bit too elaborate, her laugh a bit too shrill, her bearing a bit too dignified. She was moving up in the world—probably the daughter of a wealthy tradesman. I knew I wouldn't like her as soon as she entered the room.

Miss Grace looked just like her name. She was tall and willowy with a long neck, rich brown curls, and large green eyes. She walked sedately with a dignified air and greeted me in a soft, cultured voice without any undue emotion. Noting her creamy white skin, I was certain she never went outside without a bonnet, something which I had been guilty of many times. I was also fairly certain she was not the type to snort when she laughed. Here was a clearly wealthy, elegant, accomplished young lady—the very epitome of what my grandmother would have me be-come—and I was struck with a pang of inferiority.

Mrs. Fairhurst turned her attention to me as Lady Caroline served tea.

"Have you traveled much, Miss Daventry?" she asked, raising her eye-brows at me over her teacup.

"No, not much."

"Have you ever been to London?"

"No," I answered, feeling as if a trap was being set for me.

She looked shocked in an exaggerated way, opening her eyes wide while looking at Miss Grace, who sat next to me. "Never been to London? What a pity. You must have heard how admired Grace was last season. She was one of the most courted ladies in Town. Was she not, Lady Caroline?"

Lady Caroline smiled politely. "Was she?"

"Why, of course she was! You must remember. Where is Sir Philip? He can tell you. He danced with Grace several times himself, did he not?"

Grace nodded, and Mrs. Fairhurst went on, but I stopped paying attention. My mind had caught on one word, and I couldn't move my thoughts beyond it. She had called him *Sir* Philip. But he was not the eldest son; Charles was. Charles had the title. Not Philip. Why did Lady Caroline not correct her?

Mrs. Fairhurst laughed through her nose. "Miss Daventry, I feel so sorry for you, having never been to London. You really must see a little more of the world if you hope to become the sort of interesting lady that would attract a husband."

I knew I wouldn't like this woman. I debated what I could say to her to put her in her place, and then decided that I probably couldn't say anything since she was Lady Caroline's guest. So I lowered my eyes, took a sip of my bitter tea, and wondered what in the world she had meant by calling him *Sir* Philip.

Lady Caroline cleared her throat. "Mrs. Fairhurst, I have heard you are making some improvements on your house."

"Oh, yes, we certainly are." She began reciting a loud, detailed description of her estate while Lady Caroline listened with an air of polite forbearance.

Under the cover of her mother's talking, Miss Grace turned to me. Her eyes were kind and she smiled hesitantly. "I was looking forward to meeting you. I hope we can be friends."

I nearly choked on my tea. I studied her before answering, but found nothing but innocence in her eyes.

"I should like that," I said. I took a deep breath. Why was it so stuffy in here? Had someone lit the fire? I cleared my throat. "I heard your mother refer to Sir Philip. But is she not mistaken? Isn't Sir Charles the eldest?"

She looked surprised. "Well, yes, of course. But he died five years ago."

Chapter 14

My thoughts reeled. I felt wholly incapable of comprehending what had just been revealed to me. Miss Grace glanced at her mother, who was still talking loudly enough to drown out our conversation.

"Tell me—how do you like it here?" she asked in a low voice.

I forced myself to focus on the elegant young lady next to me. I would think of Philip later. "I like it very well," I said in a faint voice.

She lowered her voice even further. "I don't think I could be entirely comfortable here."

That caught my attention. "Oh?"

"You must know by now what an incorrigible flirt Sir Philip is. He can hardly pass by a lady without paying her a compliment. I know I should not take him seriously, but his manners are so charming that it's easy to feel flattered. Don't you agree?"

I knew what she was referring to. He was a flirt. I had known that all along. I nodded weakly.

"My mother says he leaves a trail of blushes in his wake everywhere he goes," she whispered. "As well as a trail of broken hearts. Of course he *is* the most sought-after bachelor in Town every season."

I could understand why. He had been attractive before I knew about the title and the estate and the wealth. Now, it made perfect sense to me why he would be the catch of the season.

"I haven't been hurt by him," Miss Grace continued, "but I think it has become something of a game with him, to see how many ladies he can make fall in love with him. He is a collector of hearts—hearts he has no interest in keeping." She glanced down at her tea. "And, of course, so many of them come here, hoping to ensnare him. I think for many of them it is just ambition that motivates them . . ."

She let her voice trail off and looked up at me expectantly. My brow furrowed as I realized what she was hinting at. Did she think that *I* had come here with that intent?

"I must set your mind at ease," I said. "Lady Caroline invited me, and I had never heard of Sir Philip before I arrived." In fact, I wanted to add, I had never heard of him before today.

"Of course you didn't." She rested her hand lightly on my arm. "I only wanted to warn you, right away, because I would hate to see you leave brokenhearted like all the rest."

I suddenly saw through her act. Her mother, moving up in the world, would, of course, want her daughter to have a title. She must have seen me as a threat, and thought to warn me off. But I knew something they didn't. I knew that Cecily had her heart set on Philip. If the Fairhursts thought I was a threat, they would have a conniption when they met Cecily, who was at least twice as beautiful as I was, and much more elegant. She would come with her charm and her beauty and her accomplishments, and Philip would fall madly in love with her. I had no doubt about it. Miss Grace did not stand a chance.

Nobody stood a chance.

"Thank you for the warning," I said, remembering to whisper, "but I am in no danger of having my heart broken by Sir Philip. In fact, I can safely promise you that I will never take him seriously." My heart felt as hard as ice as I said the words.

Miss Grace smiled. "I am relieved to hear it."

I thought those might have been the first sincere words she had spoken to me.

She looked at her mother, who had paused during her loud, one-sided conversation. Perhaps this was the signal that her goal had been accomplished, because at her look Mrs. Fairhurst turned to Lady Caroline.

"Well! What a delightful visit this has been, but now we must be off! I daresay we shall see you all soon enough."

The two women stood and took their leave, Miss Grace with tremendous poise, Mrs. Fairhurst with tremendous condescension. I walked to the window and watched them leave, reflecting that they had each, in their own way, stripped some of the happiness from my current state. I hated them both for it.

Lady Caroline came to stand beside me. "I hope you haven't let Mrs. Fairhurst upset you."

I shook my head. The insults meant practically nothing, compared to what Miss Grace had said. But why Miss Grace's revelation should cut up my peace so much was a mystery to me. I could not comprehend my own heart, or my own mind, and all I wanted was some time alone to try to come to some understanding of myself.

"Have you been enjoying yourself here?" Her question echoed Miss Grace's.

I forced myself to pull my thoughts away from the Fairhursts and what I had just learned. Giving Lady Caroline a quick smile, I answered, "I have. It's such a beautiful home, and I love the grounds."

Lady Caroline smiled kindly at me, and I sensed she somehow knew more about me than I guessed. "Did you know your mother visited here, before you were born?"

Now she had my complete attention. "Did she? I never knew that."

She nodded. "It was shortly after her visit that we grew apart. I've regretted that for years."

"What happened? Did you quarrel?" I had never asked my mother why the friends had grown apart.

"I wish we had. That might have been amended. No, it was something much more subtle, and something which I'm afraid I didn't understand until it was too late to do anything about it. I had my hands full with babies, you see, and she went a long time hoping for a child before she had you and Cecily." She sighed. "I think it was difficult for her to see my life because it seemed like I had everything she wanted most."

I tried to remember my mother ever hinting at such a thing. "I never . . . I never heard her say such a thing."

"No, I don't imagine she did." Her eyes grew soft with kindness and a touch of sadness.

I stood silent for a moment, thinking about my mother wanting what Lady Caroline had.

"She did a painting while she was here," she said, pointing at the wall opposite us, where the painting of Edenbrooke hung. "It is still one of my favorites."

I caught my breath. "I should have known. I admired it my first night here."

I crossed the room and stared at the painting. Lady Caroline said something about needing to talk to the housekeeper. I nodded without pulling my gaze away from the painting and hardly heard the door close behind her. I should have recognized the style; my mother's touch was all over the scene. I ached with longing for her. The ache grew until it filled me to the brim. And then, suddenly, I couldn't stand to be inside another moment.

⚜

The orchard awaited me with its quiet and stillness. I sat under a tree and thought about Miss Grace's revelation and what it meant to me. Obviously, it meant that Cecily was in love with Philip, not Charles; it was *Philip* she planned to marry. But how had I not known that Philip was the master of the house? I had been here for almost a week. Surely there had been some hint of it during that time.

I stood and paced as I recalled several instances when it should have been obvious to me who Philip was. He had spent hours one morning meeting with the steward, who helped manage the estate. Lady Caroline had asked him for his permission to hold a ball. I had probably even heard someone call him *Sir Philip*. Why had I not pieced the clues together?

The orchard did not feel cozy and secure today. Gone was the serenity and comfort I usually found within its protective space. My pacing increased, but I was still filled with a restless energy that I could not exhaust. I asked myself many questions: Why had I not recognized Philip's identity? Why did this revelation upset me so? Why was my heart such a stranger to me? But no answers were forthcoming.

In frustration, I plucked an apple from a branch above me and bit into it, but it was too tart to swallow. I spit it out and threw the apple at a nearby tree. I missed. A sudden urge swept through me, and I plucked another apple and threw it, harder, at the same tree. It hit the trunk with a satisfying smack.

It felt so satisfying, in fact, that I had to do it again. And again. Where such an urge came from, I couldn't say. I only knew I either had to throw these apples as hard as I could or risk facing some truth I didn't want to face. I hurled the apples, harder and harder, until my shoulder hurt and the ground around my target was littered with smashed fruit. When I finally stopped, the truth I had been trying to avoid lay as clearly before me as the mess of ruined apples.

Edenbrooke was ruined for me. Everything I had found here—all of the happiness I had discovered, and the pieces of myself, and the friendship, and the sense of belonging—was all ruined. My hands curled around nothing as I stared at the bruised apples at my feet. One tiny piece of information had changed everything. Philip was the eldest now. He had the title and the estate and the wealth. He was the one Cecily had set her heart on. And I? I never raced the same course as Cecily. Philip was like that beautiful doll from long ago. Cecily had claimed him first. And I would have to pretend that I never wanted him.

It was not that I wanted to marry him myself. I had not considered such a thing. (Well, except for that strange urge I had to kiss his wicked smile.) But he had become a friend to me when I had no other. And a friend who seemed to know me well, and accept me, and one in whom I could confide was a treasure. A priceless treasure. I hated the thought of giving that up. Resentment surged through me, and I was suddenly six years old again, hating Cecily for claiming that doll first. But Philip was so much more than a doll. He was . . .

I stopped myself short. It did no good trying to define what Philip was to me. All that mattered was that he was not mine.

I turned away from the orchard, restless with dissatisfaction. I wasn't hungry, and I didn't want company. What I wanted, in fact, was solitude with a purpose. Then I had the perfect idea. I ran to my room, grabbed the satchel with my painting supplies, and left the house without talking to anyone. I didn't even wait for a groom to saddle Meg, but did it myself. I didn't stop until I reached the knoll. There I dismounted, turned until I found the same view my mother had painted, and sat on the grass under the shade of the tree.

It was almost the same spot where Philip and I had sat yesterday, but everything was different now.

⚜

Hours later, I set my brush down, rolled my shoulders, and stood back to study my watercolor with a critical eye. I had captured Edenbrooke—the symmetry of the house, the bridge, the river, the orchard. All of that was in the background. In the foreground of the scene was the tree Philip and I had sat under on the knoll, and next to the tree stood a lone figure. Her back was to the viewer, and her hand rested on the tree as she looked down at Edenbrooke. In a stroke of vanity, I had painted her hair hanging long down her back and made it shimmer like honey. Even though her face was turned away, it was obvious from her posture that she ached with longing.

This was exactly what I had wanted to create: this sense of standing alone with everything I wanted in sight but out of reach. It was, without a doubt, the best painting I had ever done. My mother would be proud of this. She would be proud of *me*.

I sighed and rubbed an errant tear from my eye. Pouring my heart onto the paper so completely helped ease some of the ache I felt. But at the same time, the sight of myself standing alone and longing for what I could not have pierced my heart, and I cried. I did not cry much—I was quite skilled at burying grief and binding up wounds in my heart—but I did cry a little.

Afterward, I felt more capable of controlling my heart. It did not protest so loudly when I told it to behave. This is what I told my heart: *Philip belongs to Cecily. He can no longer be your friend, your riding companion, your confidante. He can no longer be the highlight of your day. He must be nothing more than an acquaintance. And you must make the change before Cecily arrives. You must sever your friendship—push him away. It will be for the best. And you must not ever cry over him.*

My heart would obey me, I was certain. I simply needed to be strict with it.

Once the paints dried, and my tears as well, I packed everything into the satchel, found a stump to stand on in order to mount Meg, and rode back to the stable. I had not kept track of the time, so it surprised me to see that the sun looked close to setting. The thought crossed my mind that I should not have stayed out so long by myself. I had missed tea, and my stomach growled at the realization. I dismounted in the stable yard and led Meg into the dim light of the stable, nearly bumping into Philip before I saw him.

"Where have you been, you little truant?" he asked.

I had not expected to run into him. I reminded myself of my decision to be nothing but an acquaintance to Philip. Now was as good a time as any to start. I smiled and tried to make my tone light.

"You remind me very much of my last governess. Are you going somewhere?"

"Yes, I was going to look for you." His voice was more curt than I had ever heard it. I sensed I did not want to know the reason for his tone.

This effort to sever our friendship was more difficult than I expected. I had to force myself to sound cool and unaffected. "Oh? Well, here I am."

I led Meg into her stall and started to unbuckle the saddle, hoping Philip would leave me alone. My control was already shaken, my hands trembling from our unexpected encounter.

Philip followed me and reached for the buckle at the same time I did. He grabbed my hand and pulled me around to face him. My heart escaped all its bounds and took off at a gallop.

Philip's face was half hidden with shadows. I couldn't read his eyes, but his mouth was grim. "You left with Meg hours ago, without telling me or anyone else where you were going. What if something had happened to you? What if you had been hurt? How would I have found you?"

I looked at my shoes, feeling sullen and guilty at the same time. "I'm sorry."

He waited, as if expecting me to say more, but I said nothing, hoping my silence would end this, here and now. When he spoke again, his voice was still hard with frustration.

"Marianne, you may not think much about the fact that I am responsible for you—for your safety and welfare—but I assure you I think about it every day. How could I face your father if something happened to you while you were living under my protection?"

So, he thought of me as a responsibility. Did that also make me a burden? I hated the very thought.

"I didn't think about that," I muttered.

"Do you know what I've been thinking about?"

I looked up and shook my head, dread falling through me. I had never seen him so upset.

He took a breath. "I have been wondering if you had suffered the same fate as your mother."

I flinched at his words, feeling as if I had been struck, and yanked my hand out of his grip.

"There is no need to use that against me, Philip. I said I was sorry!" I had spoken too harshly. He reeled back. I stared at the ground, feeling a dangerous swell of emotion and a prick in my eyes that warned of more tears to come. The silence was thick between us. I swallowed and tried to find control of myself again.

In a much quieter voice, I said, "I lost track of time. But I honestly didn't think anyone would worry about me."

"Anyone?"

I looked up. Anger flashed in Philip's eyes; my apology had only made things worse. He stepped closer to me. "Not *anyone,* Marianne. I said *I* was worried about you. Is that significant at all to you?"

He was looking at me—really looking—as if searching for something very important. There was no hint of teasing in him. No playful flirting. I wasn't used to seeing this side of Philip. I had seen much of his lightheartedness, but not this intensity that made me feel as if there was a fire building between us. I shrugged, knowing it solved nothing but not knowing what else to do.

He looked down and scuffed his boot against the floor, moving back a step, then forward again. I watched these signs of unrest with growing alarm. I had never seen him so uncollected.

"Marianne," he finally said, his voice thrumming low and hushed. He looked up, and his blue eyes sparked with intensity even in the low light. "Do you care for me?"

Something jumped inside of me. "What?"

"You heard me." His voice was still quiet, but strong and unbending.

His eyes would not allow me to escape. "Do you care for me? Do you care about my feelings?"

His words flew at my heart and scattered its rhythm wildly. I looked away. *Say no,* I told myself. *Say no.* It would be quick and easy. It would accomplish exactly what I needed to have happen. But my heart would not allow me to speak, no matter how I struggled to form the words. Had he just moved closer? How small was this stall? Too small. Definitely too small, because for some reason Philip felt the need to rest his left hand on the wall above my shoulder, trapping me too close to him.

I took a half-step backward, my back pressing against the wall. This stall was much too warm, and Philip was much too close. Without thinking, I put my hand on his chest, meaning to push him away. But as soon as I touched him, I froze. All I could do was watch my hand rise and fall with his breathing, while my heart evaded all of my attempts to corral it. I had to push him away. Now. I put my other hand on his chest, hoping it would give me the strength I needed, but that made it even worse. My thoughts scattered with the currents of emotion that raced through me.

He was waiting for my answer. But it was an impossible question. As impossible as the question he had posed to me my first night here, about whether or not this was normal. I had to cut these ties of significance between us before Cecily arrived. Cecily was my sister, my twin, my other half. She was the sun to my moon. She was the only one left in my family who still cared about me—who still wanted me. I could not betray her. I *would* not betray her.

I stared at the buttons on his coat and took a shaky breath. "Y-yes, of course I care about your feelings, Philip. You have been a . . . a good friend to me, and a generous host."

He held perfectly still. "Look at me, Marianne," he said in a quiet voice.

I raised my eyes to his cravat, but no further.

"My face, please," he said with a sigh of exasperation.

But I couldn't. There was too much between us in this moment, and it terrified me.

Philip raised a hand to my face and lightly slipped his fingers under my chin and nudged it up. I had to tip my head back to look at him. His fingers brushed my jaw, my blushing cheek. My heart threatened to jump out of my chest, and there was a fire spreading through me, threatening to consume me as well as my good intentions.

"A good friend?" he asked, when I was finally looking into his eyes. "And a generous host? Is that all?" His voice was husky and caused a thread of ache to pull through me.

Without warning, I was trapped in Philip's gaze. He was so close—almost close enough for me to find that great, important, beautiful truth he was hiding. It took all of my concentration to persuade myself not to slide my hands up his chest, over his shoulders, around his neck, not to curl my fingers into his hair, not to pull his head down to mine . . .

Good heavens, what was wrong with me? Philip was a friend, and nothing more. So why was that suddenly so difficult to believe? Why was it so much easier to believe I was falling into that *something* I had sensed on that rainy day in the library?

Chapter 15

I took a deep breath, trying to clear my mind. I could not fall for Philip's tricks. Never mind that so many other ladies had. Never mind that it felt inevitable. My loyalty to my sister was more important than the pull I felt.

"Yes. That is all." I forced myself to look into his eyes as I said the words so he would believe that I meant them.

Something dark flickered in his eyes, and then he looked up, above my head. I sensed a great struggle within him, and watched as a muscle jumped in his clenched jaw. He finally lifted his hand from my chin and pushed away from the wall. My hands fell away from his chest as he stepped back a pace.

Even though I had refused to succumb to the emotion I felt, I couldn't help but notice how handsome he looked with his cheeks ruddy and his eyes burning. And when he raked his hand through his hair, I couldn't help but follow the movement with my eyes, wondering what it could possibly feel like to bury my fingers in his hair.

"Very well," he said in a quiet but rough voice. "If you care about me at all—as a friend, or even as just *your host*—then don't run off like that again. Don't make me worry needlessly."

"I won't," I said in a shaky voice. "I promise."

I had to turn away. My gaze rested on Meg. I had come in here to do something with her, but now I couldn't think what. The stall was too close and too warm, and Philip was too . . . Philip.

"I'll have a groom take care of her," he said. His voice was strained but gentle.

He picked up my satchel and gestured for me to precede him out of the stall. The setting sun cast golden paths between the trees, leaving much of the area cooling in shade and the blue-gray light of oncoming dusk. When we emerged from the stable, I pulled in a deep breath of fresh air. This was better. Open spaces and fresh air should clear my head, and my heart. It should clear the thick emotions between Philip and me.

But I sensed something deep and taut connecting us. It made our silence feel uncomfortable, and I wasn't used to that with him. I was used to comfort and familiarity, not tension and awkwardness. I wondered if everything between us was really so fragile that it could be ruined in just one day.

As much as I had lectured my heart about the need to destroy my friendship with Philip, I panicked at the thought that it might have already happened. I wasn't ready. My heart had not been schooled enough to accept it. And Cecily wasn't here yet. I peeked up at Philip and found him looking down at me with a thoughtful expression.

"What did you do today?" he asked.

"Oh, I just painted," I said. "What did you do?"

"Absolutely nothing. I simply sat in my library and thought about you all day."

When I looked up at him in surprise, he winked.

I was so relieved I laughed. He was flirting with me, just like he had always done. Nothing had to change. Not yet. Once Cecily arrived, I would cut him out of my heart. But for right now, I would enjoy this moment.

"You did not," I said, because that was how we played our game.

"That's what you get for trying to change the subject. May I see what you painted?" When I hesitated, he smiled at me in the way I found impossible to resist. "Please? I want to see what was worth making me worry about you."

I glared at him. "That's a low trick."

"Yes, but effective, I think," he said, stopping and turning to me.

Philip was nothing if not persistent. Sighing with defeat, I took the satchel from him and pulled out the painting. I handed it to him hesitantly, anxious about his reaction. I watched his face carefully and was not disappointed. His immediate reaction was a mixture of surprise and appreciation. The expression that followed defied definition. I couldn't find a word for the emotion I saw in his eyes when he looked at me.

"I'm afraid I can't give this back to you."

I smiled. "What a nice compliment. Thank you." I reached to take the watercolor back from him, but he stepped away from me.

"I am in earnest. What do you want for it?"

I was sure he was teasing. "It's not for sale." I moved to take it from him, and he hid it behind his back with a grin, clearly enjoying our new game. I regarded him thoughtfully. I considered trying to wrench the painting from him, but decided I would probably be unsuccessful in the attempt. He smiled smugly at me. Now I had to try.

I reached around him, but he snared me quickly around the waist with one arm while he held the painting safely behind his back with his other hand. I was taken off guard by his unexpected touch and the warmth of his body against mine. I stepped away quickly, and he released me.

"You didn't really think that would work, did you?" he asked with a smile.

"No, but I thought it was worth a try."

"Yes, it was definitely worth that," he said with a rakish grin that made me blush. "Would you consider a trade?"

His question sparked my curiosity. "What kind of trade?"

"That's up to you. What do you want?"

There was nothing suggestive in his voice, but in his eyes I saw a host of possibilities. My face flushed hot, and I found myself suddenly tongue-tied. Wicked flirt!

"I can tell by your blush that you're too shy to ask for it," he said. "Would it help if I guessed? I would know the right answer by the shade of red on your cheeks."

It was impossible not to laugh. "You're atrocious."

I held out my hand for the painting, but he shook his head, clearly not ready to give up the fight.

"What about Meg?" he asked.

I was startled. "I couldn't take Meg."

"Why not?"

"It's a horse, Philip, that's why not. She's far more valuable than that painting."

"Not to me."

I shook my head. "It's absurd. I couldn't do it."

"Something else then."

"Why do you want it so badly?" I asked.

"Don't ask me that. Just tell me what your price is." He said it with a smile, but there was an unmistakable glint of determination in his eyes.

I sighed, knowing Philip was relentless once he set his mind on something. "There are only two things that I really want, but you can't give me either of them, so there's no sense in telling you." I held out my hand again.

Philip ignored my hand. "I want to know." The teasing was gone, replaced with utter determination.

"Very well," I said, knowing it would make no difference in our battle. "I want my father to come home, and I want the locket the highwayman took. It had a picture of my mother in it." I saw a flash of sadness in Philip's eyes; it made my heart ache. "See? You can't give me either of those things, so I must insist on keeping the painting."

He studied me in silence for a moment, then looked back at the watercolor. I felt suddenly transparent, as if he was looking at the deep recesses of my heart, and I cringed inside with the sense of vulnerability it gave me.

"It appears we are at an impasse, then, because I cannot give this up." He looked at me with a speculative gaze. "I have an idea: let's keep it somewhere we can both enjoy it until we've agreed on a price."

"The library?" I guessed. I sighed at the smile Philip gave me. "Very well. But if we can't agree on a price before I leave, then I will take it with me, and you will have to let it go without a fight."

"Agreed," he said with a smile that told me he thought he was going to win. But this was one contest he would not win. For I had painted my heart into that picture, and I would not let him have it.

The following morning was very much the same as every other morning I had spent at Edenbrooke. I once again met Philip at the stables for our early morning ride. Once again his horse beat mine in a race. And once again we talked and laughed as we walked back to the house together. But through it all, I sensed that everything we did was not part of an ongoing routine, but the final act in a play that would conclude this afternoon. Cecily was expected to arrive today, along with Louisa and William and Rachel. And nothing would be the same again.

A sense of melancholy stole over me as I changed out of my riding habit. So I stayed in my room instead of going down for breakfast and tried to find solace in my drawing. While sketching the prospect from my window, I attempted to convince my heart that there was no need to grieve over losing something I had enjoyed for only a week. It was only a morning ride with a friend, and nothing more. But my heart had become more difficult to deceive lately and accused me of being a liar.

I frowned at my sketch. Surely my heart was inferior to my mind and will. I would simply have to exercise more control over it. It had learned to obey me after greater losses than this. It would obey me again.

A knock at the door interrupted my thoughts. A servant had come to inform me that I had a visitor. Taken off guard, I quickly smoothed my hair before following him downstairs. Who could be calling on me?

I paused in the doorway of the drawing room, surprised to find Philip there; he was supposed to be meeting with his steward. I was also surprised by the swift look Lady Caroline sent me, as if she were trying to guess my feelings with a glance. But most of all I was surprised to discover that my visitor was a stranger to me.

He had golden blond hair done in the Brummell style. His collar points reached all the way to his cheekbones, his waistcoat was daring but tasteful, and I counted three fobs. He carried himself with an air of confidence and a flair for fashion that impressed me.

The gentleman bowed elegantly. "Miss Daventry?"

"Yes, what can I do for you, Mr. . . . ?"

"Beaufort. Thomas Beaufort."

I sat next to Lady Caroline, and Mr. Beaufort sat across from me. Philip stood behind him, close to the window. Mr. Beaufort held a book in his hand, which he handed to me.

"Please forgive me for being so forward as to call on you without introduction. But I was commissioned to bring this to you, and I was told it was of the utmost importance that you receive it."

I opened the book with great curiosity. My eyes skimmed over the lines: "Miss Daventry is fair and true, with eyes of such a beautiful hue . . . " I promptly snapped the book shut again. It was a collection of Mr. Whittles's poems!

Mr. Beaufort smiled. "My uncle, Mr. Whittles, charged me with the task of presenting this collection of poems, which he has dedicated to you."

This must be the nephew Mr. Whittles had mentioned on the morning I left Bath.

"I see," I said, clearing my throat with embarrassment. Did he think I welcomed his uncle's attentions? How mortifying! "Thank you, sir. I hope you have not traveled out of your way to deliver this."

"No, not far. But distance would not have deterred me. I confess I have been eager to meet the object of such . . . rapture." He waved his hand in the air as if gesturing to unseen angels.

I felt my face grow hotter. I wished Philip wasn't hearing this. He had turned his gaze to me with something of amusement and curiosity in it. He would undoubtedly tease me about all this later.

"I am sorry you had to be subjected to his poetry," I said to Mr. Beaufort. "I tried to stop him, but it was impossible."

He laughed. It was a pleasant sound. "I can well believe it. But I can hardly blame his taste, even if his poetry is not the finest." Admiration gleamed in his eyes.

My blush refused to disappear, and I cursed my inability to feel comfortable with handsome young gentlemen. For this gentleman was handsome, although in a different way from Philip. This was the sort of gentleman Cecily probably met every day in London. This was the sort of gentleman my grandmother would want me to feel comfortable with and to learn to flirt with.

Mr. Beaufort leaned toward me. "Tell me, Miss Daventry, do you plan to attend the ball at the Assembly Rooms this Friday evening?"

I glanced at Lady Caroline, who nodded slightly. "Yes, I believe we had planned on it," I said.

He smiled suavely. "And do you dance as prettily as you blush?"

My gaze darted to Philip. It sounded just like the sort of complimentary thing he would say. I thought he might appreciate Mr. Beaufort's phrasing, but his eyes were narrowed and his mouth was set in a firm line. He clearly did not appreciate Mr. Beaufort. But did Philip really think he was the only man who was allowed to flirt with me?

I smiled back at Mr. Beaufort, feeling defiant for a reason I couldn't explain. "Not quite, but much more willingly."

Mr. Beaufort laughed as if I had said something very clever. My smile grew as I realized I had just flirted for the first time in my life. It was a heady experience, and one not altogether unpleasant.

"Then may I have the honor of the first two dances with you?" he asked.

I nearly looked at Philip again, but stopped myself, realizing that *he* had not asked me for any dances, so it should not matter to him what I answered.

"Yes, you may," I said to Mr. Beaufort, feeling powerful. A handsome young gentleman wanted to dance with *me*. Not Cecily, but me.

Mr. Beaufort smiled in return, then stood and apologized for not being able to stay longer.

"I will look forward to Friday, then," he said, leaving us with a bow.

Lady Caroline looked at me, then at Philip, who was still looking unappreciative as he glowered out the window at Mr. Beaufort's retreating figure.

Lady Caroline abruptly stood. "Well, if you will excuse me, I have . . . something to do." She hurried out of the room and shut the door firmly behind her.

I only vaguely noticed her departure. Smoothing my hand over the leather cover of my book of poems, I smiled to myself. Was this how Cecily felt when she talked to gentlemen? Did she feel this strong and powerful? I could not blame her for being a flirt now that I had experienced the effect of it myself.

I glanced up when Philip came away from the window and sat next to me on the settee. He held out his hand. "May I?"

I handed him the book, which he opened to the first page. Philip cleared his throat and read the first poem out loud. I was amazed that his voice, rich and familiar, could make even Mr. Whittles's poem sound almost . . . good. I wondered what he could do with a well-written poem.

My urge to smile disappeared. My feeling of power deserted me. In its absence I felt deflated, and the lachrymose mood I had been trying to fight off earlier returned.

Philip turned the page and read another poem. Gazing at his familiar profile, I thought of the orchard littered with bruised apples. I thought of Miss Grace's insinuations about my motives for coming here. I thought about how Cecily had danced with Philip and had fallen in love with him in London. I wondered how many hearts he had collected, and how many he had broken.

He glanced at me as he turned the page. "I am surprised you never told me about this admirer of yours—this Mr. . . . ?"

"Mr. Whittles." I laughed a little in embarrassment. "He was not somebody I wanted to remember."

Philip looked up from the book, expectantly, sure I was about to entertain him.

"He was twice my age, wore a creaky corset, and had a very wet mouth."

He laughed. "It sounds like a lethal combination."

"He was perfectly repulsive. I never understood why my aunt seemed to like him."

"Did she?" Philip raised an eyebrow.

I nodded. "Yes, but he was very obtuse. It seemed a hopeless case."

Philip shut the book. "It sounds like you have some matchmaking to do."

I shrugged. "I would like nothing more, but I have never known how to go about it."

Philip considered me for a moment. "I have it. Write them each a love letter, as if from the other, and see if it sparks something."

"A love letter." I could not even begin to fathom how to write a love letter.

"You do know how to write a love letter, don't you?" Philip asked with a smile.

"Of course not," I scoffed.

"Why 'of course not'? Don't you think you might write one someday?"

I shrugged, pretending to feel nonchalant about the topic, but inside, I was squirming with awkwardness. "I've never considered it."

"Then I will teach you. But now I'm curious." He smiled teasingly. "Have you ever *received* a love letter?"

I blushed. "No, I have not. Not unless you count Mr. Whittles's poems."

"I definitely would not count those." His gaze turned provocative, his lips curved into a smile. "Seventeen, and never had a love letter? That doesn't seem right. Shall I write you one, Marianne?"

I scowled at him. He took such delight in embarrassing me. "No, thank you," I said forcefully.

"Why not?" His voice was quieter now. He had turned sideways on the settee so that he was angled toward me.

I reminded myself of several things, in quick succession: Philip was a flirt. Philip loved to make me blush. Philip stole hearts he had no intention of keeping. He was teasing me, as he always did. There was nothing more to it than that.

"You know I will leave if you tease me too much," I warned him.

He turned the book over in his hands, looking at it instead of me. "Why do you think I would tease you?"

I rolled my eyes. "Experience."

He lightly tossed the book onto the tea table and leaned toward me, his arm along the back of the settee. "But, Marianne, I am always serious when it comes to matters of the heart."

He was still smiling, but his eyes were serious. It was one of those instances—always unexpected—when I had the feeling Philip's teasing was a façade, a thin cover for deeper feelings I could only guess at. I studied his expression without success. In so many ways, this man was still a mystery to me.

I might never write a letter to Mr. Whittles as if from my aunt. But I was intrigued. I wanted to know this side of Philip—this side of him that knew how to court ladies and how to write a love letter and how to read a poem so that it melted something deep inside me. I wanted to know the side of him that Cecily knew. It was dangerous, and most likely foolish, but I had only a few short hours before everything would change, and I knew I would never have this opportunity again.

"Very well," I said, feeling nervousness tremble within me. "You may teach me. After all, it may be a skill worth learning."

Philip smiled, then stood and walked to the writing desk in the corner. He picked up quill and ink and paper, then carried everything to the round table where we had played whist with Mr. and Mrs. Clumpett last night.

"You won't learn anything sitting over there," he said. "Come here."

I joined him at the table, and he held out a seat for me. Then he moved another chair so that it was right next to mine and sat down. I looked at the closed door of the drawing room. Philip was always careful to keep doors open when we were alone, but he made no move to do so now. My heart picked up speed, and nervousness began to stream through me. He sat so close to me that I could smell a mixture of scents—soap and clean linen and something that smelled earthy, like the grass after rain. I thought he smelled like sunlight and blue skies.

"Are you ready for your lesson in romance?" Philip asked with a teasing gleam in his eye.

Chapter 16

I was not sure I was ready at all, with Philip sitting so close to me in this quiet room. But then I remembered I was supposed to be growing up, and I tried to imagine what an experienced lady in London would do. I tried to imagine what Cecily would do. I imagined I was graceful and elegant and accustomed to handsome gentlemen teaching me how to write a love letter.

I kept my voice casual and said, "Please, go ahead."

He cleared his voice and spoke in a tutorial manner. "The purpose of the love letter is to convey feelings one cannot say out loud. Here is your first exam: Why would a gentleman be unable to declare himself openly?"

Philip sounded so serious, as if he were a real teacher and I a pupil. I didn't want him to be serious. So I bit my lip, as if thinking hard, and said, "Um, because he's . . . a mute?"

Philip's lips twitched in an effort not to smile. "I see you passed the general and went straight to the specific. The answer, Miss Daventry, is that a gentleman is unable to declare himself openly if his circumstances prevent it." He raised an eyebrow. "Were you paying attention?"

I nodded. "Yes, but you spoke of a gentleman. Should you not be teaching me how a lady writes a love letter? After all, I will need to write a love letter as if I were my aunt."

He rolled his eyes. "I am not going to pretend to write a love letter to another man. You will just have to take my instruction and apply it in your own way. Now, how do you think he should begin?"

"With her name?" I guessed.

"Unimaginative." He picked up the quill, dipped it in ink, and wrote,

To my unsuspecting love.

I had to lean closer to Philip to read the words clearly. "Much more imaginative," I murmured.

"And now for the essence of the letter."

I kept my eyes on the paper, waiting for him to write more, but his hand stayed poised above the paper, until I looked up. He gazed into my eyes for a long minute, then said in a quiet voice, "The eyes are a good place to start."

Oh, no. Now he was going to start teasing me in earnest. I was sure of it.

When I look into your eyes, I lose all sense of time and place. Reason robbed, clear thought erased, I am lost in the paradise I find within your gaze.

Oh, my.

I could never have imagined such words, not from anyone, not from Philip. They burned me from within, and I think if he had read them out loud I would have been consumed by heat. I was grateful that he was silent.

I still felt his gaze on my face—he was so close—but I did not dare look at him again. Instead, I rested my chin on my hand, curling my fingers over my cheek in an attempt to hide my blush.

I long to touch your blushing cheek, to whisper in your ear how I adore you, how I have lost my heart to you, how I cannot bear the thought of living without you.

The tease! I cursed him silently. I was sure he wrote about my blush just to provoke a reaction from me. He loved to provoke me, I reminded myself. He loved to make me blush. He said so himself, that day in the library. But even telling myself that did nothing to lessen the heat of my embarrassment.

I tried to remind myself that this was only a lesson, and not a real love letter. *Not my love letter,* I repeated in my mind while I stared at the paper.

> *To be so near you without touching you is agony. Your blindness to my feelings is a daily torment, and I feel driven to the edge of madness by my love for you.*

The only sound in the room was the quiet scratch of quill on paper as Philip wrote. I stared at the letter as if it was my only anchor to reality. My heart thudded so hard it ached. Without knowing much about love myself, I knew that Philip must have once loved someone this passionately. He had once felt exactly what he had written—that he was nearly out of his mind with love. I choked on a surge of jealousy so bitter it shocked me.

> *Where is your compassion when I need it the most? Open your eyes, love, and see what is right before you: that I am not merely a friend, but a man deeply, desperately, in love with you.*

I was shaking. I gripped my hands into fists and searched for some composure. I should be able to treat this as an amusing lesson in romance—a chance for me to become a little more experienced. Then why did I feel stretched thin, so transparent and tremulous? Why did my heart gallop? Why did I feel I was coming undone?

I knew none of the answers. I only knew that I was greatly disturbed by this . . . lesson. I wanted to find something to laugh about. But the letter sat before me on the table like an intimate glimpse into Philip's heart.

And there was nothing to laugh about. Indeed, I felt strangely close to crying.

I wanted to push the paper away. I wanted to run from the room. I wanted to reverse the clock and never know that Philip was capable of . . . this. I wanted to undo everything, even coming here to Edenbrooke, rather than know this about Philip.

Finally he spoke. "Do you have any questions?" His voice caused a ripple to cascade through me. I closed my eyes and summoned my courage to stay in my chair and not cry. This was my opportunity to prove my maturity. I would not let him know how his words had disturbed me.

I cleared my throat. "How shall you sign it? Your secret admirer?" My voice sounded close to normal, which I was quite proud of.

After a pause he said, "No, that won't do." His hand moved again, writing the words

Longing for you.

He signed his name underneath. I stared at his name, my fingers curled over my hot cheek, trying to hide something from him. Anything.

"What do you think?" he asked.

I tried to breathe normally and speak normally, but there was nothing normal about this moment. "Very nice," I said in a tight voice.

Silence stretched so taut that I felt it almost like a tangible presence, humming in the small space between us. I stared at the letter, intent on not looking up, because to look up would be disastrous. I counted slowly to ten in my mind. Nothing. I counted to ten again. Was he trying to burn a hole in my face with his gaze? Could this possibly be any more awkward? No. This was undoubtedly the most awkward moment of my life. I was sure of it.

Then Philip took a breath, and I felt a switch turn in him. He said in a light voice, "Of course, one must always take into consideration the modesty of the lady. Too subtle, and she may miss your meaning altogether. Too strong . . ."

Philip set down the quill and reached up to the hand I was using to cover my blush. He hooked a finger around mine and pulled my hand down to the table. "Too strong," he said, "and she may never look you in the face again."

I heard the wry amusement in his voice and looked up sharply. His eyes were brimming with amusement, and that was when I realized he was laughing at me. He must have known all along how embarrassed I was, and he simply wanted to see what reaction he could provoke in me. *Hateful* man! Whatever feeling had prompted me to almost cry a moment before now turned to anger of the hottest kind.

I snatched my hand away from his and glared at him. I opened my mouth to tell him exactly what I thought of his atrocious teasing, when the door suddenly opened and Mrs. Clumpett walked in, looking over her shoulder and saying, "I think I left it in here last night."

When she saw us, she stopped. "Oh, am I interrupting something?" she asked with a curious look.

"Not at all," I said, but my voice came out hoarse.

I hoped Philip would say something to dispel her suspicions. But of course he wouldn't do something I actually *wanted* him to do. Instead, he said, "I was just giving Marianne a lesson in romance."

I gasped and shot him a look of consternation. He winked at me in his audacious way and flashed me his familiar grin. He was unbelievable.

"Oh, well, my book can wait. I will simply come back later to look for it," she said with a smile as she turned around and closed the door behind her.

I stood as quickly as I could and stepped away from the table. "Philip! She is probably suspecting all sorts of things now that are not true."

He stood and held out the letter to me. "Is she?" His eyes held both a question and a challenge, and I could not begin to think of how to respond. So I stood there, flustered beyond words.

Then that man just walked out of the room, leaving me angry and embarrassed and confused, with a love letter in my hand.

❦

Betsy took extra care with my hair that evening, brushing it until it shone like a ribbon of honey before pinning it up. She had been chattering nonstop about her trip into town.

"I have been asking around about James, miss."

"Who?" My thoughts were still caught on the love letter lesson.

"Our missing coachman."

"Oh, of course. James. And what have you found?"

"There is talk of someone seeing him at an inn south of here. Said he looked well enough, with a pocket full of money. Seemed to be heading to Brighton, which is a very good idea, if I do say so myself, for sea air would be just the thing for a man recovering from a gunshot wound. I think he just decided he'd had enough of that nurse and left on his own."

I thought for a minute. "I suppose he may have decided he was well enough to leave on his own. But where would he have gotten the money? And why would he leave without saying anything? His care was paid for."

Betsy shrugged and adjusted one last strand of hair. "There. What do you think?"

I looked in the mirror. Betsy had insisted I wear my new green silk gown. It was one of my more elegant gowns, but I wondered about the color.

"Should I not wear the pink?"

She shook her head decisively. "No, this one brings out the green in your eyes. And your hair looks so pretty against it."

As much as I hated to agree with Mr. Whittles, at that moment, my hair did look like amber. I had often complained about having such an indecisive eye color, with blue, green, and gray all fighting for dominance, but with the gown bringing out the green in my eyes, I was secretly pleased with the result. I may not be a classic beauty like Cecily, with her bright gold hair and blue eyes, but I thought I looked well enough tonight.

"You are right," I said. "The green is perfect."

She smiled. "I know. You should trust me with such matters." She stood back to look at me, pulled a curl out so it draped across my neck, and then nodded. "You're ready."

"Thank you. I have no idea what I would do without you."

"Do you know how you can really thank me? Tell me exactly what Sir Philip says when he sees you." She smiled mischievously.

My heart dropped. "Betsy, you shouldn't say such things."

"Why ever not?"

"Because someone might hear you and think that I desired Sir Philip's admiration." I took a deep breath. "But I don't. I don't desire anything at all from him."

She looked at me askance. "You may not desire his admiration, but you certainly have it. We've talked about it down in the kitchen, the other servants and I."

Dismay filled me. This was terrible. If Betsy thought there was something between Philip and me, chances were good that the rest of the servants shared her opinion. They didn't understand that he was only a flirt and didn't mean anything by it. Somebody would certainly tell Cecily, and the damage it could cause was appalling to consider. I reached back and tried to undo the buttons on my gown.

"What are you doing?"

"I've changed my mind. I'm wearing the pink."

Betsy protested until she saw that I was serious, and then she reluctantly helped me change. She grew uncharacteristically quiet as she did. When she finished, I turned to thank her, and found her giving me a look heavy with disapproval.

"I don't know what you think you've seen," I said, "but I can assure you that you have imagined something that is not true. Sir Philip feels nothing toward me, and I feel nothing toward him. He is a flirt, and he has had no one else to flirt with here, and that was the only reason he was paying any attention to me. As soon as Cecily arrives, though, everything will be put to rights. You will see."

As if my words had some sort of magical power, a knock sounded at the bedroom door. I opened it, and there stood Cecily, looking taller and prettier and more elegant than I had remembered. I almost didn't recognize her. But then I looked into her eyes and I saw my childhood, and home, and happier days.

"You're finally here!" I cried, hurrying to embrace her.

She hugged me tightly but briefly before pulling away. "Yes, but I have only just arrived, so I must hurry to change for dinner. Come with me if you're ready, and we can spend a few minutes catching up."

I ignored Betsy's stare as I followed Cecily out of the room and down the hall to her own bedchamber. Her maid was already laying out an evening gown. It was a blue silk that matched Cecily's eyes. I sat on a chair while she dressed.

"How was your journey?" I asked. "How was London? I have so much I want to ask you. I cannot tell you how good it is to see you."

"I have so much to tell you as well!" Cecily said, sitting in front of the dressing table. She watched her reflection in the mirror while her maid arranged her hair. "You would love London! It is so diverting. Just imagine—routs and balls and musicales and the theater. There is something different every night of the week, and nobody goes to bed until long past midnight. There is so much to do and see. And everyone is so elegant! You must have a season. Next year, surely Grandmother will allow it."

I could not tell Cecily about the inheritance and the conditions attached to it with her maid here, so I only said, "I hope so."

She glanced sideways at me. "Did you have that gown made in Bath, my dear?"

I smoothed my skirt. "I did."

"Well, don't worry about it. Nobody cares what you are wearing here, I am sure. And I will help you before you go to Town so that you will be perfectly up to snuff by the time you're presented." She smiled broadly.

"Never fear, Annie, I will save you from that horrid Bath and those dress-makers as well."

I hardly heard the rest of the speech—only the sound of my old pet name. Nobody called me Annie except my father and Cecily. Such a longing for home surged through me that I could not sit still. I jumped up and hugged Cecily. "I'm so happy you're here."

She laughed. "Yes, so am I, but you're ruining my hair."

I smiled sheepishly as I stood back from her. She inspected her image in the mirror one last time, then stood and turned to me.

"What do you think? Am I going to catch myself a husband tonight?" She looked radiant.

"I have no doubt." The words were true, but I felt as if I were choking on them.

In the drawing room, Lady Caroline introduced me to her daughter, Louisa, her son William, and his wife, Rachel. William smiled as if he knew an amusing secret about me. Rachel gave me an appraising look that was not unkind. Louisa was, at best, aloof toward me.

Cecily had asked me to enter the room ahead of her, so that I wouldn't be a distraction when she made her entrance. Now, as she walked into the room, everyone's eyes turned to her. She was beauty personified. Her hair was like gold silk, her skin like cream, her eyes like bluebells. She was as bright as the sun.

"Sir Philip," she said, looking very elegant as she curtsied to him. No doubt she had learned a lot about being elegant in London. I felt awkward and clumsy just watching her.

"Miss Daventry." He bowed in return.

"I am so happy to visit your beautiful home. And I am even happier to see you again."

He said something polite in return. I had not looked at Philip at all since entering the room, but now that I was watching Cecily talk to him, I felt I could look at him without anyone noticing. He evidently noticed, however, because as soon as my eyes rested on his face, his gaze flicked to me.

I had hidden his love letter in the drawer of my writing desk. I wished I could as easily hide it from my thoughts. His words resurfaced every other minute, tugging at me, coming to life in my mind. Cecily was saying something about how grand and beautiful everything was. I looked away, not hearing what Philip said in return.

The butler opened the doors and announced that dinner was ready. I stood back to see how we would proceed to the dining room. Lady Caroline looked from Cecily to me and opened her mouth as if to speak, but before she said a word, Cecily had linked her arm through Philip's and smiled up at him. That question was answered, then. She walked in on Philip's arm and was given the seat of honor to his right. She was the elder, after all. She had always insisted on being first—those seven minutes meant everything.

I sat to Philip's left. From my position, I could easily see Cecily as she engaged Philip in conversation throughout four courses. She talked to no one else, and she obviously knew how to flirt. She was very good at smiling demurely, and looking up at him through her lashes, and touching his arm when she laughed. After two courses, I couldn't bear the sight of her hand on his arm, so I looked at my plate and ate my dinner while attempting to shut my ears to the sound of Cecily's laugh. I had never been bothered by the sound of it before, but tonight it grated on my nerves until a headache hummed around the base of my skull.

When the footmen brought in dessert, I couldn't help but feel Philip's gaze resting on me. When I lifted my eyes, he gave me a look that was full of questions.

"You're very quiet this evening," he said, leaning toward me and speaking quietly.

I glanced quickly across the table and saw Cecily watching me. Her gaze slid to Philip, who was waiting for my response. I shrugged and looked away. From the corner of my eye, I saw Philip look from me to Cecily and back.

"Sir Philip, I understand you have some very fine horses in your stables," Cecily said. "I hope you might have one suitable for me. I love to ride, and I would especially love to accompany you."

Mr. Clumpett unexpectedly spoke up. "That filly Miss Marianne has been riding is quite a beauty, Philip. Is she a new addition to your stables? I've seen you two out riding together nearly every morning."

I silently cursed Mr. Clumpett. Who knew he was interested in horses as well as the wild animals of India?

"Yes, she is a new addition," Philip said.

Cecily looked at me with surprise. "You're riding again?"

For some reason, her question made me feel close to tears. Perhaps it was the sympathy that hid not far behind her surprise—or perhaps it was that she knew better than anyone else why it was such a momentous act for me to ride again. Whatever the reason, I felt choked with sudden emotion, and I had to blink quickly to ward off the unwanted tears.

"Yes. I am."

Cecily smiled across the table at me, and we understood one another as we always had. At that moment, there was no one between us—only understanding, and a shared grief. Then she turned her sunny smile to Philip. "I am glad to hear you have a suitable horse, Sir Philip. I shall have to try her myself tomorrow morning. What time do we start?"

I looked at my plate again and tried to contain my emotions. First I felt ready to cry, now I felt ready to throw something at Cecily for wanting to take away my horse. This was not a good start to the evening.

"The decision is not mine to make," Philip said. "I promised Meg to Miss Marianne for the duration of her visit. You will have to ask her."

I was surprised and gratified by Philip's response, and cast him a grateful smile before I remembered I was not supposed to do such a thing. Cecily had first claim to my loyalty and affection, not Philip.

152

Cecily looked at me. "I am sure *my sister* won't mind if you don't, Sir Philip."

I took a breath. "I don't mind," I said, but it was a lie. I did mind very much. Was she going to take Meg from me too? Was it not enough to take Philip? I stopped myself at the thought. Cecily was not taking Philip from me. He was never mine.

I sagged with relief when Lady Caroline finally stood, signaling the end of dinner. For once I was grateful that the men always stayed behind in the dining room. I followed the other ladies into the hall. Cecily had her arm linked through Louisa's and was whispering something in her ear. Lady Caroline stood to the side, letting everyone else pass, until I drew even with her. She rested her hand lightly on my shoulder and spoke quietly.

"You seem a little out of sorts tonight. Is there anything amiss?"

"I have had a headache. That is all."

"Why did you not tell me? I would have taken care of you." Lady Caroline turned me toward the stairs. "Come with me. You should be in your bed."

In no time, she and Betsy had me changed into my nightgown, tucked me into bed, and sent for a cup of tea. Then Lady Caroline sat on my bed and bathed my forehead with lavender water. Her touch felt so motherly, and her eyes looked so kind and full of concern that I was overcome by a fierce longing for my own mother. I had told my heart to never cry over Philip, but I had given it no instructions about crying over my mother, my father, and the home and family I had lost. The tears spilled out so quickly I had no hope of calling them back. They ran down my temples, into my hair.

Lady Caroline handed me her handkerchief. "Do you want to talk about it?"

I shook my head. No, I absolutely did not want to talk about it.

"If you ever do—if you ever want to talk about anything, Marianne—I hope you will come to me."

A knock sounded at the door. My traitorous heart, released a little from its bondage, dared to leap with hope. But when Betsy opened the door I saw that it was just a maid from the kitchen with the tea. After Lady Caroline and Betsy left, I chastised myself for loosening my hold on my heart at all. It did nonsensical things when it wasn't tightly controlled, like hoping to see Philip standing outside my door. I sipped at the tea, but I had no taste for it. When I set the cup down on the tray, I noticed for the first time the book lying there.

It was the book of poetry I had started to read the day Philip had shown me the library. A piece of paper fell onto my lap when I opened the book.

> *I am sorry you are feeling unwell. I thought you might like something to help you pass the time.*

He had not signed it, but he hadn't needed to.

Tomorrow, I would be stronger, I told myself. Tomorrow, I would have better control over my heart. Tonight, I would indulge myself a little. I lay back against the pillows and turned to the first poem. My headache retreated and my heartache ebbed while I read the poetry Philip had sent me. I fell asleep with his note curled in my hand.

Chapter 17

Cecily came to my room early the next morning before breakfast. I sat at my writing desk, composing a letter to Grandmother. Betsy had not yet come up to help me with my hair, but I had to do something to stay busy so I would not think about Cecily and Philip and their morning ride together.

"I came to see how you're feeling today," Cecily said, sitting on my bed. "I'm sorry you were unwell last night! I would have come to see you myself, but I thought you would do better with some peace and quiet. And I know you don't like to be the center of attention, so I want to set your mind at ease: we did not talk about you at all last night. We played whist, and Sir Philip was my partner, and he was so droll! I vow, I was laughing all night."

I could easily believe that, considering how much she had laughed during dinner.

"I'm glad you enjoyed yourself," I said, trying to make myself believe the words.

"I knew you would be happy for me. You always were an unselfish sister that way." She lay back on my bed with a yawn. "That is why I didn't bother inviting you to ride with us this morning. Of course, it did little good, since Sir Philip invited his brother to come with us. Still, any time with him is better than none."

"Oh? You have already gone riding?" I tried to smile. "How did you like Meg?"

She frowned. "She was a bit spirited for my taste, but I was able to keep her in check. I think you must have given her too much freedom, though. When she belongs to me, I will make sure she is properly trained."

I clenched the quill I was holding so hard it snapped in two. I dropped the pieces on the desk and stood to look out the window. I would accept Philip's offer to trade my painting for Meg before I would let Cecily ruin that horse. She could find another horse—one that suited her better.

"I have wondered something," Cecily said in a casual voice. "Why did you not write to me that Sir Philip was here, this whole time? If I had known, I would have come sooner."

I turned from the window and looked at her in surprise. "What do you mean, you didn't know?"

"I was told he went on a trip, and that we should stay in London and enjoy the masquerade ball since he would be away. But I wasn't informed that he had cancelled his trip until I heard it from the servants here."

I had no answers to give her. I realized how foolish I had been to never question Philip's presence at the inn. Of course he must have been on his way to somewhere. It was one more mystery to add to his collection of secrets.

"I don't know anything about his trip," I said. "In fact, I must admit, Cecily, that I didn't even know it was Sir Philip whom you referred to in your letters."

She gave me a quizzical look. "How could you not know?"

I sat on the bed across from her, feeling nervous, and chose my words carefully. "It was the strangest thing, but I never heard him addressed by his title, and nobody told me that Sir Charles had died. I suppose everybody thought I knew. So I didn't know that Sir Philip's presence here would be significant at all to you."

"Hmm."

I did not like the speculative look she was giving me.

"What?" I asked, feeling defensive.

"I hope you will not have anything to regret," she said.

I sat up straighter. "What do you mean?"

"You. And Sir Philip."

I willed myself not to blush. "Nothing happened between Sir Philip and myself."

She laughed. "No, I did not suppose anything had *happened*. But you would not be the first lady to fall for his charms." She looked at me expectantly.

"He is, of course, very charming, but I knew all along he was a flirt, and so I was never in danger of taking him seriously. He has been a friend to me, and that is all." I leaned forward and rested my hand on hers. "But, Cecily, even if I had been in danger, you should know that I am loyal to you, first and always."

She smiled and squeezed my hand. "Of course, I know that. But I would hate to see you brokenhearted when Sir Philip offers for me."

I looked down at the blanket and picked at a loose thread. "You seem very . . . optimistic. Has he . . . said something?"

"No, not yet, but I am certain it will not be long before he does. I know the signs of a man in love, and I have no doubt that Sir Philip is well on his way to falling in love with me, if he has not already."

I bit the inside of my cheek as I struggled to keep my feelings in check. "Well, then," I finally said, looking up with a weak smile, "I am sure it will be no time at all before you have won his heart and hand and everything else you want."

"Do you really think so?"

"Yes." It was the truth. Cecily had always gotten everything she wanted.

"Lady Cecily sounds so elegant, don't you think?" She looked around the room with a sigh of pleasure. "And I have really chosen well, have I not? I doubt I have ever met a better combination of good looks and great wealth. Not to mention the estate. Of course, I will want to spend most of the year in London. I can't imagine staying in the country after knowing the entertainment to be had in Town." She glanced at me quickly. "And I am violently in love with him, you know."

What could I possibly answer in return? I nodded and looked away from her happy face. My heart felt cold and heavy, and I wanted to sink onto my bed and stay there for at least a week.

"You seem very dull," Cecily said, sitting up suddenly. "I think you need to get out of the house. Sir Philip said he has some business to attend to with his steward and he will likely be busy all morning, so Louisa and I are going to walk to Lamdon. You may come along. I am sure she won't mind your company, and you will love her, I know."

I hesitated, not sure if I wanted to spend the morning with Louisa, who had not been friendly at all to me last night. "If you're sure . . ."

"Yes, of course." She stood up and looked down at me. "You will do something about your hair, though, yes?"

I rolled my eyes. "No, I am going to walk to town looking like I just rolled out of bed."

She laughed and ruffled my hair as if we were still children.

I could not help but smile in return. When she left, I sat at the writing desk to finish my letter with a new quill. The letter was to the point.

> *Dear Grandmother,*
>
> *Here is what I have learned from Cecily so far: an elegant young lady should touch a man's arm and laugh at everything he says. I suppose this is called flirting. I find it loud and annoying.*
>
> *Sincerely,*
> *Marianne*

⚜

"Oh, look how charming your bonnet is," Cecily said as I joined her and Louisa after breakfast. I carried my letter to Grandmother in my reticule, and I had allowed Betsy to fuss over my hair a little more than usual.

I hoped to impress Louisa—or, at least, to not embarrass Cecily. "Isn't it nice, Louisa?"

Louisa said nothing, but she didn't look like she was about to go into raptures over my bonnet. Cecily linked one arm through Louisa's, and the other through mine, and we set off in this manner for Lamdon, which was but a few miles away.

I looked past Cecily to ask Louisa, "Was this your first season as well?"

She nodded.

"How did you like it?"

"It was very diverting," Louisa said. She looked at Cecily. "Do you remember the ball at Almack's when Mr. Dalton—"

They burst out laughing. "And then Miss Hyde told him to—"

More laughing. I looked on and wished I knew what was so funny. "What happened?"

Cecily waved a hand. "Oh, I don't think you would find it humorous. You would have to know the people involved."

I nodded.

We walked on a few more steps, and then another laugh escaped from Cecily. "What was it that Lady Claremont said that night? Something about freckles—"

Louisa giggled. "Ruining a lady's chances more than a tarnished reputation. And I quite agree. There is nothing so unattractive as a freckled face."

I bit my lip as I thought of my own freckles, which had grown in number since I had been spending so much time out of doors. Hopefully Louisa would not notice them.

"I don't know about that," Cecily said. "I saw plenty of things more unattractive. Remember Mr. Baynes?"

Louisa shuddered. "How could I forget?"

They talked the entire way about the people they had met in London. It appeared my attempt to befriend Louisa had done no good at all. When we reached Lamdon, we stopped first at the post office, where I mailed my letter to Grandmother.

"You know you can just ask Philip to frank that for you next time," Louisa said.

I knew that. But I liked having my own money to spend, and something to spend it on. I liked not being dependent on someone for everything. It satisfied the demands of my pride a little.

Cecily announced that she had to buy some new ribbon for a bonnet she was trimming, so we found the ribbon shop and started browsing. She picked three ribbons, all different shades of blue, and turned to me.

"Which do you think?" She held them up to her face, opening her eyes wide. "Which most closely matches my eyes?"

I looked at the three colors and secretly thought that it didn't make a difference which shade of blue she chose. But knowing that wasn't the answer she was looking for, I said, "That one. The darkest one."

She looked at it, her brow wrinkled. "Really? Because I did not think my eyes were quite this dark. But this other color has a touch of green in it, which I don't have in my eyes at all. Louisa, what do you think?"

"Definitely not that one," she said, pointing to the one I had chosen.

Cecily put it down immediately. I tried not to care. It was just a ribbon, for heaven's sake. But there was a time when my opinion would have been the only one that mattered to Cecily. I turned my attention from them and stood in the doorway, looking out into the street.

I was in this attitude of bored surveillance when I spied a familiar-looking figure across the street. He lifted his hat to me in recognition and I reeled back in surprise. I imagined I could see the smirk on the Nefarious Nephew's face, even at this distance. I thought of backing up and shutting the door, but it was too late. He had seen me and was crossing the street, languidly swinging his walking cane as he did.

"Good morning, cousin," Mr. Kellet said, bowing a little and looking very pleased with himself.

I frowned at him. "What are you doing here?"

He waved at the general surroundings. "Visiting this charming town. What are you doing here?"

I gestured just as nonchalantly at the ribbon shop. "Shopping for ribbon."

"Alone?" he asked with a glint in his eye that worried me. It worried me that he was here at all, actually. I could not believe he had chosen, by coincidence, to come to Lamdon on a whim. Was it paranoid of me to suspect that I was the reason he was here? Had he followed me from Bath?

"No, I am not alone," I said, nodding toward the inside of the shop.

Mr. Kellet stepped toward me, and I was forced to either retreat into the shop or come in closer contact with him than I wanted to. I stepped inside and he followed me, his eyes darting around the room. They rested on Cecily, who stood at the counter with her ribbons, her back to us. She turned just then with her purchase and walked toward us, Louisa trailing behind her. When her gaze landed on Mr. Kellet, Cecily's eyes widened, and a self-satisfied smile turned up her lips before she pressed it down.

Mr. Kellet bowed. "Miss Daventry. Miss Wyndham."

Why could he not call me Miss Daventry? Cecily was just as much his cousin as I was.

"Mr. Kellet," Cecily said, sounding a little breathless. "What a welcome surprise." She looked up at him through her lashes. "What brings you to this area?"

He took her hand in his and raised it to his lips. "I have been following my heart, and it has led me here, to you."

I frowned at them. Cecily's gaze rested on Mr. Kellet's face as he kissed her hand. I recognized the look on her face—excitement and admiration, with just enough suggestiveness thrown in to bring a man to his knees. It was the very same look she had used on Philip the night before, when she had captured his attention all throughout dinner.

I could not believe her. She had always acted foolish around Mr. Kellet, but this was beyond the pale. She should know better than to encourage a man of his reputation. I had not had a season in London, yet even I could judge by his haphazard mode of dress and the appraising look in his eyes as he swept his gaze over her figure that he was not a proper gentleman. Besides that, we had heard of his escapades for years. Why would Cecily want to flirt with him?

"Excuse me, Mr. Kellet, we were just leaving," I said, moving closer to Cecily.

He turned his languid gaze on me and smirked. "Are you? Well, I hope I may call on you soon, cousin."

"No, you may not. And stop calling me cousin." I knew I sounded rude, and I was glad of it. He only laughed.

Cecily frowned at me, then turned with a bright smile to him. "Mr. Kellet, you must excuse my sister's behavior. *I* hope you will come see us all, *very* soon."

My face was hot with embarrassment as I followed her and Louisa out of the ribbon shop.

As soon as we were out of earshot, she said, "Marianne, I can't believe how rude you were toward Mr. Kellet."

My mouth fell open in shock. *She* was censuring *me*? "I can't believe how encouraging you were." I took a deep breath, trying to calm down. "You know what he is. He is a self-serving rake and the worst kind of scoundrel there is."

She looked at Louisa and they both burst into laughter. They were clearly not taking me seriously.

Louisa smiled condescendingly. "You are very naïve, aren't you?"

I felt as if I had been slapped.

"No, hush, Louisa," Cecily said. "Don't be cruel. She has simply been sheltered. We must help her grow up." She turned to me. "Listen, dear, of course we're aware of Mr. Kellet's reputation. But there are some very good reasons to have a man like him around." She leaned close and said quietly, "The rakes are the best kissers."

I stared. "How would you know?"

She looked at Louisa and they giggled. I would never have suspected

Cecily of such behavior! But I saw the knowing smiles they cast at each other, and I was forced to accept the idea that maybe—just maybe—Cecily did know something about rakes and kissing. But I couldn't believe, after our conversation this morning, that she would really behave this way.

"Cecily, do you really intend to flirt with Mr. Kellet when you have a different goal in mind?" I asked. "With a different gentleman?"

She was clearly surprised. Louisa coughed in a way that sounded like she was trying to cover up a laugh.

"Everyone knows it's perfectly acceptable for a lady to flirt," Cecily said, "as long as she is discreet. And her husband will appreciate having the same freedom." She leaned closer, putting her arm around my shoulder, and said quietly, "Please don't say anything like this when you have your season. I understand, as your sister, but others will not be so kind to you, and I'm afraid you will be very embarrassed."

She moved away from me and gave Louisa a look of long-suffering that made my face burn with shame. I said nothing more as we walked along, but my thoughts raced. How could Cecily think about kissing a rake when she was supposed to be violently in love with Philip? And how would Philip feel if he knew this about Cecily? Others might behave immorally, but Philip never would. I knew him, and I knew how deeply he wanted to be like his father—a gentleman in every sense of the word. Never mind what behavior passed as "elegant" in London. Philip was different. I was certain of that.

Chapter 18

At dinner that afternoon Lady Caroline mentioned the ball that would be held at the Assembly Room that evening. "Speaking of which," she said, "we still have a lot to do to prepare for our own ball. It is only a week away, you know."

"Thank heavens I won't have to be a part of the planning," William said. "I can't stand hearing talk of colors and flowers." He looked at Philip. "You haven't changed your mind, have you?"

I glanced at Philip. I hadn't spoken to him since the night before, and I found myself missing him much more than I had anticipated. Just now, letting my gaze rest on his familiar face, I felt a unique sense of relief.

"No, of course not," Philip said.

"Good. I've been looking forward to this trip these past six months."

Trip? What trip? I looked in confusion from one to the other, but before I could ask anything, Lady Caroline said, "We won't need your help with the planning, but I do expect you both to be back in time for the ball."

William threw Rachel a pleading look, but she only smiled and said, "Don't look at me like that. You know I want you at the ball."

He groaned, and I had to smile a little at his pained expression.

"We can't help with the ball plans today," Louisa said. "I'm going to introduce Cecily to the Fairhursts. You won't mind if we take the gig, will you?" She looked at her mother, who turned worried eyes to me. The gig would not hold three passengers, which meant I was excluded from their plans.

"You can take the carriage," Lady Caroline said, "so that both of our guests will be able to join you."

She seemed to put extra weight on the word "guests." Surely everyone at the table knew what Lady Caroline was doing—she was trying to force Louisa into taking me along. But I refused to be the object of charity, and I would not go along if I wasn't wanted.

"Thank you for considering me," I said, "but I would love to stay and help you plan the ball instead. I have already met the Fairhursts."

I felt Philip's gaze and knew my face was red with embarrassment, but I didn't glance his way. I pulled my pride tight around me like a cloak in winter and kept my pretense in place. Louisa might not want my company, but that didn't mean it had to hurt. Cecily caught up with me in the hall as I left the dining room.

"I'm so sorry," she said.

I stopped and looked at her. My smile felt forced.

"I didn't feel like I could ask Louisa twice in one day to let you accompany us. But I would have invited you if I could have. I hope you understand."

Another forced smile. "Of course."

She hugged me, and the scent of lilacs enveloped me. "I knew you would." She pulled away and threw me a smile before going upstairs to get her bonnet. I stood in the foyer, feeling lost and alone. Lady Caroline had to speak with the housekeeper, so she wasn't ready to talk with me about ball plans. Before today, I would have been making my way to the library to meet Philip for that chess game he kept promising me. But there was to be no more of that, now that Cecily was here.

Still, I wandered toward the library because I had nothing better to do. I was sure Philip was doing something with William. Just as I expected, the room was empty. I sat on a chair in front of the window and looked out at the orchard. This was the same place where I had sat the day Philip told me all about his Tour. Smoothing my hand over the leather armrest, I tried not to think of the days gone by that would never return. But it was no use. I missed Philip. I missed our afternoons together. I missed the days we had before Cecily had arrived and changed everything. And I missed Cecily too—the sister I had known and loved all my life, who had always had time for me.

I lay my head against the back of the chair, closed my eyes, and tried very hard to tuck my sadness away. It was threatening to escape its proper bounds and spill out of my heart. Even using all of my concentration, I was unable to find any real security of my emotions. They wavered close to the surface, and I kept feeling the urge to cry.

I felt a stir in the air around me. Opening my eyes, I found Philip sitting on the windowsill directly in front of me, with his arms crossed, as if determined to wait there a long time if he had to. For some reason, I wasn't surprised to see him. We looked at each other in silence for a moment before the emotions I saw in his eyes became unbearable. There was sadness and gentleness and more pity than I wanted to see.

"Did you need something?" I asked.

"Yes," he said, reaching out and taking my hand. My heart thumped hard at his touch. I told myself I should pull my hand away, but I couldn't make myself do it.

"What did you need?" My voice was little more than a whisper.

"Your smile. I haven't seen it all day."

I looked at my hand in his and wondered how to respond. I didn't think I could conjure up one more false smile to save my life, so I just sighed and didn't say anything.

"Why don't you join William and me? I'm going to show him the work I've had done on the estate since his last visit."

I met his gaze. "I don't want your pity."

His grip on my hand tightened, and his voice sounded exasperated. "I am not offering you pity, Marianne. I want you to come with us."

He looked sincere, and I wanted to believe that he wanted my company. But I didn't want to know for sure, because I didn't think I could bear it if I found out that he didn't mean it—that he was only being polite. Besides that, I had still chosen Cecily. I had committed my loyalty to her. I knew it was still the right decision, even if it made me unhappy.

"Thank you for the invitation," I said, slipping my hand out of his. "But I can't accept it."

He lifted an eyebrow. "Can't or won't?" His question reminded me of my question to him the first night I was here.

Smiling a little, I answered, "Both."

He looked away.

I stood and walked to the door, but turned back when I remembered something. "Thank you for the poetry."

He looked at me again, but said nothing in return.

❧

Lady Caroline was ready to plan the ball when I met her in the drawing room. Mrs. Clumpett and Rachel were engaged in the sorts of activities that elegant ladies do—sewing and music and reading. They were clearly resigned to their roles as elegant ladies; I should resign myself to mine as well. But after sitting with Lady Caroline for an hour and a half discussing every aspect of the ball, I ached with restlessness.

She looked up from her lists and saw me shifting in my seat. "I think this is enough for now. Thank you for your help."

I stood and looked around the room. What to do now? Mrs. Clumpett sat practicing the pianoforte, reminding me that I should try to be accomplished. I sat next to Rachel on the settee and picked up the embroidery I found there. But my mind was not on my work. Something was bothering me, but it was just beyond the edge of my awareness, and I couldn't pull it to the surface. After several minutes, it came to me. It was the trip that William and Philip had mentioned, and which I had heard nothing about. Had it been my imagination, or were they all keeping it a secret from me?

Rachel glanced at me. "Good heavens! What are you doing to my embroidery?"

I looked down and realized that it was not mine, and that I had just embroidered random stitches all over the cloth. I dropped it abruptly.

"Pardon me."

Rachel picked up the embroidery and began to pick out threads. The pianoforte was loud, assuring me that the others would not overhear.

"William seems to be looking forward to this trip," I said nonchalantly. Rachel frowned at the tangle of a French knot that I had made, trying to pick it apart with a needle.

"Yes," she sighed. "I have resigned myself to it, because they enjoy it so. But my father would never have approved of it." She gave me a look of long-suffering. "He was a rector. Thank goodness he is in his grave."

I stared at her as she pulled out the stitches I had so clumsily made. What were Philip and William going to do that a rector would disapprove of?

Rachel went on. "But such are the ways of men. I know I couldn't stop William if I tried. So I don't. I have decided that the less I know about what they do, the better I feel about it. Sometimes ignorance is the best defense, you know."

I was stunned. I tried to think of some other explanation, but all I could think was that the only reason a woman would *not* want to know what her husband was doing was if he was doing something improper.

Although I had never been to Town, I knew enough that I could fit the pieces of the puzzle together for myself. After all, I had heard rumors about Mr. Kellet's scandals enough times that I understood the gist of what he was doing. Betsy had told me plenty, too, about what people in London did. But I could hardly believe they could all talk about such things so casually! Why, they had spoken about their trip in front of Lady Caroline!

I suddenly saw the Wyndham family in a new light, and I was horribly disappointed in the whole lot of them. But I couldn't say anything, or react in the way I wanted to. It would only bring further embarrassment upon me, just as it had with Cecily and Louisa.

Of course, I didn't know William well at all. But Philip! I had thought he was such a gentleman. He seemed so noble. I had thought he would somehow be above such things. How could I have been so mistaken in my understanding of his character?

I felt ill, and knew that I must escape, at once. I said something about needing to get something from my room and fled as quickly as possible. But I did not go to my room, for I knew there was no peace to be found there. Instead I roamed the house in a distracted state, trying not to imagine Philip doing things a rector wouldn't approve of, until my face was hot and my heart was sick.

In my distracted wanderings, I ended up on the third floor and stopped in front of the paintings there. Perhaps if I had something beautiful to occupy my mind, I would be able to push aside the sick feeling that roiled within me.

I had examined only a few of the landscapes, however, when I realized I was hearing an odd noise. It sounded like the clang of metal on metal, and it gradually pulled me from my concentration until curiosity drove me to explore the source. I followed the sound until I came to the room I had seen once before, on my tour of the house.

The fencing room. The door was slightly ajar, and I could look in without being seen. The sight that greeted me caused my heart to leap into my throat. It was Philip in his breeches and shirt, fencing with William. Philip looked lithe and strong and graceful and powerful. My throat went dry, and I stood still, afraid to make a noise, unable to tear my eyes away. He drove William hard against the wall, but William held him off, foil against foil.

"Rein it in, Philip. I'd rather not be injured."

Philip stepped back and muttered, "Sorry." As he turned, I saw his face clearly for the first time and caught my breath. I had never imagined he could look so impassioned. He looked as if he had a fire burning within him, and that if he ever unleashed it, it would consume everyone around him.

"I assume this mood has something to do with your . . . assignment," William said, seeming to put stress on the last word. He looked amused.

"You know it does," Philip said curtly.

"Is it really that bad?" William was definitely amused.

Philip raked a hand through his hair. "Worse than ever. I don't know how much longer I can tolerate it." William chuckled and Philip scowled at him. "You find this humorous, I see."

"After all the women you've run away from, yes, I do find this humorous."

Philip did not smile in return, though. I suddenly wondered if it was appropriate for me to listen to their conversation. How embarrassing if they were to catch me listening outside the door! I was about to back up and try to escape undetected when William spoke.

"Her grandmother arranged the visit, didn't she? Why can't you just send her back to Bath?"

I froze at his words. They were talking about me!

"I would if it were possible," Philip said. "Anything would be better than having her here. But it's out of the question. Her grandmother was very clear on that point—she doesn't want her in Bath." He sighed. "I want nothing more than to be rid of my responsibility toward her, and yet she has nowhere else to go."

My heart pounded so hard it hurt.

"We're leaving tomorrow," William said. "Perhaps her father will come back while we're gone and take her home. Then all of this will be resolved easily."

"I wish you were right, but I doubt it." Philip tapped his boot with his sword. "He has stayed away for more than a year now, and is unlikely to return any time soon."

"Then it looks like you will have to suffer it out." William grinned and lifted his foil. "Just try not to take out your frustration on me."

Philip muttered something that I couldn't hear, giving William a dark look. William just laughed.

As they began to fence again, I stepped back and turned numbly from the door. I walked slowly, very slowly, down the hall, around the corner, down the stairs, and to my bedchamber.

I closed the door and crossed the room to look out the window, fighting to keep from my heart the truth that had been thrust upon me. I may as well have been trying to blot out the sun. There was no escape from being unwanted. And that was the truth that struck at me the most deeply. Nobody wanted me—not my father or my grandmother or the Wyndhams. Not Louisa. Maybe not even Cecily. And certainly not Philip.

I had grown accustomed to my father's abandonment. And I had suspected that my grandmother had not welcomed being responsible for me. But I had never doubted Philip's friendship—not since that day we had spent together in the library. I had felt so sure of it, convinced that not even his horrid flirting could diminish the strength of the bond I felt between us.

Now, to discover that I had been wrong about everything—about Philip's character as well as his regard for me—was a blow so great that I reeled from it. Philip was not a gentleman, and he was not my friend. It was all an elaborate pretense. There was nothing real and nothing true for me to stand on.

I felt like I did the first time I had been thrown from a horse, with the reins yanked from my hands and the ground rushing up at me. Then, as now, there was nothing I could do to prevent the pain that was coming.

Chapter 19

I lay on my bed and stared at nothing. I tried to think of nothing as well, and wished that nothing could be all that was within and around me. Betsy interrupted my exercise in nothingness—the ultimate avoidance—by standing beside my bed, hands on hips.

"Aren't you going to the ball tonight?"

"No." I closed my eyes and tried to resume my state of nothingness.

But even with my eyes closed, I could feel her looking at me. Then she said, "You look just like my father did when his favorite dog died."

I opened my eyes at that. "Excuse me?"

"It's true. He had that same look about him—as if nothing else in the world could make up for what he had lost." She sighed as she sat down on the bed. "And nothing ever did."

I groaned. "Thank you, Betsy. That is very comforting." I turned away from her, hoping she would leave me to my misery, but she reached out and touched my shoulder gently.

"Do you want to tell me what happened?"

I considered lying to her. I considered remaining silent. But the knowledge I had acquired today filled me to the brim, begging for an outlet. I had never confided in Betsy before, but she might be the closest thing to a friend I had here. And she might know something that would help me understand why I had been so fooled.

"I found out that my grandmother arranged for this visit—I wasn't invited at all." My voice caught on the words. I could not tell her the rest. I could not tell anyone the most shameful part of it: I wasn't wanted here either.

"Oh, is that all?" she said breezily. "I could have told you that weeks ago."

I sat up. "What? What do you mean?"

She picked something out of her teeth. "Well, I knew all along that your grandmother arranged this, but she threatened to cut out my tongue and eat it for breakfast if I did so much as breathe a word of it to you, and I don't know what I would do without a tongue."

I rolled my eyes. "Betsy, I am sure she would not have eaten it for breakfast. You know she only eats meat at dinner," I muttered.

Betsy frowned. "I hadn't thought of that. Well, yes, she did send you here, only she didn't want you to know, so she arranged it with Lady Caroline. I'm not sure what part Miss Cecily played in it all, but my guess is Lady Caroline asked her to extend the invitation so you wouldn't be suspicious. And truthfully, I think it was a famous plan, for Sir Philip would never have looked at you twice if you had met in London, and this has worked out very much to your advantage, if I may say so."

"To my advantage? Why do you think that?" I couldn't find anything advantageous about being thrust upon an unwilling host.

"Why, so that you could ensnare him, of course."

My mouth fell open. "*Ensnare* Sir Philip?"

She swung her leg back and forth. "Yes. What other purpose could there be for this visit? And what luck that we happened to stop at that inn so that he was forced to come back!"

I could not keep myself from asking, "What do you mean, he was forced to come back?"

"Well, you know he was running away when we met up with him at the inn. Running away from you, I mean. Can you imagine, a grown man willing to spend months away from home just so he wouldn't have to meet you? But look how fate managed everything, what with James getting shot and Sir Philip stopping for a bite to eat before continuing on his journey." She looked at me, her expression turning sharp. "You must have known that."

I shook my head. "I did not."

"But what did you imagine he was doing at the inn that late at night?"

"I didn't even think about it."

"Well, from what I heard, as soon as he got word that you were coming, he flew out of here as if the devil himself were chasing him."

As if the devil himself were chasing him. I recalled my conversation with Miss Grace—how she had assumed I was just another ambitious female with my cap set at Philip.

"Betsy, does everyone think I came here to . . . ensnare Sir Philip?"

She shrugged. "I imagine so. That's the talk in the kitchen, at least."

"I hope you set them straight."

She bit her lip and looked away.

"Betsy!"

"Well, it would be difficult to make anyone believe otherwise, considering how you've been carrying on."

I choked. "Carrying on? How have I been carrying on?"

"You know—spending so much time with him. And the way you look at him . . ."

"How do I look at him?" I asked as dread filled me.

She waved a hand in the air. "As if he . . . created happiness."

I groaned and lay back on the bed, covering my face with my hands. I felt consumed by embarrassment. All of those hours I had spent with Philip in what I deemed to be innocent companionship had been noted and gossiped about by all the servants. They seemed like tainted hours now, and I regretted every one of them.

"What will you do about the ball?" Betsy asked.

"Will you give me a little time? Alone?"

"Of course." She left the room quietly.

I stood and paced in front of the window. I had to leave. I couldn't stay where I wasn't wanted. But where could I go? My grandmother had sent me here, and it seemed she didn't want me to return to Bath. My father hadn't answered my last three letters. And I had no other close relatives that I could impose on.

In desperation, I sat at my writing desk and took out a piece of paper. My father might not want me any longer, but I had a right to call on him for help. I scrawled a message to him, worried that if I thought too much about my words, I would cry and ruin the letter.

> *Dear Papa,*
>
> *I am sorry that my horse balked at the jump that morning. I am sorry that Mama's horse threw a shoe and so she took mine instead. I have thought and thought and thought if I might have prevented the accident, but I cannot think how, and it is too late to undo it. What I must know is if you blame me, and if you still love me, and why you have abandoned me when I have needed you so much.*
>
> *Love,*
> *Marianne*

I quickly folded the letter, biting my lip to keep myself from losing control of my emotions. If I started to cry now, I didn't know how I would ever be able to stop.

I opened the drawer of the writing desk to retrieve the wax and seal, but my fingers froze as I spied the two letters tucked in the back of the drawer—Philip's love letter and his note. I pulled them out, carefully unfolded them, and read each one. My heart ached and then throbbed with anger and resentment. How dare he deceive me? How dare he pretend to be my friend when all along he wanted to be rid of me?

I knew what I had to do. I tore the love letter in half, then half again, then half again. I could still see some words though: *torment, adore, desperately.* Each word stabbed me with the pain of betrayal. I ripped the words again and again, wishing I could obliterate every feeling in my heart as easily. I didn't stop until there was nothing left but tiny, unreadable crumbs of paper. Then I did the same with his note, swept the pile of broken words into my hands, and threw them all into the fireplace.

When Betsy came back a few minutes later, I handed her the letter addressed to my father.

"Will you see that this gets mailed as soon as possible?"

She nodded and tucked the letter into her pocket. "But what about the ball?"

The ball. Philip would be at the ball, but so would Mr. Beaufort. Mr. Beaufort was interested in me. He might even want to marry me. I checked my heart again, and felt nothing from it. It was dull and empty—lifeless. That was exactly the way I wanted it.

"Yes, I am going. But I want to look more beautiful tonight than I ever have before. Are you up to the challenge?"

She clapped her hands. "Leave it to me. You will look ravishing, I am sure."

I smiled grimly.

When I stood before the mirror after Betsy had finished with me, I studied myself with an objective eye. I wore the green silk gown, and I did not look like a very young girl anymore. Perhaps it was the hairstyle and the jewelry and the gown, but I thought it had just as much to do with the glint in my eye.

Betsy stood back to look at me, critically, from head to toe. She finally nodded with approval.

"You won't even need to pinch your cheeks tonight," she said. "They're already rosy."

I thanked her and pulled on my long gloves as I left my room and walked down the hall. I paused before I reached the stairs. Hiding in the shadows, I breathed deeply and tried to prepare myself mentally for what was coming. My only hope for success tonight was pinned on my being able to remain immune to Philip's charm. I had to keep my heart shut away and silent. If he disassembled my defenses it was possible I might lose the dignity I was working so hard for. And then I might do something unpardonable, like cry in his presence or tell him that I knew he didn't want me here.

Therefore, I built up my armor, chink by chink, against him. I repeated to myself all that I held against Philip. I thought of his many faults as I walked with careful dignity down the stairs. He lied, for one. He told me I was welcome here when I was not. He led me into a false sense of security by making me feel certain he was my friend, when all along he wanted to be rid of me.

He was arrogant, for another, if he thought I would come all this way in the hope of ensnaring a man I had never met. What an assumption! Did he think every woman who glanced his way was pining for him? Would sacrifice her dignity for the chance of securing him as her husband? Well, he was much mistaken, for I would never sacrifice anything for him.

The butler opened the doors to the drawing room, and I stepped inside. The rest of the family was already assembled, but I hardly noticed them. I only noticed Philip, as he quickly looked my way, and I saw something flash in his eyes that looked like admiration. But I must have been mistaken, for he did not admire me. He wanted to be rid of me. I remembered my task at hand and moved to the other side of the room where I could continue to list his faults to myself without having to be near him.

He was too handsome. Much too handsome. Especially tonight, in his formal black, with his waistcoat and cravat snowy white and his hair gleaming in the candlelight and his eyes meeting mine across the room with a question in them. I turned away so I would not have to see his much-too-handsome face. It was a great fault of his, for it led feeling young ladies to want to forgive his other faults for the sake of his eyes and his smile.

He was persistent. I added that to my list of his faults when he crossed the room to me even though I obviously wanted nothing to do with him.

"What have I done to deserve that look?" he asked in a low voice so that nobody else could hear. It was a deceptive thing to do, for it made it seem like we were coconspirators instead of an unwilling host and an unwanted guest.

"You have done nothing, sir."

"Sir?" He said it as if it was an insult. "Now I know it's serious. Tell me at once so that I may apologize."

I laughed lightly, but I felt nothing but hardness inside. "You're imagining things."

Philip frowned as the butler opened the door and announced that the carriage was ready. As I turned to the door, I saw Cecily watching me with a suspicious look. It didn't bother me, though. She could have Sir Philip Wyndham. They would make a perfect pair, the two of them. She would flirt with Mr. Kellet while Philip went away to do things a rector wouldn't approve of, and they could live a happy, deceitful, immoral life together.

I made sure I did not sit next to Philip in the carriage, but the way it turned out was worse, for Philip sat directly across from me, with his knee brushing mine when the carriage swayed around a turn, and his gaze fixed on me so completely that I felt my face burning. To distract myself I continued my list.

He was too perceptive. I did not like that about him at all. He always said I had an expressive face, but the fault was his for seeing too much. I did not want him to know anything of my heart tonight, so I kept my face averted, choosing to look out the window and paying no heed to the conversation of the others.

I nearly had my list and my armor complete when we stopped in front of the Assembly Hall. Philip stepped out of the carriage first, then turned to me and offered me his hand, which I was forced to accept or else risk tripping and falling to the ground. His grip was strong and dependable and familiar. My defenses trembled at his touch.

Too handsome, I repeated to myself. Too perceptive. Too charming. I had added that last one to the list during the carriage ride. Too familiar, too moving, too persistent. Of course, I could not forget the most important: too deceitful.

I dropped his hand as soon as I touched the ground and felt both relieved and disappointed at the same time. I must work harder at schooling my heart, I told myself. I must not let it override the rational workings of my mind.

I saw Mr. Beaufort as soon as I entered the ballroom. He began to make his way across the crowded room toward me. Philip stood at my side, and even though I intentionally did not look at him, his closeness was making me very nervous.

I tried to find my smile and my poise as Mr. Beaufort drew near, but I could hardly breathe with Philip standing so close. Then I saw Mr. Kellet smirking at me from across the room, which made the evening even worse.

"Will you dance with me tonight?" Philip asked in a quiet voice.

My heart skipped at least three beats. I pulled up my gloves, feigning interest in them.

"No, thank you," I said, striving for nonchalance in my voice.

Mr. Beaufort was only a few steps away when a group of women moved between us, blocking his path.

"No, thank you?" Philip asked, disbelief in his voice.

My heart was pounding, my face flushed. I dared a quick glance up at Philip. He was searching my face as if for clues, his brow contracted, his mouth a tight line. "What has happened?"

I shrugged and looked away from him. "Absolutely nothing."

Philip was clearly upset. The thought gave me a mean sort of pleasure. He *should* be upset. He was, after all, the cause of everything that was wrong about this evening. He was the deceiver, not I. I ignored the quiet voice inside of me that reminded me of the lies I had told tonight.

Mr. Beaufort had maneuvered around the group of women and was now but a few paces away from me. Philip stood so close that I could feel his warmth even though we were not touching. I gripped my hands together. He was too close. His warmth, his intensity, and his familiarity were all working against my defenses. But before I could step away from him, he leaned down and spoke low in my ear, so low that nobody else could have heard.

"You look beautiful tonight."

A shiver spread through me and I blushed furiously, for Philip's quiet voice had made the words sound sincere. In the next instant, he straightened and walked away without looking back.

I tore my gaze away from Philip's broad shoulders to see Mr. Beaufort standing before me and bowing.

"Miss Daventry. You have grown in beauty in just the few days since we met."

I tried to feel flattered, but his words fell on my ears with a hollow ring. Nevertheless, I smiled and murmured, "Thank you."

A dance was beginning. I gave Mr. Beaufort my hand and allowed him to lead me to the dance floor, where couples were lining up across from each other. I focused my gaze on him and tried to forget the warring emotions of the day. I tried to quiet my heart, which had been bounding at a furious pace ever since I had seen Philip tonight. Taking a deep breath, I told myself to focus on the task at hand. Tonight was an exercise in learning how to be an elegant lady. I would do everything I could to forget that Philip was even in the room. It would be easy to do, especially since I had already refused to dance with him.

I smiled brightly at Mr. Beaufort, ready to try my hand at flirting, until seconds before the dance started. That was when I noticed Philip standing on Mr. Beaufort's right hand. I looked at him with surprise, then to my left and saw that Cecily was his partner. Her smile had that tinge of suggestiveness that made me think of what she learned in London about kissing rakes. A surge of jealousy rose so swiftly within my breast that I lost my breath for a moment. I turned my gaze back to Mr. Beaufort, but

I had to work very hard to remember that I didn't care what Philip or Cecily did.

The music began. It was a lively dance, which was fortunate, because it left little opportunity for speaking. I tried to smile at Mr. Beaufort and not look at Philip, but it took so much effort that by the end of the dance I was exhausted.

I hardly had time to catch my breath before another gentleman stepped forward and asked me to dance. This time Cecily danced with Mr. Kellet. I saw Philip down the line dancing with Miss Grace, even though I was not looking for him. I thought I should practice my flirting, to keep my mind off of Philip, but I was hardly successful. My smile was forced and my attention kept wandering to Philip and the words I had heard him speak to William.

After a few more dances, the musicians took a break. I stood by an open window and allowed my gaze to sweep the crowd. Without effort, my eyes caught on Philip. I was not trying to find him among the crowd. He just happened to be the sort of man who stood out among other gentlemen. And there he was, near an open window, talking to Mr. Beaufort.

Both gentlemen were standing stiffly, and neither of them was smiling. It almost looked as if they might be arguing, but I couldn't imagine what they would have to argue about since they hardly knew one another.

It was difficult to not compare the two men as they stood together. Mr. Beaufort was certainly dashing, with his stylish golden hair and the flair of his dress. But seeing him next to Philip, his appeal faded greatly in my mind. For it was obvious, comparing them side by side, that Mr. Beaufort was like a set of paste jewels—flashy on the outside but really an imposter, with nothing of great value within.

Philip, on the other hand, shone like a real gem—without even trying. His clothes were just as well-made as Mr. Beaufort's, but he wore them with a natural, athletic grace, and he didn't employ any extreme fashions to create an impression. He was purely elegant, naturally, without thought or planning, and upon looking at them, I found that I would infinitely prefer the real gem to the imposter.

I felt sick with disappointment and disgusted with myself. There was no comparison to make. Philip did not want me; Mr. Beaufort did. That was the only thing that mattered. And besides that, I did not want Philip—that handsome, incorrigible, charming tease who stole hearts he had no intention of keeping.

I was not aware of Mrs. Fairhurst's presence until she spoke, and then I was startled to hear her so close. "Sir Philip is certainly a great catch, is he not?"

She was looking in the same direction I had been, and I blushed, embarrassed to have been caught watching Philip, especially by her. I turned my back to the man in question and said, "Is he?"

She laughed through her nose. "Oh, come, Miss Daventry. You cannot deceive me. I know you are perfectly aware of his . . . attractions."

I looked at her with barely concealed loathing. She smiled at me with her lips but not her eyes.

"If I am," I said, "how is that any concern of yours?"

"Oh, it's not my *concern*. I am simply doing you a favor, my dear, since you obviously did not heed my Grace's warning to you when you arrived." She opened her fan and waved it briskly. "He has half the ladies in London violently in love with him every year. Elegant, accomplished ladies of rank and fortune." She lifted an eyebrow as her gaze swept over my figure. "Clearly you cannot comprehend how far you fall beneath his level."

Anger burned away my embarrassment. I knew she was right, but I would not give this atrocious woman the satisfaction of appearing cowed. "Half the ladies in London are in love with Sir Philip, you say?" I asked with an innocent look.

She nodded, her smile now quite smug.

"Hmm. He would be very disappointed to hear that, for he assured *me* it was closer to three-fourths."

Her smile froze.

"I wonder which one of us is right," I said. "Shall I ask him?"

She snapped her fan closed, her eyes blazing with anger. "That will not be necessary."

Suddenly Philip was standing before us, and both Mrs. Fairhurst and I jumped a little. He ignored Mrs. Fairhurst entirely. Holding out his hand to me, he said, "I believe I have the next dance."

Chapter 20

Philip most certainly did *not* have the next dance, but I was not about to admit that in front of Mrs. Fairhurst. I had no choice but to put my hand in his and let him lead me to the dance floor.

This was most unexpected. As he led me to the line of couples, I frantically searched my memory for the list of his faults I had compiled earlier. But I couldn't think clearly while standing across from him, waiting for the music to begin. I was nervous—very nervous. I had never danced with Philip before, and having him watch me with those familiar eyes was making my heart race. I took a deep breath and decided I would pretend he was any one of the ordinary men I had danced with that evening. In fact, I wouldn't even look at his face. I would look at his cravat and say nothing.

The music started. I stepped toward Philip as he stepped toward me. I kept my eyes fixed on that perfectly tied cravat. I could do this. I could pretend he was a stranger and never meet his eyes and never feel anything at all while dancing with him.

But I had not taken into account one important fact: Philip did not dance like any ordinary man I knew. When he touched my waist, he did not rest his hand passively and lightly. Rather, he pulled me toward him, his hand pressing on the small of my back, so that in a step I was so close

I could feel him breathe. A shock raced through me, and I looked up in surprise. I looked into his eyes, which I had sworn I would not do.

Oh, my. Perhaps an experienced lady in London would know what to do with the smoldering look he gave me, but I did not. And I found, quite to my dismay, that when I looked into Philip's eyes I could not remember a single fault on that list. He said nothing, and I said nothing as we turned. When he released me, my legs felt weak and my hands shook. I turned in a daze to follow the other steps in the dance.

Before I was prepared for it, it was time to meet in the middle again. I could not believe I had ever danced this way before without realizing how intimate it was. My hand clasping Philip's, his other hand on my waist, pulling me close while we gazed into each other's eyes—it was all too much. And still he said nothing to me. I began to think it would be better if he did say something, if only so I could say something flippant in return and dispel the emotion that was building between us.

I saw, when he released me, that Lady Caroline stood just behind the line of dancers, watching us, and that Rachel, who was dancing with William several couples down, was also looking our way. My face burned and I wondered what they were thinking. Did I look like I was trying to ensnare Philip? And where was Cecily? What was she thinking?

Just when I thought things couldn't be worse, Philip spoke. He pulled me close and said in a low voice, "Half the ladies in London?"

So he *had* overheard! "Yes, that seems to be the general consensus."

His eyes narrowed and he watched me as we moved apart and down the line of dancers. When we met again, he asked, "Is that what you're holding against me?"

"I'm not holding anything against you." I spoke stiffly, then tried to smile so he would believe the lie.

Philip shook his head. "You're a terrible liar. You shouldn't even try."

I glared at him, wracking my brain for the perfect reply. Nothing came to mind, however, which may have been because I could never think clearly when I was this close to him.

"You know, your glare is not quite the punishment you think it is," he said.

His breath brushed my neck and made another shiver run through me. I lifted an eyebrow.

"And why is that?" I tried to keep my voice frosty.

The steps of the dance took us apart, and I had to wait, tense with anticipation, to hear his answer. Philip never looked away from me. When we finally met in the middle again, he said, "You are even more beautiful when you're angry."

I shot him a dark look. "Don't be absurd."

"I'm not," Philip said. His eyes were still smoldering, and I sensed again that restrained passion within him that I had witnessed in the fencing room. "You should see yourself, with that flash of fire in your eyes. And when you press your lips together like that, a dimple appears in your left cheek, right next to your mouth. I find it . . . maddening."

I burned with embarrassment and anger and severe discomfort. Philip was *flirting* with me, and it was very wrong of him. I had always known that his flirting was a game to him, and so that wasn't what made me angry. What angered me was that his flirting made me realize that all of those other gentlemen I had danced with did not know how to flirt at all. Not one of them had made me feel as if I were turned inside out and set on fire all at once. And how could I ever be happy with another man when Philip was around to outshine them all?

Besides that, it was apparent that Sir Philip Wyndham was the most infuriating man alive, for now I couldn't even give him an angry look without knowing he enjoyed the sight. I was left, in fact, completely defenseless.

There in the middle of the dance floor my armor was undone and the unthinkable happened. I remembered that Philip didn't want me, and never had. My sadness flared to life, burning through my anger, melting every defense I had. Then I made a terrible mistake. At the height of my vulnerability, I looked into Philip's eyes. Time seemed to slow, the music faded away, and the other dancers disappeared. There was nobody in the world except for Philip and me, and I was finally close enough to discover the secret I had sensed in his eyes.

It was there, shining so clearly, so obviously, that I wondered how I had never seen it before. I was so stunned I stopped dancing, appalled, while the truth I had discovered burned devastatingly bright within me. The most surprising part of my discovery was that it wasn't Philip's secret I had seen in his eyes, but my own.

I was in love with Philip Wyndham.

A second thought immediately followed the first: Philip was certainly not in love with me.

Dread dropped through me. Oh, what had I done? How had I been so great a fool?

"Marianne?"

I blinked and tried to focus on Philip's face. His eyes were tight with concern. "You're very pale," he said. "Are you unwell?" He gripped my elbow tightly, as if to hold me up.

I nodded. I was unwell.

"Excuse me," I said, turning away from him. I was surprised that he let me go so easily. Perhaps I wrenched myself free, though. I was too dazed to know how it happened, but suddenly I was free of him and pushing my way through the crowd of dancers. They were turning and smiling and talking and laughing, arms and hands and faces and legs and noise and ribbons and lips. I was jostled, and I pushed back harder, desperate to escape the tumult, when a hand snatched at mine.

It was Philip's, and looking over my shoulder I saw his lips move—he said something—but I couldn't hear what. Everything was too loud and too whirling and too hot. I tripped over dancing feet, and then an arm was around my waist, and Philip pulled me out of the dance, where his mother waited with a worried expression.

187

I sat in a chair by a window. Philip leaned over me, looking very worried, and Lady Caroline was there, too, fanning me and asking what had happened.

"She nearly fainted in the middle of the dance," Philip said.

What an absurd thing to say. I never fainted—well, almost never. But I did feel strangely detached from my body. I couldn't feel my legs or arms. I was floating, groundless. I looked down and was surprised to see Philip's hand gripping mine. I couldn't feel that either. Cecily was suddenly by my side, smelling like lilacs and exuding such soft beauty she looked like an angel.

"Oh, dear," she said. "I thought you looked terribly pale. Where are my smelling salts?" She took my free hand and rubbed it between hers. "Are you feeling faint now? Perhaps we should find a place for you to lie down. Or a drink."

A sense of clarity came back to me as I looked into her familiar blue eyes. They were my mother's eyes. And this was Cecily, my twin sister, who was in love with the same man I was, and who would undoubtedly be able to win his heart. And why shouldn't she? After all, he didn't want me.

"I'm fine," I said, pulling my hand away from Philip's, but not Cecily's. I did not look at him. "I think it was the heat. Please don't give me another thought. I'll sit here by the window for a few minutes and be as good as new."

"I'll stay with you," Philip said, but his solicitude only fired an anger deep within me. How dare he continue to try to deceive me? How dare he continue to toy with my heart?

"No," I said, harshly, and saw out of the corner of my eye how Philip's head jerked back with surprise. "You should finish the dance," I continued, trying to soften my voice. "With Cecily."

I was sure Philip was looking at me, but I did not return his gaze. It was part of the defenses I had raised. After a moment, I saw him bow his head and offer Cecily his hand. As soon as they walked away, I turned to Lady Caroline.

"May I go home? Please?" I couldn't even think of an excuse to give her.

Concern touched her eyes, but she said nothing more than, "Of course. I am growing tired of dancing myself. I will accompany you."

I waited at the door while she had the carriage brought around. I kept my back to the dancers so I would not have to watch Philip and Cecily dancing together. Lady Caroline was very considerate and only spoke a few times in the carriage about the ball and the weather. She didn't ask me to confide in her, and I was grateful for that. I think if I had been given a chance, I would have burst into tears. As it turned out, I was able to keep my emotions in check until we reached the house.

Betsy was surprised to see me back so early, but I said nothing to explain myself, and after a few minutes, she stopped asking questions. As soon as I was out of my gown and into my nightgown, I dismissed her and crawled into bed. I lay awake, examining the workings of my heart. It was a painful and embarrassing exercise, but I needed illumination more than I needed shielding.

This is what I discovered: I had loved Philip all along. I had kept it a secret, even from myself, and I had shied away from that secret over and over again.

I supposed I had sensed intuitively that once I acknowledged the secret, I would also have to acknowledge the fact that Philip would never feel the same way about me, and that would ruin everything. And my intuition was right—Philip didn't feel the same. In fact, he would do anything to be rid of me. Well, I would make sure he got what he wanted. He would be rid of me, as soon as possible. This paradise was ruined for me. As soon as Lady Caroline's ball was over, I would find a way out of Edenbrooke, even if it meant going back to Bath.

At that decision, I broke all of my promises to myself. With a great, wrenching sob, my heart broke open, and I cried as I had not cried since my mother died.

Chapter 21

Philip was gone when I awoke. Betsy announced it to me in her breathless voice, elated about having new gossip to share. I sat in bed holding the cup of chocolate she brought me, feeling conflicted. The defensive part of me did not want to hear Philip's name at all. The weak part of me wanted to hear of nothing else. I also had a throbbing headache from crying so much through the night. I said nothing as I listened to Betsy's ramblings, as I was involved in a battle between my mind and my heart.

"I saw them before they left—Sir Philip and Mr. Wyndham, that is. I was coming from the kitchen and they were standing in the foyer and Sir Philip happened to see me. Imagine my surprise when he came and spoke to me!"

I nearly dropped my cup. "He spoke to you?"

"Yes. He said, 'You're Miss Daventry's maid, are you not?' And I said that I was, and he asked me how you were feeling. 'Well enough, I daresay,' I told him, and then I remembered that I still had the letter you had asked me to mail in my pocket, so I gave it to him and asked him to frank it. He said he would take care of it, and he took it with him. Now he and Mr. Wyndham are gone, but they will be back in a week, I've heard, for the ball."

I stared at her. "You gave my letter to Sir Philip?"

"Yes. Wasn't it a good idea?"

I did not want Philip to have my letter. It was personal. What if he somehow accidentally opened it and read it? I knew that was a far-fetched idea, but it was within the realm of possibility. I felt vulnerable knowing he had my letter, and I did not like the feeling one bit. But there was nothing I could do about it.

After dressing, I found Cecily lying in her bed, recovering from her late night. My good intentions were firmly in place when I asked her how she had enjoyed the remainder of the ball.

"It was not as enjoyable as I had hoped," she said, covering her yawn with a dainty hand. "Sir Philip was in a strange mood. He hardly spoke two words to me when we danced together, and as soon as the music ended, he walked away. I didn't see him again until the carriage ride home. But luckily Mr. Kellet was very attentive." She flashed me a sly smile. "*Very* attentive."

I was taken aback by her look. "What do you mean?"

She rolled her eyes. "Marianne! I thought you were a little bit wiser now." She leaned forward and whispered, "He told me to meet him outside, and when I did, he grabbed me and kissed me."

My smile froze. "And how was it?"

She leaned back against her pillows, grinning. "It's like I told you—the rakes are the best kissers."

"Cecily!" I stood abruptly. "How can you . . . how can you act like that and talk like that? How can you even *think* of another man when you're supposed to be violently in love with Sir Philip?"

"Well, *he's* not trying to kiss me, now, is he? So I might as well find my pleasure where it's available until he does act on his feelings." She raked her hands through her hair. "And there is plenty of pleasure to be had from Mr. Kellet."

I reeled back, shocked. And then I remembered that Philip was off seeking the same type of pleasure. I turned away from her in disgust and walked to the door.

"Where are you going?" she asked, sounding surprised. "Don't you want to hear more about the ball?"

"No," I said, opening the door. My good intentions had fled. "I have no desire to hear anything at all about rakes or . . . or kissing . . . or whatever it is you elegant people do in pursuit of pleasure. You may talk to Louisa about it." I slammed the door shut behind me.

Mr. Beaufort called on me later that morning. I had a talk with myself as I walked downstairs to meet him. Here was a handsome, respectable young gentleman who seemed interested in me, and I told myself I should do all that I could to encourage him. After all, a little encouragement from me might lead to an offer of marriage. And right now, when it appeared nobody in the world wanted me, an offer of marriage seemed like a light in the darkness.

Lady Caroline sat with Mr. Beaufort in the drawing room. He still looked dashing and handsome, but now that I had a chance to really look at him, I saw a dullness in his hazel eyes that disconcerted me. But that didn't matter. He wanted to be with me. I focused on flirting and encouraging, and set to it as if it were an arduous task. After half an hour, Mr. Beaufort stood, looking pleased, and bade me good-bye.

"I hope I may call on you again soon," he said.

I watched him leave before I glanced at Lady Caroline, who had kept us company while we visited. She set aside her embroidery and turned to me with a smile.

"I am going to cut some roses in the garden. Will you join me?"

I wanted to refuse—I was exhausted from my attempts at flirting— but she smiled at me with such warm affection that I couldn't find it in my heart to tell her no. I went upstairs to get my bonnet, and when I returned, she was waiting for me with two baskets and two shears. We walked to the rose garden. I tried not to remember the time I had spent wandering through the gardens with Philip. I tried not to think of Philip at all, actually. Not what we had done, and certainly not what I assumed he was doing right now. *That* thought made me feel as if I had plunged the shears right into my heart.

I started cutting roses and laying them carefully in my basket. After a moment of companionable silence, Lady Caroline said, "There is nothing in my life that makes me happier than to see my children happy. Especially Philip."

Oh, no. She was going to talk to me about Philip? That was the last thing I wanted to hear about.

She went on. "It has been so nice—no, more than nice—it has been a real joy to see Philip so happy lately, to see him laughing again."

I looked at her in surprise. "He didn't laugh before?" The idea seemed absurd—incomprehensible even.

"Oh, no, he used to laugh. He just hasn't recently." She brushed a bee away from the rose she was cutting. "As a boy, Philip was lighthearted and carefree. He had a talent for charming someone out of the sulks or turning a fight into a comedy. There was always a new energy when he entered a room—as if he carried a ray of sunshine with him wherever he went."

She sighed. "But he seemed to lose that part of himself when he took on his father's role. I think the weight of his responsibility made him take himself too seriously. And then, being flattered and pursued by so many ambitious women . . . well, I fear it ruined him." Her mouth set in a firm line. "He became an arrogant boor." She snipped a rose.

I thought of my first impression of Philip at the inn. "I know what you mean. I encountered that arrogance when I first met him."

Lady Caroline smiled. "Insufferable!"

"Yes, he was," I agreed with a laugh.

"But he's not like that anymore, is he?"

I shook my head. I hadn't thought of it before, but Philip's arrogance was a distant memory for me.

"That's what I meant when I said it was a joy to see him happy again," Lady Caroline said. "It is as if we have our Philip back—the Philip we all love, the Philip we have all missed these past few years. And having him back has made the whole family happy in a way we haven't been since my dear husband died." She stopped cutting and turned to me. Putting a gentle hand on my arm, she said, with utter sincerity, "We all feel so indebted to you, my dear."

I was so surprised that I snipped off a large white rose too close to its head. Feeling like I had just beheaded something, I shoved my shears into my basket. "You think this change in him is because of me?" I asked in disbelief.

"Why, I know it is."

She continued cutting roses as if our conversation was at an end. I watched her in suspense, wanting her to convince me that she was right even though I knew she was wrong. My heart had not yet succumbed to my will. It wanted to hope, even though hope was futile and foolish. I tried to bite back the words, but finally, in a moment of weakness, I blurted, "How do you know?"

Her lips twitched as if she were fighting back a smile. It reminded me of an expression I had seen on Philip's face more than once. She put her shears in her basket and gestured to a bench set in the shade of a tree. Sitting beside her, I wondered if this was the most foolish thing I had done yet.

"Did you know that Philip was running away the night you two met?"

I nodded, remembering what Betsy had told me.

Lady Caroline sighed. "I'm afraid I am partly to blame for that. Philip had returned from Town a few weeks before. He can't stand staying in London for the whole season. I thought it was an accomplishment that I had gotten him there for any part of it. Well, I didn't send him word that you and your sister were going to visit. I left the girls with my son and his wife and came here myself, to warn Philip and prepare for your visit.

"He had reacted poorly in the past, you see, when young ladies came to visit, and I thought surprising him with it might be the way to go. But I was wrong. He assumed it was another case of ambitious young ladies after his wealth or his title, and he couldn't bear another visit like that. There have been so many, you know. He left that evening without a word to me."

She looked closely at me, as if trying to convince me of something by the force of her gaze. "But then he met you at the inn, and he came back." Her smile warmed her eyes. "He came back, my dear, that very night, late in the night. Now, I must confess to a little meddling on my part. When he returned and told me what had happened to you, and how he had met you at the inn, I had a suspicion. So I wrote to Rachel and told her to keep the girls an extra week in London, using the masquerade ball as an excuse. Your first evening here, when Philip came into the drawing room and saw you . . ." She breathed deeply, shaking her head a little as if in wonder. "He lit up, Marianne, just like he used to do." She rested her hand on mine and squeezed it. "I had my Philip back."

I watched in surprise as her eyes filled with tears. But when she smiled, I realized they were tears born of joy.

"Forgive me if I have been too personal," she said, gracefully wiping a tear from her cheek. "But after losing my dear husband, and my son Charles, it felt like more than I could bear to lose Philip too."

Dismay filled me. She was giving me too much credit for whatever change she had seen recently in Philip. I was certain I was not responsible, for it was in direct opposition to what I had heard from Philip with my own ears. He didn't want me here. Something else must have made him happy. It certainly wasn't me.

I wanted to tell her how mistaken she was, but I couldn't. "Thank you for sharing that with me," I said, attempting to smile. "I feel like I understand your family a little better now."

She looked at me in her keen way. "I hoped it would help you understand Philip a little better."

"Yes, that too," I said to placate her, and then I quickly excused myself. Her hope was too painful to witness. If she thought that my relationship with Philip had sparked the change in him that had made her so happy, then she would be very disappointed when I left Edenbrooke next week.

Halfway to the house, my steps faltered, then stopped. A gentleman was walking toward me across the lawn, coming from the direction of the woods. Mr. Kellet. I thought of turning and running in the other direction, but he called out to me.

"You're not thinking of running away from me, are you, cousin?"

Why would he not stop calling me that? I stood my ground and frowned, refusing to let him think I was afraid of him. "No, I am not. I am only going to take a turn around the lawn. You are welcome, of course, to join me."

He smiled as if that had been his plan all along and he had just manipulated me into doing what he wanted. Which was probably true. He seemed to delight in vexing me. We began to walk—me quickly, and he with a strolling gait that made me want to yank his walking cane out of his hand and break it over his head. He *would* try to prolong my suffering.

"How is the old bird?" he asked, referring, I gathered, to my grandmother.

I gave him a haughty look. "Still in good health, I believe."

He sighed and looked up at the sky. "Will she never die?"

I shot him an angry look, ready to berate him, but he laughed and said, "You are so easily taken in, cousin. You should do something about that."

I hated thinking that he had the upper hand. And I was through with politeness. "Stop calling me cousin. Why are you here?"

"Visiting my dear cousin, of course."

I stopped and turned to him. "No. I mean why are you here, in Kent? Did you follow me?"

He laughed. "You flatter yourself." He stopped and leaned on his walking cane. "But I did receive some interesting news. Evidently your grandmother has decided my scandalous behavior has shamed her long enough, and she has cut me out of her will."

"Oh?"

His eyes narrowed. "And I thought to myself—who would she name her heir if not me? Not that old maid, Amelia." He pointed his walking cane at me. "You."

I decided to meet his challenge head on. "You are right. But the inheritance is conditional. She can still cut me off without a penny, just as she did to you."

"Conditional on what?"

"That is none of your concern, *cousin.*"

He laughed lightly and raised an eyebrow. "Touché!" He studied me for a moment with narrowed eyes as if debating a course of action. I watched with a sense of misgiving as a slow smile spread across his face. "Well, this has been very enlightening. But now I have somewhere else to be." He bowed casually and turned away to saunter toward the road. Several leaves clung to the back of his coat, and one was even sticking out of the top of his boot.

Good riddance, I thought. But I couldn't help wondering why he would come all the way here to ask those few questions. And what had he been doing in the woods? A movement out of the corner of my eye caught my attention. It was Cecily, walking from the direction of the woods. She was brushing off her skirt, and, as I watched, she pulled a leaf out of her hair.

I stared at her, feeling sick. This was the kind of conduct she had learned in London? This was considered acceptable behavior for an elegant young lady? I turned away, disgusted at the sight of her disheveled hair and happy smile.

When I reached my room, I wrote two letters. The first was quick and to the point.

Dear Grandmother,

I have had the misfortune of seeing Mr. Kellet in the area. I have also lost James, the coachman you hired. Also, I know that you arranged for this visit and made everyone lie to me about being invited here. If you didn't want me, you should have just told me so instead of letting me impose on someone else. And I am not impressed with elegant ladies at all. I think I would prefer to milk cows for the rest of my days.

Sincerely,
Marianne

I meant exactly what I wrote. I had no desire to become like Cecily. And if that was what was required to earn a fortune, then I would simply not earn that fortune. I was not destitute, after all. My father was well enough off, and I would have an inheritance from him. But I would not waste any more of my time trying to become someone I was not.

After I finished my letter to Grandmother, I saw Mr. Whittles's book of poems in the drawer and thought of another letter I had been meaning to write for some time. The second letter took more thought, but when I finally finished with it, I was pleased with the result. There was so much waste in hoping for something that could never be yours, I decided. It was better to seize happiness where it was available. I addressed the letter to Mr. Whittles.

Chapter 22

The next morning Mr. Beaufort called on me again. As soon as he entered the drawing room, he addressed Lady Caroline.

"Is there some place I might speak with Miss Daventry in private?"

Oh, no.

Lady Caroline said something about needing to speak with the house-keeper and shut the door behind her as she left.

I was not ready for this conversation. It had happened too quickly, and I had given no thought as to how I might respond.

I gestured toward the settee. "Would you like to sit down?"

"Only if it pleases you," he said with a smile.

I sat on the settee and folded my hands in my lap, wondering what to say to him.

Evidently he did not need my contribution, though. He sat next to me and said, "Miss Daventry, I have not been able to stop thinking of you since the moment I laid eyes on you. You have captured my heart, and I cannot restrain myself from declaring that I love you!" He grasped my hand and knelt before me. "I have little in the ways of the world to offer you, but what I can offer you is my undying affection, my esteem, and my relentless adoration of you. Will you do me the honor of accepting my hand in marriage?"

I wondered how I had ever thought him handsome. His eyes seemed like shallow pools—nothing like the depth I always saw in Philip's eyes. Of course, I was not choosing between Mr. Beaufort and Philip, because Philip had not offered for me. But I was choosing for myself, and even if nobody else wanted me, I did not want to spend the rest of my life looking into those dull, shallow eyes.

"I am sorry," I said. "I cannot accept you."

Mr. Beaufort's smile dropped, and his eyes flashed with something like anger. I leaned away from him, surprised by the sudden turn in his emotion. But he abruptly returned to smiling, and said, "Perhaps you need time to consider my offer." He took my hand and pressed his lips to it. "I will be happy to call on you again."

He left before I could tell him not to bother. I was sure I would not be changing my mind. I would rather grow into an old spinster than marry a man I did not love, now that I knew what it meant to love.

I walked across the room and stood in front of my mother's painting. Had Lady Caroline been right about my mother? Had she felt like Lady Caroline had everything my mother wanted? If so, I understood perfectly why the friendship had ended. I think I would hate Cecily forever if she had everything I wanted—Edenbrooke and Meg and Philip. Especially Philip. I touched the frame and leaned toward the painting, wishing fiercely for my own mother.

"My dear, are you unwell?"

I lifted my head. It was Mrs. Clumpett, with her perpetual smile. Even now, with her forehead creased with worry, her mouth still turned up.

"No, I am well," I said. "Only a little . . . homesick."

She nodded. "I can well understand that feeling. Mr. Clumpett and I have missed our own home. The birds around here are just not the same. And the library is so disorganized."

I smiled. "You're right."

"In fact, now that I think of it, I believe it's time for us to go home.

Oh, wait, I forgot." She glanced at me quickly, then looked away. "We will have to stay a little while longer." She sighed. "Unless . . . tell me, do you think *you* might be leaving any time soon?"

I thought of my letter to my father. "Perhaps," I said. "I hope so, but it's hard to know."

She nodded, and for once she didn't look like she was smiling. Was her decision somehow tied up in my plans? Why would that be so? Was this one more person who didn't want me here?

"Let me know when you have your plans settled," she said. "I do miss our birds."

It was such a little thing to say—"I do miss our birds"—but it touched me deeply. It reminded me of everything I missed about my own home, and the happiness I had once felt there.

※

Time in Philip's absence did terrible things. Clocks slowed, the sun stood still in the sky, even the nights stretched longer than normal. I felt as if entire months had passed since the ball, though it had only been four days. I went about my normal activities. I ate food and I slept and I spent my days in the company of the other women. But through it all I felt as if an important part of me was absent. Perhaps it was my heart.

Cecily and I had hardly spoken since I had stormed out of her room the day after the ball. She and Louisa were as thick as thieves. They were always going off on walks together and whispering to each other. I did not attempt to join them. Instead, I focused on my new project.

Rather than trying to fulfill my grandmother's assignment, I spent my free time painting scenes of Edenbrooke. Five days after Philip left, I had half a dozen paintings of some of my favorite views of the estate. I wanted to record as much as I could of this place, which, for a time, had been the closest thing to paradise I could have imagined on earth. I mourned the thought of leaving this place forever. When Cecily married Philip, I would not come back here. I knew it. My mother never came back, and now I understood why.

I was sketching the view from my bedroom window when Cecily came into my room.

"Only three more days until the ball," she said.

I nodded, keeping my gaze on the bridge as I worked on making the angles of the arch look just right. If I looked at just the angles and stones, I could train myself to not think of Philip riding toward the bridge with a whistle on his lips. It was hard work, but I was subduing my heart a little more every day.

"I don't know what I will do if Sir Philip doesn't come back in time for the ball," she said, flopping down on my bed. Her golden hair fanned around her face as she pouted at the ceiling. "I have spent hours planning exactly how I'm going to make him declare his feelings for me, and if he isn't here I will be so disappointed I will die. You don't know what it's like to have all of your hopes for your future happiness pinned on one man. The suspense is excruciating!"

I rolled my eyes. "I'm sure you will not die of disappointment, Cecily. And if Sir Philip is going to declare himself, he will probably find an opportunity to do so without your scheming."

I thought I had my heart firmly under control, but the words I spoke caused sharp stabs of pain. The thought of Philip declaring himself to Cecily was too much for me to contemplate.

"Perhaps Mr. Kellet will come and keep you entertained if Sir Philip isn't here in time," I said. I couldn't keep the touch of malice out of my voice, but Cecily didn't appear to notice.

"I hope so," she said, rolling over onto her stomach. "I made sure he was on the guest list."

"See? You will have plenty of . . . pleasure to look forward to."

She smiled with a faraway look in her eyes, as if remembering something enjoyable.

"I wonder who is the better kisser—Sir Philip or Mr. Kellet?" She looked at me. "Who would you rather kiss?"

"Neither," I lied.

"Hmm. I don't know either. But I'll be sure to let you know when I find out."

Resentment surged within me. "If you do find out, please don't tell me. There are some things I would rather not hear."

"By the way," she said, "whatever happened with Mr. Beaufort?"

I was surprised to realize I hadn't told her. But then, I had hardly talked to Cecily at all since Philip left.

"He offered for me, and I rejected him. That is all."

"Good. I didn't want to tell you at the time, but I think there's something not quite right about him."

I thought of his shallow eyes and had to agree with her assessment.

Before she left, she looked over my shoulder at my drawing. "You have a real gift for art. You're much better at it than I will ever be."

"Thank you." What a nice thing to say. I looked at my drawing, then up into my sister's face. I had let my feelings for Philip come between us, and I was sorry for it. I set down my pencil and turned to her. "Cecily, can I ask you something?"

"Yes, of course."

I took a deep breath, gathering my courage, and asked, "Did you want me to come to Edenbrooke? Or was it Lady Caroline's idea?"

She tilted her head. "What made you ask that?"

I held her gaze. "Just tell me, please."

Cecily tucked a strand of my hair back into its twist. "It may have been Lady Caroline's idea, but of course I wanted you. You're my sister."

She said it so matter-of-factly that I believed her. My heart lifted and I smiled. It felt so strange to smile, and such a relief at the same time, that I had to stop and think about the last time I had smiled. I couldn't remember a single instance of happiness since Philip had left.

"I think we need to spend more time together," Cecily said. "I've missed you."

"I've missed you, too." I felt a real fondness for her in that moment, and after she left, I continued to smile.

꒰꒱

The next afternoon I was sketching the view from the library window when Rachel found me. I almost had the orchard complete. When I painted it, I would make the sky look overcast, as it looked the day Philip and I spent in here.

"Oh, here you are," she said. "I've been looking for you."

I looked up from my drawing. She came toward me with a smile. "I have just received a letter from William."

I stared at her. Did men really write home to their wives while they were off . . . carousing?

"I knew you would want to hear it," she continued, as she closed the door and came to sit next to me, "as it mentions Philip."

Dread made my heart pound hard. I shook my head. "No, I don't. I can't imagine there is anything in there I am interested in hearing."

"Come now, you can be honest with me. I've seen how you've been moping around the house, and if it's not Philip you're pining for, it's William, and that would not suit me well at all."

I frowned at my drawing. "I am not pining for anyone."

"Nonsense. Of course you are." She smiled brightly at me, then looked at her letter. "Let's see. It sounds like they are really enjoying themselves. Oh, here is the part I wanted to read to you: 'Philip has fallen in love with a real beauty, with nice legs and beautiful lines. He thinks the price is too dear, but I would not be surprised if he brings her home in the end.'"

I felt as if I were being strangled. "I have no wish to hear about Philip's . . . conquests," I choked out.

Rachel looked up. "No, dear, you know they aren't participating this year."

I could not look her in the face. They weren't participating? What did that mean? I didn't know *that* much about these things.

"They're . . . not?"

She looked at me curiously. "No, because Philip gave that horse to you to ride instead. I thought you knew."

"That horse?" Some part of my mind was not working properly, obviously, because I could not fathom what a horse had to do with any of this. "Do you mean Meg?"

She waved dismissively. "Whatever the name is."

I was working hard to assemble this puzzle, but without success. "What does Meg have to do with whether or not they . . . *participate*?" I blushed saying the word.

She stared at me as if I were daft, then set the letter down on her lap and spoke slowly and carefully. "Well, my dear, they need a horse in order to participate in the races. And they didn't take a horse this year, because Philip gave you a racehorse to ride and then didn't want to take her away from you."

I gaped at her. "Races? Horse races?"

"Yes. They're at Newmarket. I thought you knew that."

"But—but you told me that your father would not have approved of what they were doing."

"No, it's true, he never did approve of racing." She sighed. "But there are a lot worse ways for a man to spend his free time, so I don't stop William from going." She smoothed her hand over the letter in an affectionate gesture. "It has been a dream of his, all along, to breed racehorses, but of course it's not financially possible for us. To be honest, I have suspected that Philip might be doing all of this more for William's sake than for his own interest." She smiled a little wistfully. "He never has forgiven himself for inheriting everything, you know."

A surge of emotion was struggling against the bands I had placed around my heart. It beat hard. I felt it awaken, stir, and stretch. My hands trembled.

"I didn't know," I murmured.

She laughed lightly. "Well, what did you think they were doing?"

I looked away in embarrassment. "Um . . . I thought . . . I assumed . . . they were involved in a different sort of . . . behavior."

Rachel suddenly gasped. "Conquests? You didn't really think—" She burst into laughter. "Oh, it's no wonder you've been acting so miserable since they left! You poor thing." She put an arm around my shoulder as she laughed, but I was too mortified to join in.

After a moment, she pulled away and said gently, "But how could you suspect Philip of such behavior? Considering how close you two are, I would have thought that you would know his character better than that. Don't you know what sort of gentleman Philip is?"

I dropped my head into my hands. "I don't," I mumbled. "I don't know anything."

"Well, I have known Philip my entire life, and I can tell you what sort of man he is." I looked up. "The very best kind," she said, watching me carefully. "And he deserves the very best kind of lady for his wife. But I don't think Cecily fits that description. Do you?"

I looked at her sharply. Guilt for secretly agreeing with Rachel battled with loyalty within me. Loyalty won.

"No, you're mistaken. Cecily has some wonderful qualities. She is well-suited for the sort of elegant lifestyle Sir Philip can provide."

Rachel smiled kindly. "It's obvious what you're doing, and you are very noble to try to step out of the way for your sister. But she's not the one Philip wants."

I regarded her in silence, wanting to believe her. But what if she was just meddling, like Lady Caroline? How could I dare allow myself to hope? My will battled with my heart, and I . . . I sat, stunned, with my heart begging me to hope.

"Do you know what I think?" Rachel asked.

I shook my head.

She held up the letter from William. "I think that Philip has been just as miserable as you since he left, which leads me to believe that something has come between you two."

I touched my cheek, trying to smooth away my blush. "There was nothing to come between us. We have been friends. That is all."

She raised both eyebrows. "Philip does not look at you the way a man looks at his friend."

I looked away, embarrassed and miserable. "That's just because he's a flirt. He doesn't mean anything by it."

"A flirt? Whatever gave you that idea?"

I blinked in surprise. "I thought it was common knowledge. Miss Fairhurst led me to believe that everyone knew about his reputation."

Rachel looked astonished. "You believed Miss Fairhurst? Really, Marianne, I thought you had more sense than that."

I stared at her. "You mean, he's *not* a flirt?"

She looked at me for a long moment, as if debating what to say. "I won't deny that many ladies have fallen in love with him, but I will tell you this: I have never seen Philip behave toward anyone the way he behaves toward you."

My thoughts spun as every assumption on which I had built my understanding of Philip dissolved. I looked at my hands in my lap and saw them trembling.

"Rachel, I am willing to admit that I have been fooled, and confused, and very naïve. But if Philip did feel something for me, why didn't he say anything?"

She leaned toward me, speaking urgently. "Marianne, you must understand that Philip has a very strong sense of what it means to be a gentleman. And, according to his principles, he couldn't court you, considering the circumstances."

I was confused. "What do you mean? What circumstances?"

"You have been in a very vulnerable position, with your father far away and without another man to protect you. Philip took on a guardian's role when he took you in as his guest. Indeed, he told your grandmother that he would act as your protector while you stayed here.

"How could he declare himself while he was in that position of responsibility toward you? Don't you see how his sense of honor as a gentleman would have prevented that, unless he was sure of your feelings? He wouldn't take advantage of your vulnerability by declaring himself while you were so obligated to him."

I twisted my hands together while my thoughts reeled. Why had I never considered any of this? Probably for the same reason I had hidden my feelings for Philip from myself. I didn't want to face what could potentially break my heart. And then there was the issue of Cecily's feelings.

"Of course," Rachel said, "if he *was* certain of your feelings, he probably would have said something."

I laughed a little. "*I* wasn't even certain of my feelings. And then there was the fact that Cecily had claimed him first."

Rachel nodded. "I thought as much. But if Philip had loved Cecily, or had even been interested in her, he would have courted her in London. So I think you can put aside that doubt. The real question is, what are you going to do to encourage Philip to declare himself to you?"

My mouth fell open. "Do? What do you mean? I'm not going to do anything! I don't even know how Philip feels about me."

Rachel scoffed. "Philip has been wearing his heart on his sleeve for the whole world to see. He obviously loves you. But everyone needs some encouragement, and I think you need to be prepared to offer some encouragement when Philip returns."

She left me after that, smiling as if she was very pleased with herself.

Standing, I paced back and forth in front of the fireplace. My thoughts tumbled furiously. Philip and William were at Newmarket at the horse races, not off carousing. I wondered how I could have misunderstood Rachel when we had first discussed the men's trip. I couldn't remember the exact words we had exchanged, but I had felt certain that I knew what she had been talking about.

Words were such slippery things. I could take Rachel's words and understand them in one way, and then look at them again from her perspective and understand them in a completely different way. The same thing had happened when I had listened to her read from William's letter. I'd felt certain he was referring to Philip falling in love with a woman, not a horse.

Was there something flawed about my thinking? Or had one wrong assumption led to another? Words alone were ambiguous, unreliable. But what could be reliable, if not words?

I was so caught up in trying to understand how I had made my mistake in judgment that I almost overlooked a significant part of my conversation with Rachel. I had been right about Philip's character. Rachel had confirmed what I had initially thought—that Philip was a gentleman and that he would not participate in the sorts of activities I had suspected him of.

Perhaps I was right about something else, too. Perhaps I was right when I thought that Philip really did care for me, if only as a friend. Maybe—just maybe—I had misinterpreted what he had told William in the fencing room.

Maybe he felt honor-bound not to declare himself while he was responsible for me and that's why he said he wanted to be rid of his responsibility toward me. I turned from the thought. It was too much to hope for.

As far as whether or not he was a flirt, I gave that some thought as well. It occurred to me that I had never seen Philip flirt with anyone besides me. He had certainly never flirted with Cecily, or Miss Grace. I had observed him at the ball, and he had not smiled at any other young lady the way he had smiled at me. He had never had that teasing gleam in his eyes when he looked at anyone else.

I shook my head in wonder. It was possible. It was just possible that I had been mistaken before. I wanted to believe that I was mistaken now, and not just for my own sake. I desperately wanted to believe that I really knew Philip. I had fallen in love with the man I thought him to be, and I wanted to believe that man existed.

My heart and mind battled until I could no longer think and rethink everything. I understood Philip's love letter now, when he wrote about being driven to the edge of madness by love. I was at the edge of madness myself, and I had to do something to distract myself.

I walked outside and made my way to the stable. I stepped inside Meg's stall, picked up the currycomb, and began to groom her. I had always enjoyed grooming horses. There was something about the shushing sound of the brush against their coat, and the warmth of their flank against my hand, that soothed me.

The repetitive action and quiet calm allowed me to ponder what Rachel had told me. I had no clear answers about Philip. But I had hope, and I was willing to wait and find out for myself what was true and what was false.

A thought rose to the surface of my mind as I brushed Meg. I was not entirely unwanted here. Lady Caroline liked me—I was sure of it. And Rachel seemed to like me too. She went out of her way to talk to me and give me hope about Philip. And Cecily was a devoted sister. She wanted me here too.

The joy that realization granted me was overwhelming. Leaning my head against Meg's neck, I sniffed as tears of relief and happiness streamed down my cheeks. Then I laughed at myself, lifted my head, and wiped my cheeks. Surely I had cried enough in the past week to last a lifetime. I was turning into a watering pot, and that was unlike me.

"So you're a racehorse," I said to Meg as I continued to brush her. "You should have told me. If I had known, I would have pushed you harder. We could have beaten that black horse of his."

She whinnied in response.

Chapter 23

William and Philip had told their mother that they would return in time for the ball she was hosting. But it was the day before the ball, and neither of them had made an appearance.

I sat in the drawing room dutifully working on some embroidery while Cecily and Louisa played a duet on the pianoforte. From my position near the window, I was the first to notice the carriage pulling up the drive. I tried not to give in to the hope and excitement bounding through me, but I recognized the carriage. It was the same one Betsy and I had ridden in to come here.

It was Philip's carriage.

He had come home, after all, just in time for the ball, just as he'd promised. My hand shook, causing me to make an uneven stitch. I set aside my embroidery and took a steadying breath. What would I say to Philip? How would I know his feelings for me? And could I dare to offer him some encouragement, as Rachel had suggested?

I heard men's voices outside the door; then the door opened and William walked in. He looked around the room and said something in greeting, but I hardly heard his words, I was so distracted by wanting to see Philip.

Lady Caroline looked up from her writing desk, and Rachel crossed the room to her husband with a smile. Cecily and Louisa stopped playing the pianoforte. I craned my neck, trying to see beyond William. What was taking Philip so long?

Then William asked, "Where is Philip?"

I stared at him.

"Philip?" Lady Caroline said. "Is he not with you?"

William frowned and looked at me, then quickly looked away again. "No. He said he had something else he had to do. But I thought he would have returned by now."

We could give him no answers, as none of us knew that they had separated.

William shrugged off the mystery, saying, "I daresay he'll be home tomorrow. I think he planned on being back for the ball."

That he could dismiss Philip's absence without telling us anything about where he might be or what he might be doing was completely un-satisfactory. William didn't even offer any explanation as to why he looked at me and frowned. I worried that Philip had stayed away because he didn't want to see me again. It was an unbearable thought.

I left the drawing room and asked the butler to find Betsy for me and send her to my room. I was pacing back and forth in front of my fireplace when Betsy threw open the door and ran into the room.

"What is it, miss?" she asked, out of breath.

"I need you to find out where Sir Philip is, and why he did not return with his brother."

Her eyes lit up with a gleam of excitement mixed with determination. "If there is something to be learned, I will learn it, never fear, miss!" She flew out of the room.

Less than half an hour had passed when the door opened and Betsy ran back into the room. I was accustomed to her dramatic entrances, so it didn't alarm me.

"What have you learned?" I asked.

"Nobody knows where Sir Philip has gone, miss." She pressed a hand to her chest as she panted, trying to catch her breath. "The coachman said that he left Newmarket four days ago. He said that Sir Philip was acting strangely, hardly paying any attention to the races, and after two days of it, Mr. Wyndham said to him, 'I can't bear any more of your moping. Go win her.' And that's when Sir Philip left, not saying anything about where he would go or what he would do." She stared at me with wide eyes. "What do you think of it all?"

I shook my head, dumbfounded. "I have no idea." But I did know one thing. If Philip was going to win someone, I wanted it to be me.

⚜

Later that day, I left the house with my sketchbook and made my way to the orchard; I was restless with impatience to see Philip and I could not sit inside with the other ladies another moment. I couldn't bear to listen to Cecily fretting about her plans for Philip to propose at the ball, and how they would be ruined if he did not return in time.

I still didn't know what I would say when I saw Philip again. But I had come to a conclusion: I would not run a different race simply because I was afraid of losing to Cecily. If Philip truly was the gentleman I thought him to be—and the one Rachel swore he was—then Cecily did not deserve him.

Sitting with my back against the trunk of a tree, I sketched a cluster of apples hanging from a thick branch. Concentrating on my subject, I initially did not notice the sound of footsteps in the grass. But suddenly a flash of a dark coat from the corner of my eye caught my attention. My heart leaped. It was Philip. He had come home in time for the ball, just as he had promised. And he had found me here, in the orchard, because he knew me so well.

What would I say to him? What would he say to me? I set aside my drawing and stood up, smoothing my skirt, then my hair. I didn't need to pinch my cheeks, because my face was already warm with the nervousness that flooded me. He had to be nearby. I heard more rustling, and then I saw him emerge from the trees. I turned to him with a hesitant smile.

My smile immediately faltered. "Mr. Beaufort," I said, disappointment coloring my voice.

He bowed. "Miss Daventry. You look so beautiful here, among the blossoms."

"What are you doing here?" I didn't mean to sound rude, but I had no patience for polite conversation right now.

He walked toward me, smiling, and said, "I have come to change your mind." He grabbed me around the waist, pulled me to him, and pressed his mouth against mine.

I pulled my head back and pushed against his chest. "Unhand me at once!"

I was no match for his strength, though. He only pulled me more tightly against him.

"Listen to me carefully," he whispered, his mouth too close to my face. "We are madly in love and we are going to run off together. By the time we're discovered, your grandmother or father or whoever it is that cares about you will be happy to have me marry you. And then we will live very happily together on your fortune."

I froze. He knew about my inheritance? "Fortune?" I laughed. "There is no fortune."

His eyes glinted. "You think to make a fool of me? I know very well there is a fortune of forty thousand pounds waiting for you to inherit. My good uncle, Mr. Whittles, overheard your grandmother say as much while he was in her house."

I remembered the day my grandmother had told me about the inheritance, and how I had found Mr. Whittles outside the door.

I shook my head. "It has not been made official. My grandmother will leave me nothing if you ruin my reputation."

He smiled. "I think she will. But there is no need to ruin your reputation. Just accept my offer. Think of the enticements, my dear. I will shower you with gifts, give you everything you want, even your freedom, as long as you allow me my freedom in return."

"You'll give me everything I want with my own money?" I laughed at him. "You're absurd."

His hand gripped my waist so tightly it hurt. "Do not speak to me like that."

I suddenly recognized that this was no game and that I was literally in the grip of an unscrupulous man.

"You don't need to do this," I said, fear pounding with every beat of my heart. "My grandmother will give you money, like a ransom. You don't need to take me anywhere." I smiled at him, but his eyes stayed hard.

"Whatever amount she offers, it cannot be more than your inheritance, and so I will have to reject that idea. Now. We are going to hold hands and run off to the carriage I have waiting down the road. If anyone sees us, they will believe we are two young people desperately in love."

I shook my head. "You're mad. I won't go with you."

He reached into his coat pocket and pulled out something gold, which he let slip through his fingers so that it dangled from a chain.

I gasped. "My locket!" My thoughts went reeling as I tried to make sense of what was before me. "*You* were the highwayman? The one who shot my coachman?"

He smiled and cold chills ran down my spine.

"What did you do to James? Why did he leave the inn?"

"Don't worry about him. Once I learned from him exactly where you were going, I convinced him to leave the area and seek other employment. He was sensible."

The terror of that night, of the masked highwayman, the pistol, and James bleeding in the road, rushed back to me. My knees trembled and my voice shook. "What did you want from me that night?"

"I wanted the same thing I have always wanted—a fortune. I admit that my first attempt was a little unpolished. I thought only to run away with you by any means necessary. But when your maid shot at me, I abandoned that endeavor. I was certainly not going to risk my neck when there were other ways to get what I wanted. I had hoped to convince you to marry me based on my own merits. But you were unable to appreciate what I had to offer. And so it has come to this."

He put the locket back into his pocket and then pulled something else out. "You remember this, do you not?"

It was a pistol. I nodded my head, very carefully.

He smiled. "Good." He slipped the gun back into his pocket. "Now, let's be off, my love!"

He grabbed my hand and started to run through the orchard. I tried to pull my hand out of his grip and opened my mouth to scream. He stopped abruptly, clamped his hand over my mouth, and whispered, "It will be much simpler if you go along with the plan. You see, I have some-body waiting for you in the carriage, and I believe she is the one who shot at me last time. You do not want her to be hurt the way your coachman was hurt, do you?"

He had Betsy. More than my own life depended on my actions right now. I carefully shook my head.

He smiled. "I knew you would be able to see reason." He pulled on my hand again, and this time I did not resist. Just beyond the orchard was a short path that cut through the woods. After several minutes, we emerged onto the road where a closed carriage stood, with the horses tied to a tree.

Mr. Beaufort opened the carriage door and bowed. "I hope you have a comfortable journey."

I saw immediately that the carriage was empty.

"You lied to me!" I tried to pull away from him, but he grabbed me around the waist and threw me into the carriage. He leaned in and said, "I would not try to jump out if I were you. People have been known to have their brains dashed on the rocks when they try it."

"Wait!" I lunged for the door, which he was already closing. "Where are you taking me?" I shouted.

He smiled at me through the window. I was beginning to suspect that he was mad. "To Dover, my love!"

I felt the carriage sway as he climbed up to the coachman's box. He was going to drive, which meant there was not even a coachman who might come to my rescue. I flung myself at the door and yanked on the handle. It was broken. I tried the other door, but it did not have a handle at all.

I screamed in frustration and beat at the door. Mr. Beaufort had only been tricking me with that comment—giving me the hope of escape if I but had the courage to take the leap. I thought I heard him laugh, and then the carriage swayed, and I was being driven away, swiftly, with no one to hear my screams.

Chapter 24

It did not take me long to understand what would happen to me if I did not escape. To be ruined by reputation was just as damning as to be ruined in actuality. No one would want me if I passed the night with Mr. Beaufort, no matter what he did or did not do to me. Fear ballooned in my chest at the thought. I tried to break the window, beating at it with my fists, but the glass held. After a while I dropped to the bench, exhausted. I could no longer hope for rescue from anyone, nor escape. I tried not to cry while my hopes raced away from me.

I kept watch out the window in an attempt to make sense of where we were going, but since I was not familiar with the area, the road we traveled on meant nothing to me. It felt as if we rode for hours. I was sick twice and left all of my breakfast on the floor of the carriage. And then, utterly wretched, I lay on the bench and tried not to breathe through my nose.

The sky was gray and colorless when the carriage finally stopped. It felt like we had been traveling all day long. When Mr. Beaufort opened the carriage door, he reared back, holding his hand over his mouth and nose. It gave me a tiny bit of satisfaction.

I sat up and stepped over my breakfast, holding my gown out of the way. He grabbed my elbow and helped me down. I was too weak and ill to try to run from him, and besides that, I didn't know where I would run. The fresh, salty air I breathed in was a welcome relief, though.

"What happened in there?" he asked.

"I get sick in carriages."

He looked disgusted, then a frown creased his brow. "What about boats?"

"I've never ridden in one. But I assume I would get sick on a boat as well." I almost smiled at his expression.

He muttered something under his breath, then pulled me toward an inn. "We're going to eat supper here. I don't want to have anyone else involved, and I am sure you do not either. If you will recall, I have no compunction about shooting someone who gets in my way."

I understood him perfectly. Anyone who might be in a position to help me in the inn would be risking his life to do so. Just like James. I looked up at the inn and the wood sign bearing the words "The Rose and Crown." I felt a strange sense of having been in this moment before. The last inn I had stopped at—the night James was shot—had also been called the Rose and Crown. To be sure, it was a common name for inns, but it still seemed strangely significant.

Inside the inn, Mr. Beaufort asked for a private parlor and supper. A few people sat in the taproom, but Mr. Beaufort's tight grip on my arm reminded me of his threat, and I held my tongue. Besides that, I felt too weak and nauseated to fight him.

The small parlor we were led to offered a startling contrast to how I felt. A bright fire crackled, a table was well-lit, and the furniture was clean and nice.

Mr. Beaufort gestured toward a chair. "Please, make yourself comfortable."

I wished he wouldn't pretend to be a gentleman. It made his course of action all the more appalling. I considered refusing to do what he wanted, but I quickly dismissed that idea. It would be best for me to placate him as much as possible. So I sat at the table and watched him carefully. He took the chair closest to the door, leaning back with his legs crossed.

"You can't possibly imagine you'll get away with this," I said. "My father will never agree to this marriage."

He opened his snuffbox and took a pinch. When he was done, he looked at me languidly and said in a bored voice, "Your father cares so little about what happens to you that he abandoned you to the care of a feeble, old woman who can't even take care of herself. You have no other male family members. No one to protect you; no one to fight for you." His lip curled. "You, my dear, are the ideal victim. And since we are going to France, I think it will be a long time before your father finds you."

"France?" I said in surprise.

"Yes. France. We sail as soon as the tide turns." He smiled coldly. "You understand, of course, that I couldn't let anyone find us until you were safely mine."

Did he know my father was in France? I doubted it, considering the fact that he thought going there would put us out of my father's reach.

I laughed, hard and short. "I will never be yours."

His gaze swept over me. "You will, and probably sooner than you think."

A shiver of revulsion rolled down my spine, and fear quickened my pulse, but I lifted my chin. "I am a lady, sir. I may agree to marry you, if forced, but you will not be permitted to touch me." My voice only shook a little.

He smiled. "And what will you do if I try? Fight me?"

"Yes." I met his gaze boldly.

He laughed softly, and even I could see how humorous my claim was. I was half his size and surely had less than half his strength. Besides that, he had a weapon in his possession. Well, then my superiority would simply have to come from my wits.

The innkeeper brought in a tray of food and a decanter of wine, which he set on the table. Mr. Beaufort piled food on his plate and poured himself a large glass of wine.

"Please eat if you'd like."

I couldn't eat. It was impossible. The sight of the food was enough to make me gag. And yet I wanted to allay suspicion and make him believe I would be submissive. I chose the least revolting dish and methodically spooned it into my mouth and swallowed while watching Mr. Beaufort carefully. He paid no attention to me, just ate and drank his wine as if he were dining alone. That was good. It gave me an opportunity to look around the room.

I didn't see much in the way of weapons. Along with the table and chairs and fireplace there was a low bench by the window and a writing desk in one corner. I couldn't see anything heavy enough to hit him with except the chairs, and those were too large for me to wield. The prospects were discouraging. Even the knife I was given to eat with would not be of any use, dull and blunted as it was.

I had to be more creative. I looked again at the furniture in the room, and my eyes rested on the writing desk. I saw a quill, an ink stand, and a small stack of paper. I hoped somewhere on that desk would be a penknife for sharpening the quill. A plan formed in my mind. I considered my other choices, quickly realizing I had no other choices, really, other than trying to run out the door or letting Mr. Beaufort do what he wanted to with me.

The thought made me so nervous that my hand shook and I had to set my fork down. I suddenly recalled my first evening at Edenbrooke, when I had walked to the dining room on Philip's arm. What had he said to me? "Try taking a deep breath. It might help you relax."

The memory lightened my heart a little. I took a deep breath, steadying my nerves, and watched Mr. Beaufort. He was drinking, but not eating much. He poured himself three glasses, and at the end of the third glass, he set it down clumsily on the table. This was probably the best time for me to make my attempt. I smiled shyly at him.

"I didn't realize how hungry I was. It's hard to think clearly when you're hungry, don't you agree?"

He raised an eyebrow. "I've never considered it."

"Well, that's how it always is with me." I lowered my eyes meekly. "I couldn't think earlier about what a . . . pleasure it might be to be married to such a man as you." I glanced up through my eyelashes and saw a look of gratification pass over his features.

"You're coming to your senses, are you?" He laughed. "It never takes them long."

"Oh, I can believe it. Why, just watching you here, in the candlelight . . ." I let my voice trail off.

His eyes lit up with interest. "Go on."

"I was just admiring the way the light brings out your handsome features, your strong jaw, the way your eyes . . ." I looked down and willed myself to blush. I felt my face grow warm. At least I could always count on that skill.

"Don't stop now."

"I'm too shy," I said quietly.

"You don't need to be shy," he coaxed. "Soon there will be nothing to be shy about. We will know everything about each other."

I inwardly cringed but kept my face lowered so he couldn't see my expression. "Perhaps I could write it down instead. Like a love letter."

He sat back in his chair. "Well, this is certainly a novel experience." He contemplated me for a moment, and I waited tensely. "Why not? The night is still young." He gestured toward the writing desk.

Mr. Beaufort poured himself another glass of wine while I walked to the desk; my legs felt unsteady with nervousness. I carefully sat down and angled my body to hide what I was doing from him. I searched the writing desk, and I was not disappointed. The penknife rested next to the quill. It had a small blade, no longer than my fingernail, but it was wickedly sharp. It would have to do.

I took a piece of paper from the stack and dipped the quill in ink. I wrote quickly.

> *Dear Philip,*
>
> *I don't imagine you will ever read this. If you do, it is because something dreadful has happened to me. I find myself in the hands of a dangerous man. I am determined to fight him, but before I do, my heart demands that I write this note to tell you that I love you. I am sending my heart to you in this letter so it will be kept safe from whatever may happen to me tonight. I don't know if you want it or not, but it has always been yours.*
>
> *With all my love,*
> *Marianne*

A tear or two dropped onto the paper, blurring some of my words. Mr. Beaufort cleared his throat. I hurriedly folded the paper into a small square, writing *Sir Philip Wyndham, Edenbrooke, Kent* on the outside. I wondered where I could hide the letter. My bodice? No, that might be the first place Mr. Beaufort would find it.

My stomach lurched at the thought, and I was afraid I would be sick again. I took another deep breath. I had to think. I leaned down and shoved the paper into my boot. It was such a small comfort—hardly anything in the face of what awaited me if I was unsuccessful—but I had to do it.

I took another piece of paper and thought quickly about the lesson Philip had given me. I had to make this look authentic.

> *To My Adventurous Love—*
>
> *Your brilliant eyes hold secrets that entice me. I can see in them a power and strength that sets you apart from every other man. When you look at me, my heart flutters with the knowledge that I will soon*

belong to you. You cannot imagine how strongly I feel about sharing my
life with such a man.

"Aren't you done yet?" Mr. Beaufort asked.

"Almost. It's my first time, you see." My voice shook a little, but I finished the letter.

I hope I will be able to give you everything you deserve.

Longingly,

Marianne

That would have to do. It would appeal to his ego, at least. I stood and smiled shyly at him.

He looked up. "Well?"

I hid the penknife in the folds of my skirt with one hand and held out the letter to him with the other. He stood and grabbed it from me.

"Oh, I can't watch you while you read it. It would be too embarrassing," I said. "You'll have to turn around."

"Aren't you a modest thing?" he said with a leering smile.

I crossed the room while he bent his head over the letter. I stood near the door—not so close as to make him suspicious, but close enough to be in range if my plan worked.

He turned to me with an eager light in his eyes. "You are more surprising with every moment," he said, walking toward me. He grabbed me around the waist. I tried not to pull away. His breath reeked, and I realized it was brandy and not wine he had been drinking. He swayed slightly on his feet. I didn't know how his drunken state would factor in to what I was going to do. I hoped it would help.

I put one hand on his cheek, gripping the knife with my other hand. "Close your eyes," I whispered.

He smiled and closed them. "A new game. I never expected this from you."

I braced myself, held the penknife to his throat, and called on my courage. I found it lacking. I couldn't do it. I couldn't stab him like this.

His hand moved from my waist to my hip and I flinched.

"If you move I will slit your throat," I hissed.

His eyes flew open, and he looked at me in shock. I stared at him with all the hatred I had in me. He moved his hand. I pressed the knife against his skin until it drew blood. "I will do it," I warned him through clenched teeth.

He withdrew his hand from my body, his countenance dark with fury.

I reached into his jacket and felt around until I found the pistol. I pulled it out and took a step away from him, pointing the pistol at him. My hand shook.

"Now let us understand each other," I said. "I am going to leave, and you are going to disappear. If you're smart, you will leave the country as you had planned and never come back. Are we clear?"

He sneered. "Perfectly." In one swift movement, he knocked the pistol from my hand. It skidded under the table. The next instant, his hands gripped my shoulders and he pulled me toward him.

"You think I'm strong?" he whispered. "You think I'm powerful? I'll show you what real strength is. I will show you what happens when you try to make a fool of me."

Panic gripped me, obliterating all my thoughts and plans. I twisted and turned in his grip, but he only held me tighter and pressed his vile lips against mine. I turned my head to the side and spit out the taste of his kiss.

He laughed and lunged for me again.

The sound of his laugh cut through my panic, clearing my thoughts enough that I remembered the penknife I still held in my hand. I stabbed blindly at his hands. He swore and his grip loosened. I abruptly let my knees buckle, and my weight broke his hold on me. When I fell to the floor, I kicked against his knees with both feet, hard enough that he lost his balance and staggered backward against the door. I rolled to my knees and crawled quickly under the table.

My hand hit something solid. The pistol. I came out on the other side of the table, stood, and pointed the gun at him.

"Let's stop this now," I said.

He sauntered around the table toward me. I backed up, keeping the gun aimed at him. My hands started to shake, betraying the fear that raced through me. I tightened my grip.

"Stop or I will shoot."

He smirked and said, "You don't have it in you."

I wavered for a minute, believing him. *Did* I have it in me? I noticed the blood on his hands from where I had stabbed him. It was very red. My vision blurred for an instant, and I had to blink quickly. Then I saw Mr. Beaufort reaching for me.

I suddenly thought I heard Philip shouting my name. It startled me so much that I squeezed the trigger. The sound was deafening in that small room. I jerked backward from the force of it.

Mr. Beaufort flinched, crouched down, then stood back up and smirked harder than ever. I had missed.

He reached out and grabbed the pistol from my hand. I ducked down and crawled under the table again, as fast as a crab. He grabbed at my foot, and I screamed as I kicked back and freed myself, emerging from beneath the table on the side by the door. I wrenched the door open but was immediately knocked to the floor by a tremendous force.

My head hit something hard on the way down. I gasped, rolled onto my side and curled into myself instinctively as the room grew dark. I was so stunned, all I could do was cover my head with my hands as violent sounds erupted around me.

When a hand grabbed my wrist, I fought blindly, too terrified to open my eyes and see my attacker. Through my panic, I heard a voice yell, "Marianne! Open your eyes!"

My terror immediately died, for it was a voice I knew as well as my own. My eyes flew open in surprise, and I saw the face of the man I loved so well. But it was raw with pain, so twisted in anguish and grief that my heart broke open at the sight. I sobbed as if I would never be able to stop.

He scooped me up in his arms as though I were a child again and held me securely against his broad chest. "You're safe now, sweetheart. I have you."

I cried into my father's neck as he carried me from the room.

Chapter 25

Voices surrounded me, but I could not make sense of them. I was crying too hard to make sense of anything. When my father bent over and set me on a chair, I refused to let go of him. He knelt beside me and patted my back while I buried my face in his chest. He loved me. I knew it. I knew it as soon as I saw the look in his eyes. I did not know why he was here or how he had found me, and I did not, in this moment, care. All I cared to know was that he *was* here, and he *had* found me, and that he loved me.

When he asked me if I was hurt or needed a doctor, I shook my head and wiped away the tears so I could see him more clearly. We were in the taproom of the inn, but I ignored everything else around me while I took in the sight of my father's face. His hair was grayer than I remembered, and there were more wrinkles around his eyes, but he looked healthy.

I had so many questions I didn't know which one to ask first. Before I had a chance to say anything, though, the door of the inn flew open and William strode in. When his gaze landed on me, he stopped.

"You found her," he said to my father with obvious relief in his voice. "Where is the scoundrel?"

My father gestured toward the parlor. "In there. Sir Philip is taking care of everything."

Sir Philip? *My* Sir Philip?

"Alone?"

My father nodded. "He insisted."

I looked from one to the other. I knew what this meant. My honor and reputation had been compromised when Mr. Beaufort abducted me. And now it was within my father's rights to challenge him to a duel. But it was not Philip's responsibility to risk his life for me.

I could not sit by knowing what was happening in the next room. It was not a woman's place to witness a duel, but I nevertheless hurried across the taproom and pushed open the door of the parlor, intending to stop the duel immediately. I froze in the doorway.

I didn't dare make a sound. Mr. Beaufort was standing very still with his back to the fireplace. Philip stood with the tip of a sword pressed into Mr. Beaufort's throat. I saw another sword on the floor. Neither gentleman looked toward the door. Philip looked perfectly in control, his sword bending the skin of Mr. Beaufort's neck without piercing it. When he spoke, though, his voice sounded so fierce I hardly recognized it. "Tell me what you did to her."

"I made sure you wouldn't want her anymore."

"I will always want her," Philip said in a quiet, furious voice. "Always! There is nothing you could do to change that."

Mr. Beaufort sneered. "Then why do you want to know?"

"Because I would never make her say the words. And because I want to know how much I should enjoy running you through."

"Stop!" The word felt ripped from me.

Both men looked at me. I nearly started sobbing again at Philip's expression, for it matched my father's. I turned my gaze to Mr. Beaufort, because I couldn't bear to look at Philip. I walked toward them, trembling so much that I had to clench my hands into fists.

"He's a liar," I said, stopping next to Philip. "I will not allow him to ruin me in reputation after I kept him from ruining me in truth. He did nothing but kiss me." I lifted my chin and thought of how disdainful

Grandmother could look. I hoped I looked just like her. "And it wasn't even a good kiss—it was vile. But it was all he did."

Mr. Beaufort's face turned dark red, and he looked as if he would love nothing more than to have his hands around my neck. But after a moment, he dropped his sullen gaze in a gesture of defeat. I wanted to laugh with triumph, but I was afraid I might end up crying instead. I looked up at Philip.

"Even if he does deserve to be run through, I don't want his death on my conscience. Just hurt him a little, if you please, to remind him of this night."

Philip looked at me for a long moment. There were so many emotions in his eyes that I couldn't begin to decipher them all.

"He kissed you?" Anger threaded through his voice.

I nodded. His gaze rested on my mouth. The look of leashed fire returned, as if Philip was barely holding his passions in check. I couldn't help noticing that he looked very handsome with that flash of danger in his eyes.

With hardly a glance at Mr. Beaufort, Philip flicked his wrist, his sword moving so fast there was just a blur of steel and then a dark red line appeared on Mr. Beaufort's face, drawn from his chin, through his lips, to the side of his nose.

He swore and pressed the cuff of his sleeve to his mouth. The lace immediately turned crimson.

I stared, a little appalled at what I had caused.

"Is that sufficient?" Philip asked me, and I saw, over everything else waging for dominance within his eyes, a gleam of admiration.

"Yes. Now can you make sure he leaves the country?"

"I will. Is there anything else you want?" He was smiling now, smiling into my eyes, as if I held the whole universe in my hands. I was close enough to see everything, and I discovered in his eyes, and in his smile, that Philip had his own secret. One that was shining so brightly—as brightly as sunlight over water—that I caught my breath, dazzled by the brightness.

Just as I had been sure of my father's love when I had looked into his eyes, I was sure of something else in this moment. I was certain that Philip cared for me. It was so obvious—in his eyes, in the warmth of his smile, in the way he looked at me, and the way he fought Mr. Beaufort to defend me. Philip cared for me. I could not say whether or not he was in love with me, but I was certain that the friendship I had treasured so much was real. A slow smile curled across my lips. Yes, there was still so much that I wanted from Philip.

But I only said, "That will do. For now."

⚹

Philip and William left to escort Mr. Beaufort onto his ship. I gathered they would also talk to the innkeeper and help him remember the events of the night differently. And there would probably be some cost associated with the damage I caused from the bullet I had fired. On top of all of that, my head throbbed from when I had been knocked to the ground. But none of that mattered right now. I sat in the taproom with my father and took advantage of the quiet to discover some answers.

"Papa, I am so happy you've come back to England. But tell me—what has brought you home now? Has something happened? Is Grandmother—?"

"No, no, nothing has happened." He patted my hand. "I should have come home long ago." He drew in a breath, and his eyes crinkled with worry. "Is it true that you hated Bath?"

I blinked back tears, nodding because I couldn't speak.

"I'm so sorry. I only stayed away so you would have opportunities to get out in society—to meet other young people, and have a chance at a good marriage. I had hoped you were enjoying yourself."

I leaned my head against his shoulder. "I don't care for society. I want to take care of you." It was only right, now that Mama was gone, for me to run the household and see to my father's comfort.

"Your heart is in the right place, but before long you would have realized that your years of opportunity were gone. I would hate to be the cause of your losing a chance for future happiness. I had no idea until Sir Philip told me how unhappy you were."

I lifted my head to look at him. "Sir Philip? What does he have to do with this?"

"He arrived a few days ago, quite out of the blue. He gave me your letter, and said that he was determined to bring me back so that you could go home. He can be very persuasive, can't he? Of course, I didn't need to be persuaded, once I read your letter."

Philip had gone to France? For me? I could hardly believe it. "But how did you know I was here? And that I was in danger?"

"It was the greatest coincidence. We had just arrived, and were on our way to find an inn, when we crossed paths with Mr. Wyndham and his groom, who had followed you here after someone informed him of your abduction. There was no time for more explanation. We split up to check the different inns." He rubbed a hand over his face. "When we heard the gunshot, and then your scream, I feared the worst."

He exhaled a shaky sigh. "I am so relieved we found you. What would I have done if something had happened to you?" Papa pulled me close and kissed the top of my head. "You are my *raison d'être*."

I was his reason for living? I felt as if I was a cup filled to overflowing. One more drop of joy and my soul would spill right out of me.

"You must believe that I would have come back at any time," he said. "All you had to do was ask. And, no, Annie, I never blamed you for your mother's death. Never, my dear. Never."

I leaned my head against my father's shoulder and let my tears run freely. I had kept my heart so tightly contained for so long that now I couldn't seem to stop the emotions that poured from it. Oh, but they were healing emotions. With each beat, my heart was growing stronger than it had been in a year.

By the time William and Philip returned, my father's shoulder was damp from my tears, but I was happy. They told us that everything was taken care of and that we could leave right away. William would return with his groom in the phaeton he had driven, and Philip would join my father and me in a carriage they had hired to take us back to Edenbrooke. I thanked them for rescuing me, and they both waved it off as if it was just one of many heroic things they did every day.

It was dark when we left the inn. I sat in the carriage beside my father with Philip across from us. For a fleeting moment, I wished I was sitting next to Philip. Then I berated myself for my lack of loyalty and decided to be happy to have my father next to me.

There was so much that I still wanted to talk to my father about. He would surely laugh at my report about Mr. Whittles and his poetry. And there were things I wanted to ask him about France and how he had spent the past year. But Papa seemed very tired. He yawned several times while he and Philip were exchanging some casual remarks. After a few minutes, silence settled over us, and Papa leaned his head against the back of his seat.

I looked out the window and watched the moon travel with us. Another inn, another moon, another carriage ride, but everything was different now. *I* was different now. I was changed, irrevocably. And it was a change for the better. I felt it in the strength of my heart.

Soon snores came from my father. I couldn't sleep—my mind was too busy thinking about everything I had learned this evening. I repeated to myself the words Philip had said to Mr. Beaufort about how he would always want me. They fell on my tender heart like drops of balm, feeding my hope.

Philip sat across from my father, and I could see nothing of him in the darkness of the carriage, but I knew he was awake because I felt his gaze on me. And then, just when I thought we would spend the carriage ride in silence, he spoke in a quiet voice from across the darkness.

"Are you certain he didn't hurt you?"

I shivered as the sound of his voice washed over me. "Yes, I'm certain."

I heard him sigh and settle back in his seat. Then he spoke again. "Will you tell me what happened?"

So I did. I told him everything from Mr. Beaufort's proposal to the love letter I wrote at the inn to firing the pistol. Philip listened to it all, but I felt him growing tense and at one point I heard him swear under his breath.

At the end of my story, he was quiet, and I strained to see his expression, but it was in vain. The dark blanketed us. Talking like this, in the dark, with only words to connect us, felt as strange and intimate as watching Philip write that love letter.

After a long moment, Philip asked, "Why did you never tell me about your inheritance?"

The question surprised me. When I told him about the events of the night, I hadn't realized that I would be telling him about my inheritance as well. I hesitated, trying to find the right words.

"My grandmother warned me not to. And besides, I haven't actually earned the inheritance. I have to first prove myself an elegant lady to my grandmother, and I doubt that will happen." I paused. "But would it have made a difference? If you had known?"

"No," he answered decisively and immediately. "But I still wish I had."

"Why?"

"So that I could promise not to love you for your money," he said, and I heard a smile in his voice.

That day in the library when we made those promises to each other felt like a lifetime ago. I smiled at the memory. "Well, it's not too late."

Philip chuckled, and a thrill of pleasure rolled down my spine. How I loved the sound of his laugh! And then I realized what had made him laugh. I had flirted with him. I had never flirted with Philip before—not once—until tonight.

"I promise, Marianne Daventry," he began. His voice was serious and sultry at the same time, and my heart skipped in my chest. "I promise that I do not love you for your money."

A shock shuddered through me. I could not miss the change in his wording, nor the depth to his voice. Did he mean that he loved me? *Did he love me?* It was not a declaration, and Philip had always been an outrageous flirt. But just as I was ready to dismiss his words along with all of his other flirtatious comments, I remembered something he had said to me during our love letter lesson: *"I am always serious when it comes to matters of the heart."*

Could he be serious now? Rachel's advice to encourage him came to my mind, making my heart skip with nervousness. I did not know how to encourage a man to declare himself. I didn't even know if Philip had anything to declare! What if my attempt to encourage him sounded as awkward as I felt?

My father shifted beside me, mumbling something in his sleep, and I started a little. I had forgotten for a moment that he was sitting next to me. His distraction served as a timely reminder that this was neither the time nor the place for an important, personal conversation with Philip. My father could awake at any moment. So I sighed and gave up the thought of learning anything about Philip's heart or intentions tonight. I would have to wait a little longer.

But there was something I still needed to say to Philip. "Thank you for bringing my father home. It was very generous of you to go all the way to France for me." I paused, then said with a smile, "I suppose I will have to give you the painting now."

Philip chuckled lightly. "No, I have something better in mind for the painting."

I waited for more, but he stayed mysteriously silent. Philip had always enjoyed his secrets.

"Why did you bring him home, then?" I asked.

"Because you wanted him."

The statement was so simple, but it spoke volumes about Philip's intentions. I closed my eyes and smiled as the hope inside of me grew ever brighter.

"You should try to rest," Philip said. "You've been through a lot tonight. I won't keep you awake."

I was too tired, and my heart too tender, to say anything more. So I rested my head against the window and allowed myself to hope while the horses carried us across a moonlit world.

Chapter 26

When we finally arrived at Edenbrooke, I stumbled upstairs in an exhausted daze. The night sky was just beginning to lighten toward dawn when I dropped into bed. I didn't bother to undress or even take off my boots.

I awoke hours later to the sounds of Betsy trying to wake me without actually shaking me awake. She was moving about the room, rattling my cup of chocolate on the tray she carried, bumping into furniture, and whistling. I was still tired, but I could see there would be no putting her off. I turned toward the window and the afternoon sunlight that streamed through it.

When Betsy saw me stir, she nearly dropped the tray on top of me in her haste to set it down.

"Oh, I am so glad you're finally awake!" She threw herself on my bed. "I have been so impatient to know what happened yesterday! You wouldn't believe the uproar that happened here when Mr. Clumpett came stumbling into the house claiming you had been abducted."

I sat up and reached for my cup of chocolate. "Mr. Clumpett? How was he involved?"

"He said he was looking for insects in the woods when he heard shouting and saw a man throw you into a carriage. He tried to run after you, but he tripped over a tree root and twisted his ankle. He did, however, hear Mr. Beaufort say something about Dover. It took Mr. Clumpett half an hour to limp back to the house with his bad ankle and tell Mr. Wyndham what had happened. I can't even describe how exciting it was! I vow I nearly swooned when Lady Caroline gave Mr. Wyndham the dueling swords to take with him. Now I have to hear what happened or I shall die of suspense!"

I told her all of it, from Mr. Beaufort's arrival in the orchard to Philip's duel.

"He fought a duel for you?" She clasped her hands together. "Was it horribly romantic?"

I thought I should discourage her romantic fancies, but after a brief struggle, I gave up and smiled. "Yes," I admitted. "It was."

She squealed. "I knew it. I knew he was the one for you. I don't care what you say about Miss Cecily—it's you he loves, and that means I will get to be a lady's maid." She looked as if she was about to go into raptures. I had to stop her.

"Betsy, nothing happened between Sir Philip and me, so don't start planning your future life here."

She waved aside my words. "Nothing has happened *yet*. But something will. I'm sure of it. Oh, I'll make you look so beautiful for the ball tonight that he won't be able to restrain himself any longer."

My feelings wavered between nervousness and excitement, hope and doubt. I had to agree with Betsy: something would happen tonight. I felt it. I asked Betsy to draw a bath for me, and then stood up and stretched. I noticed my boots by the side of the bed, but I couldn't remember taking them off.

"Betsy, did you take off my boots?" I asked when she came back to tell me that the water was being readied.

"Yes, earlier this morning when I checked on you. I thought you would be more comfortable without them."

I stared at the boots and a warning went off in my mind. There was something important about them that I had to remember. I gasped when I recalled what it was: the letter I had written to Philip at the inn last night. I lunged for the boots and turned them upside down. There was nothing.

"Did you find a piece of paper when you took off my boots?" I asked.

"You mean the letter addressed to Sir Philip? Yes, I saw it."

Dread filled me. "What did you do with it?"

"I set it down right there on your table."

She picked up the tray she had put there, but there was no note underneath. I searched all over, even checking the bottom of the tray, then the floor, and under the bed, and even in the bed. The letter was nowhere to be found.

"We have to find it, Betsy!" I yelled in utter panic. My letter was a declaration of love, and if Philip read it, it would ruin everything. A woman never declared her feelings first. Never! What if he had no intention of offering for me, and then he read my letter and felt obliged to? What if he had only been flirting when he had made me that promise in the carriage last night? I sunk to the floor, head in my hands, and groaned with embarrassment. I would never live this down if he read that letter. Never.

A knock sounded at the door. A moment later, Cecily rushed in and threw herself at me.

"Oh, you're safe! I've been so worried about you!" She hugged me tightly, then pulled away and held me by the shoulders. "Did he hurt you?"

I shook my head and tried to smile. "No, I'm fine." She mustn't know about that letter either. She mustn't think I would ever willingly betray her by throwing myself at the man she loved.

"I can't believe it," she said. "To think of the peril you were in! I should have never left you alone. You must have been so frightened! You have to tell me all about it." She took my hand and pulled me to my feet. She seemed determined to not let me go.

We sat on my bed, and Cecily listened with wide eyes while I told her almost everything that had happened. I left out a few important details, like what Philip had said to Mr. Beaufort about always wanting me. I kept those words close to my heart like a sacred treasure.

Cecily insisted on feeling responsible for my kidnapping, and vowed to me to be a better sister and to never leave me alone again.

I felt so happy and so guilty at the same time. She couldn't guess that I was in love with the man she hoped to marry.

⚬⚬

I was a bundle of nerves by the time Betsy finished my hair and proclaimed me ready for the ball. The letter had not turned up, even though she had asked among the other servants if they had seen it. I blushed with embarrassment every time I thought about that letter ending up in the wrong hands. Or even the right hands.

I stood and regarded myself in the mirror. My cheeks were rosy, thanks to my state of embarrassment and nervousness. I smoothed my hands down the front of my white muslin gown. Betsy had cut miniature white roses from the garden and pinned them among my curls. Taking a deep breath, I turned toward the door and this fateful evening.

Pausing at the top of the staircase, I surveyed the scene below me. Papa stood in the foyer, talking to Lady Caroline. Louisa and Cecily were whispering to each other, their heads bent together. Mr. and Mrs. Clumpett stood near William, and they appeared to be talking animatedly about something. Judging from the motions Mr. Clumpett was making, I guessed it had to do with birds. I noticed he was using a walking cane tonight, but appeared to be in good spirits. And away from the others, near the door to the drawing room, stood Rachel and Philip.

Rachel appeared to be talking to him in a low voice, for he had his head bent as if listening closely. She glanced up and saw me, then said one more thing to Philip. He turned and met my gaze. He looked more handsome than any man had a right to look. He walked to the bottom of the staircase and smiled up at me. The evening had begun.

Philip's attention made me so nervous I had to grip the railing tightly to ensure I did not trip and fall down the stairs. He did not pull his gaze away from me the whole time I descended the staircase.

When I reached the last step, Philip held out his hand to me. I put my hand in his. "I didn't think it was possible," he said in a low voice, "but you look more beautiful than ever tonight."

My heart skittered. "Thank you," I said, feeling breathless.

He lifted an eyebrow in a look of surprise. "*Thank you*? Have you learned to accept compliments, Marianne?"

I tried to suppress a smile without success. Feeling a little proud of myself, I said, "I suppose I have."

Philip looked down at my hand, which he was still holding, and smiled as if at a secret thought. Then he bowed his head and brushed his lips across the back of my hand. A shock raced up my arm all the way to my heart and set it pounding.

"I am glad to know it," Philip murmured, looking up at me through his eyelashes.

Oh, my. I had seen this look before—the night of the last ball. This was the smoldering, determined look that Philip had used on me when we had danced together. This was the look that had disassembled all of my defenses. I gripped the banister with my free hand, feeling as if my legs could not hold me.

My father walked toward us just then, saving me from the disgrace of falling at Philip's feet from a severe case of weakened knees.

"You look lovely, my dear," he said, as Philip released my hand and stepped aside.

I was grateful for my father's interruption, for it brought clarity back to my thoughts, and I remembered I was still missing a very embarrassing letter. Betsy had promised to keep looking for it and to notify me as soon as she found it. I hoped that she found it soon, before it had a chance to be read or—heaven forbid—delivered.

When people began to arrive, I stood next to Cecily in the foyer and greeted the guests along with Philip and Lady Caroline, since the ball was held in our honor. Cecily looked like an angel, with her golden hair shining in the candlelight. She squeezed my hand and smiled at me, excitement glittering in her blue eyes.

I could hardly focus on the guests who flowed through the foyer as I was so preoccupied with wondering about that letter. I did notice Mr. Kellet, though, because he was the only person who smirked at me. He kissed Cecily's hand and said something in her ear that made her blush and giggle. I gave her a reproving look, but she appeared not to notice.

"What did Mr. Kellet say to you?" I asked.

She smiled secretively. "I doubt you want to know."

Remembering her comment about his kissing, I agreed with her.

She looked sideways at me. "Sir Philip looks very handsome tonight, does he not?"

"To be sure." I tried to make my voice sound breezy, but I felt my cheeks grow warm. My blush was sure to give me away if Cecily ever paid attention to it. "I suppose you will want to dance with him first."

"No, I think you should."

I looked at her with surprise. "I thought you had a plan for tonight."

Her secretive smile appeared again. "I do."

Before I realized it, the musicians were warming up and Lady Caroline was telling us it was time to take our places in the ballroom.

The ballroom was crowded and noisy. I could hardly say a word to Philip during our country dance, which was just as well, since I was so busy worrying about that missing letter that I would have had a hard time concentrating on a conversation.

Glancing down the line of couples, I saw Cecily dancing with Mr. Kellet, and she seemed to be enjoying herself immensely. When the dance ended, I reluctantly accepted the hand of my next partner while Philip bowed and walked away. I saw him throughout the ball, dancing with various ladies. There he was with Miss Grace, her mother watching from the side with a hawkish look in her eager eyes. There he was dancing with his mother like a dutiful son. And all too soon he was dancing with Cecily.

When the musicians paused for a rest, some of the guests drifted out of the hot ballroom through the French doors and onto the cool terrace. I watched Cecily and Philip from across the room. They stood close together; he bent his head to her as she whispered something in his ear. I could see his surprise even from a distance. I wondered what she had said to him. Then she whispered something else, and he offered her his arm. They left the ballroom together, but they did not follow the other couples onto the terrace.

With a surge of jealousy, I wondered where she was taking him and what she would do with him. I forgot completely about the earlier, benevolent feelings I had toward Cecily. I wanted to scratch her eyes out.

Someone tapped me on the shoulder. I turned around and was surprised to see Louisa.

"I need to speak with you," she said.

She never wanted to speak with me. "About what?"

"Just come with me."

I followed her out of the ballroom and through the throngs of guests. She grabbed my elbow and pulled me into the hall that led to the library. It was quiet here, and she stopped just outside of the library doors and turned to me.

"I know about the letter," she said. "The one you wrote to Philip."

My heart fell. No. No, no, no. "I don't know what you mean," I lied.

She rolled her eyes. "Yes, you do."

Louisa had never been my friend. She was Cecily's friend, and clearly she wanted Cecily for a sister, not me.

"I want to know if you meant it," she said. "Do you really feel that way toward Philip? Or was it something you wrote because you were in a desperate situation?"

My face was on fire. I felt like I was choking. "Why do you care if I meant it or not?"

She stepped closer. "Because I care about my brother. And he's in the library right now reading your letter. So if you didn't mean it, you had better tell me now, before you break his heart."

I stared at her in dismay while my heart threatened to stop. "He's reading it? Right now?" Panic streamed through me. I wanted to run away. I had declared my love in that letter, but I had no assurance that Philip felt the same way toward me. It was beyond forward—it was unheard of—and I was going to die from the shame of it all.

A smile lifted Louisa's lips. "You meant it."

She tapped on the library door. Cecily opened it and stood in the doorway, smiling at me. "There you are." She grabbed my arm, pulled me inside, and walked out, shutting the door behind her.

The room was dark except for a low fire burning in the fireplace and the moon shining through the large window at the other end of the room. Philip was standing next to the fireplace, with one shoulder leaning against the mantel and his head bent over a piece of paper. He looked up when the door closed, but the room was too dark for me to see his expression.

My heart was pounding so hard that I pressed a hand to my chest to keep it from bursting through my skin.

Philip was looking at me from across the dim room with that condemning letter in his hand, and he wasn't moving or saying a word. We both stood there, as if on the brink of a cliff, and I didn't know if I moved if I would fall to hell or soar to heaven.

Then he finally spoke. "Did you mean this?"

My heart was in my throat. Here I stood, between something and nothing. I could answer either way. But my heart was stronger than it had been in months, and it was begging me to hope, to believe, to take a chance. So I stepped toward him—a step toward *something*—and whispered, "Yes."

Philip moved, the firelight shone on his features for a split second, and I saw everything. That day I had watched him fence with William, I had been surprised to see how impassioned he looked—as if he was leashed fire. Now, by the light of the fire, I saw the leash snap.

He crossed the room to me and grabbed me by the shoulders. In three steps, he had me backed up against a bookcase. Before I could do more than catch my breath, he took my face in his hands and kissed me.

I had never really been kissed before. But I did not need experience to know that Philip's kiss was, in a word, devastating. His lips were firm and insistent, gentle and caressing. His fingers threaded in my hair, holding my head exactly how he wanted it while he kissed me one way, then another, until I trembled in his arms.

And then it finally occurred to me that Philip was kissing me—*Philip was kissing me!*—and I was doing nothing about it. I quickly remedied that situation, sliding my hands up his chest, over his shoulders, burying my fingers in his hair. His arms surrounded me, pulling me close, holding me as if I was infinitely precious. I burned and trembled in his embrace.

And then, just when I was sure that Philip's kiss could not get better, it slowed and softened and became achingly tender. His gentleness tugged at my heartstrings until I was completely undone. My heart broke open and quiet tears streamed down my cheeks. I tasted the salt of my tears on Philip's lips.

He pulled away from me, just enough to rest his forehead against mine. His breath came as quickly as mine did, and through his shirt I could feel his heart pounding. A slow smile curled my lips.

"How could you not know?" His voice was throaty and a little shaky. "How could you not know that there is nothing in the world I want as much as I want you?"

I shook my head in wonder. It was all too much to believe.

"It seemed too remarkable," I said, "for you to love me, instead of Cecily. And then . . . I heard you, in the fencing room, tell William you would do anything to be rid of me . . ."

Philip groaned and pulled away to look into my eyes. "Is that why you were so angry the night of the ball?"

I nodded.

"I wanted you out of my home, away from your sister, and free of the constraints of my honor—but I never wanted to be rid of you," he said.

"I was going to follow you—I would follow you anywhere—and court you as I wasn't free to court you here. But then, when your maid gave me that letter to your father, I thought following you to your own home might be the best solution. I had no hope . . ." He bent his head to mine, and kissed me again as if he couldn't help himself. "I had no hope, darling, that I had already won you."

"How could you doubt that?" I asked. I couldn't imagine *not* falling in love with Philip.

"Very easily! Every time I attempted to woo you, you either scowled at me, or laughed, or ran away. Or you told me you only cared about me as a friend."

I smiled sheepishly. That was exactly what I had done. There was so much to explain to him—about my heart, and my fears, and my loyalty toward Cecily. But all that could wait for another time. For now I said, "I was very confused, and rather blind, I think."

He cupped my face in his hands. "Then listen to me, my blind, stubborn, *darling* friend. You stole my heart the night we met, when you sang that ridiculous song and dared me not to laugh. And every moment I have spent with you since then, you have stolen more and more of me until when you're not with me . . ." He drew in a breath. "When you are not with me, I am left with nothing but longing for you."

My heart swelled until I felt as if it might take over my entire being. I had landed in heaven. This was heaven.

"I tried to tell you," he said. "So many times I came close. I even wrote that love letter, hoping you would know it was for you."

I thought of the beautiful words he had written, and which I had torn up. "Will you write me that love letter again?"

He pulled me close. "I will. I'll write you dozens of love letters—hundreds, if you want them."

"I do. I do want them." I wanted everything I could get from Philip. But this seemed too wonderful to be true. Even now, with all the evidence I had of Philip's sincerity, I couldn't help wondering why, out of all of the ladies he could have chosen, he had fallen in love with me.

"But are you certain you want me?" I asked. "I am not elegant or accomplished, and I always do the most embarrassing things—"

He stopped me. "You don't know yourself, but I do, so I will tell you what you are, Marianne Daventry." He looked intently into my eyes, as though he would write the words on my heart if he could. "You are bright and fun and delightfully unexpected. You are brave and compassionate and selfless. And you are lovely beyond measure. I want you, all of you, just the way you are." He drew in a breath. "If you will have me."

Something happened to me in that moment. Doubt was banished and hope became certainty. It overwhelmed me, and I found myself laughing and crying at once.

I was clearly unraveled, but Philip did not seem to mind at all. He wiped my tears, and he kissed me again, and again, and whispered things too sublime to repeat, until I was thoroughly convinced he was madly in love with me, Marianne Daventry, a girl with no great figure, too many freckles, and a propensity for twirling. And then I knew I had met my match.

Chapter 27

Much later, after I had pulled myself out of Philip's embrace and Betsy had fixed the damage he had done to my hair, I found Cecily on the terrace. She smiled at me as I walked toward her.

"I hope you don't mind that I read your letter," she said. "I went to your room this morning while you were still asleep and saw it on your table. I confess I couldn't contain my curiosity."

"I don't mind, considering how everything has turned out."

She took my hand. "I hope you're very happy."

"I am," I sighed, unable to restrain my smile. I wondered if she could tell that I had just been thoroughly kissed. "But, Cecily, I'm sorry if it comes at the cost of your happiness."

She waved a hand in the air. "There are plenty of other wealthy gentlemen for me to choose from. And, to be perfectly honest, I knew Philip wasn't interested in me. I saw that as soon as I arrived. There is no scheming that can help a lady's cause when the man is in love with someone else. What I didn't see, though, was how you felt." She looked seriously at me. "Why didn't you tell me?"

I shrugged. "You said you were in love with him."

"Yes, I did say that. But I think I must have been very self-centered not to recognize your feelings. I'm sorry if I wasn't the kind of sister you deserved." She gripped my hand.

We stood in silence, listening to the strains of music floating through the ballroom windows. I thought of my fairy-tale childhood with my twin sister. There once were two girls born to parents who had wished dearly for a child. The girls were the sun and the moon to them. I had spent my life being the moon, reflecting Cecily's light and allowing her to shine. But here, with Philip, I was the sun. I couldn't imagine a better beginning to the rest of my life.

"I hope we will always be close," I said, thinking of my mother and Lady Caroline.

"Of course we will be." She pulled me to her and we hugged. I held her until she pulled away. Looking over my shoulder, she said, "I have someone I need to talk to."

I turned and saw Mr. Kellet standing at the edge of the terrace. "What are you going to say to him?"

She bit her lip. "I'm not sure. But it may take a while."

She flashed me a sly smile before she walked away. Mr. Kellet disappeared around the corner of the house and she followed him.

⚜

I was the last one to enter the dining room for breakfast the next morning. Philip and William and my father all stood at my entrance. In Philip's eyes was such a look of warm affection that I blushed to have everyone see it.

As I sat down, I noticed the stares of everyone present, and then Rachel suddenly said, "Oh, have you two finally worked everything out? Thank goodness! Now we can all talk openly."

Philip chuckled, and I blushed even harder. Every person in the room, from Lady Caroline to the footman standing behind Philip, smiled. Louisa's smile was more tentative than the others', but I was happy to see any sign of friendliness from her. I was also happy to see Cecily there, and not off somewhere in Mr. Kellet's arms. I would not put it past him to run off with her, but Cecily had more sense than that, it seemed.

Congratulations were offered, and Rachel and Lady Caroline began discussing the glorious task of planning a wedding. Philip, I discovered, had already spoken to my father, who looked very happy as he smiled at me from across the table. My home was only one county away from here, which meant we would be close enough to visit as often as we wished. Cecily would return to London and our cousin Edith, where she could enjoy the diversions of Town life.

A footman appeared at my side with a letter on a silver salver. It was from Grandmother. I opened it and read it over my breakfast.

> *Dear Marianne,*
>
> *You little ninny. Of course I sent you to stay at Edenbrooke, and you should be thanking me instead of calling me to repentance. A rich heiress needs a man to protect her, and how else could I be sure of your protection while your father was away? I only kept it a secret because I knew you would not go if you suspected the truth. Silly girl. You were fortunate that Sir Philip was willing to take on the assignment of protecting you while you were living there.*
>
> *By the way, I have heard from Lady Caroline that Sir Philip is besotted with you. He must not mind the way you run wild like a farmer's brat. If you manage to make such an advantageous match, I suppose I will leave you my fortune whether or not you ever become an elegant young lady. I look forward to meeting him, and I think I may even come to Edenbrooke to see you married.*
>
> *Sincerely,*
>
> *Grandmother*
>
> *P.S. Mr. Whittles has offered for Amelia, and she has accepted him. I suspect this is your doing?*

I breathed a sigh of relief. My meddling had worked. And thinking of what my grandmother had written about Philip's assignment, an idea suddenly occurred to me. I looked across the table at Philip's aunt and uncle. Mr. Clumpett had a book propped open in front of his plate, and Mrs. Clumpett was smiling as Lady Caroline talked about the success of the ball.

I turned to Philip. "Did you ask Mr. Clumpett to protect me while you and William were gone?"

"I did. Why?"

I smiled. "He has been miserable here with your disorganized library, you know. And Mrs. Clumpett has missed her birds."

Philip laughed. "Well, they will be free to go home now to their own library and birds. I will have to look for some books on India to send to him as thanks for protecting you so well while I was gone. I can't imagine what would have happened if he hadn't been wandering through the woods that day."

I glanced at the Clumpetts again, reminding myself to thank them for all they had done for me. Both of them.

I reread my grandmother's letter and realized with a deep sense of contentment that I had not had to change at all in order to have every hope for happiness in life. I had not had to learn to sing for company or to behave like Cecily or to stop twirling. I could be myself and be loved deeply. I was, in fact, a lot like Meg, who had always been a racehorse. I just hadn't known it.

After breakfast, I escaped to the orchard. I was so happy to be here that I felt the same way I had upon arriving at Edenbrooke: as if I had come home to paradise. Mixed with the feeling of homecoming was the great surge of joy I felt about my future with Philip.

I closed my eyes and tipped back my head and felt the sun warm my face and head and outstretched arms. And then I did it. I twirled. I twirled and twirled with my eyes closed and my head back and my arms outstretched.

I suddenly heard a crunch of branches and felt a scratch on my cheek. I stopped moving and opened my eyes to find myself within an inch of having my eye poked out by a branch. I tried to move away from the branch but found my hair was stuck.

Oh, when would I ever learn to not twirl?

I pulled at the branch without success. I tried to untangle my hair, but I could tell I was making a huge mess of it as more of it got tangled. In frustration, and with aching arms, I said, "Oh, drat!"

I heard a rustle of leaves and looked toward the sound. Philip ducked beneath a tree limb and walked toward me. I blushed hard and wished I was not attached to this tree. But I had to stand and wait while he walked toward me, looking so well put-together I couldn't imagine him ever being caught doing something as embarrassing as being stuck in a tree. Why hadn't I learned my lesson the last time?

"Don't laugh," I told him, noticing the amusement building in his eyes.

His eyes darted to the branch and my tangled hair and his lips twitched. "How did this happen?"

"I was twirling."

I could tell Philip was working hard to keep back a laugh. "Have you ever considered twirling with your eyes open?"

"It's not something I plan in advance." I reached up and tried again to pull my hair loose, then winced with the pain.

Philip stepped right up to me, took my hands in his, and lowered them so that they rested against his chest.

"Allow me," he said. Then he moved his arms around me and began to untangle my hair. If someone saw us from a distance, I suspected it might look as if we were embracing. I could feel him breathe, and I watched my hands move with the rise and fall of his chest. I could smell him—that mixture of clean linen and soap and something that reminded me of the woods on a sunny day. Something inside of me melted.

I felt a gentle tug and his fingers brushed my ear, my neck. I was getting hot and rather breathless. To distract myself, I asked a question I had had on my mind for quite a while.

"Philip, why did you keep your identity a secret from me when we met at the inn?"

He paused to look into my eyes. "Fate handed me a rare opportunity to talk to a lady without wondering if she was only interested in my wealth or title. And not just any lady." He smiled crookedly, and my heart skittered in my chest. "I couldn't pass up that opportunity. Your candor was worth the risk of your anger."

It was as if his words had turned on a light. I understood Philip now in a way I never had before. I thought of how he had not wanted me to call him "sir," even though that was exactly what I should have called him. And the day we talked in the library, he had gone to the kitchen himself to get us our food instead of sending a servant to do it. I thought of the promises we had made to each other. And I thought of how he had tried to run away from Cecily, who *was* only interested in his title and wealth. Philip wanted to be loved for who he was, without consideration of his inheritance.

He gave one last tug and all of my hair fell free, cascading down my back. Philip had taken out all of my pins, and I felt undone. He stroked my hair from the top of my head all the way down my back. Then his hands circled my waist and he pulled me closer.

"You know, we have some unfinished business," he said. "I still want that painting, and now I have something of value to offer for it."

"What is that?" I was having a hard time focusing on his words because my gaze had caught on his mouth, and the line of his jaw, and the way the corner of his lips twitched when he was trying not to smile. I wanted to kiss it all.

He touched my chin, lifting my face so that my eyes met his. "I will give you a title for it."

I chewed on my lip, regarding him with misgiving. This was wrong.

In light of my recent understanding, I couldn't accept his offer. I shook my head. "I've never cared very much about having a title."

His eyebrows drew together, and his gaze turned questioning. "Then what about everything around you? Would Edenbrooke be enough?"

I pushed away the lock of hair that fell across his brow and sighed. "No, as much as I love it here, I can't sell it to you for your land."

He looked utterly solemn now, and more than a little worried. "You don't need my money."

"That's correct."

He bent his head. I felt bad for the distress I was obviously causing him, but I knew this needed to be done.

"I have nothing more to offer," he whispered.

I grasped his lapels and stood on my toes so I could look clearly into his eyes—so he could not mistake my meaning. "I do not want anything you can offer me. Remember our vows?"

He nodded. His hands rested on my waist, pulling me closer.

"I just want you, Philip. You. I will give you the painting in exchange for your heart."

He looked away quickly, and I sensed a great struggle within him. When he finally looked back at me, his eyes were shining with amazement and admiration and that great secret I had seen at the inn after his fight with Mr. Beaufort. It was shining just as clearly now as it had that night, but now I knew what to call it. Philip loved me.

"Marianne," he said in a throaty voice that made my heart thud hard in my chest. He lifted a hand from my waist and stroked my blushing cheek with the back of his fingers, his touch as light as a breeze. His skin felt cool against the heat of my blush.

"You darling girl," he murmured, tilting my chin up as he lowered his lips to mine. This time I knew enough to kiss him back. He caught his breath, and then I felt his lips curl up into his wicked grin. It was delicious.

A few minutes later, he moved his lips from mine to kiss my cheek and the corner of my jaw. "I have a proposal," he said, his breath tickling my neck.

"Another one?" I smiled, leaning into him, my heart pounding so loud I was sure he could hear it.

"This one is for after the wedding. How would you like to go to the Continent? I could give you your very own Grand Tour."

I couldn't speak.

"You're welcome to twirl if you need to," he said with a laugh.

"You don't mind?"

He shook his head. "I've been dying to see it, actually."

So I twirled for Philip, with my hair flying around me, feeling like I could break into flight at any moment. He grabbed me around the waist when I was close to colliding with another tree. "That was lovely," he said, pulling me close. "But perhaps you should keep your eyes open in the future."

"Good idea," I murmured, smiling into the eyes of my best friend, who did not mind my twirling at all.

"I just remembered," Philip said, reaching into the pocket of his coat. "I forgot to give you this."

It was my locket, which Philip had demanded from Mr. Beaufort. I had forgotten about it after the drama of the events at the inn. Now Philip clasped it around my neck, and I felt it settle like a charm about me. I put my hand over the locket, pressing the precious reminder of my mother against my chest. My own heart beat strong and sure beneath it, and I felt that everything that had been missing was restored and that all was right in the world.

Then Philip and I walked hand in hand back to the house and made our way to the library, where we finally played that game of chess.

Acknowledgments

I started dreaming of Edenbrooke five years ago, when I didn't have the first idea of how to write a novel. The fact that Marianne's story has made it this far is the fulfillment of my wildest dreams. I owe my eternal gratitude to the many people who have helped make it happen.

First, I want to thank the team at Shadow Mountain for falling in love with my story and providing such a wonderful home for it. In particular, I wish to thank Heidi Taylor and Chris Schoebinger for their vision and encouragement. Lisa Mangum is a fabulous editor and a genuinely nice person. Heather Ward created the gorgeous cover.

I couldn't ask for a better agent than Laurie McLean. She wows me every day with her brilliance, her contagious optimism, and her dedication to making great things happen.

I have to thank my best friend and husband, Fred. If I know anything about real love, I have learned it from and with him. He has been a constant support to me and has believed in me in my hours of self-doubt and disappointment. I am so happy to have him at my side and that we can celebrate our dreams coming true together.

My children—Adah, David, Sarah, and Jacob—are some of my favorite people to hang out with. They bring me great joy, and, at the end of the day, remind me that family is more important than books.

257

I want to thank my parents, Frank and Ruth Clawson, for letting me grow up with my nose in a book and for teaching me to work hard. I'm thankful for my sisters, Kristi, Jenny, and Audrey, for laughing, telling stories, staying up late, and watching girl movies. I'm grateful that Nick joined the family and taught my kids how cool a skateboarder and biker could be.

I want to give a special shout-out to some of my extended family from the Donaldson side: Christine, Jinjer, Jennie, Sarah, Emma, Heather, Louise, Johanna, Joan, and Lavina. I love you all. (I love the Donaldson boys, too, but this is a girl's book.) Thanks to the Clawson clan, the Hinmon clan, the Donaldson clan, and the Hofheins clan for being interested in my dreams and applauding my successes. A girl couldn't ask for a better extended family.

I owe a very special thank you to my friend Jaime Mormann. She went to England with me, dreamed with me, talked through writer's block with me, edited with me, and loved accents with me. Through every up and down, I knew I could call her and she would either laugh or rant or rejoice with me, as needed. I feel richly blessed to have such a devoted and talented friend.

I am indebted to my fellow writers for their help and feedback: Julie Dixon, Pam Anderton, Ally Condie, Erin Summerill, and Jessie Humphries. I want to thank every friend, neighbor, and relative who helped watch my kids so I could write. You are too numerous to list here, but you are listed in my heart! I am also grateful for Tracy McCormick Jackson, who introduced me to and encouraged me to love the Regency period. It has changed my life.

Last, but certainly not least, I must acknowledge that I could not have written this book without God's help and His generous gifts. I hope that He is pleased.

Discussion Questions

1. What does Marianne want at the beginning of the story? How does this desire shape her actions? How does her desire change during the course of the story? How does Marianne get what she really wants by the end of the story? How do you relate to Marianne's longing to be loved for who she is?

2. What do we learn about Marianne from her interactions with the highwayman and, later, with Mr. Kellet? What would you have done in her situation?

3. Most romance novels present the hero as the only significant man in the heroine's life. Were you surprised that it was Marianne's father who saved her at the inn? Why was that scene significant? How would the story be different if it had been Philip who had saved her? What role does Marianne's relationship with her father play in her relationships with others? How do our relationships with our fathers shape our romantic relationships?

4. Why do you think Philip wanted Marianne's painting? What is Philip's motivation for keeping his identity a secret? What does this tell us about Philip's character?

5. Before Charles died, Philip would have had a plan for a future career. Many men in this time period who did not inherit the family

estate went into careers in the military, the clergy, or academics. What do you imagine Philip would have done with his life if he hadn't inherited Edenbrooke?

6. There are several deaths mentioned in this story. How does the death of Marianne's mother change Marianne's life? How does the death of Charles change Philip's life? In what ways has the death of a loved one changed your life?

7. Marianne struggles with comparing herself to her twin sister, Cecily. How do we compare ourselves to other women? How is it helpful? How is it detrimental? What do you think about the resolution between the sisters at the end? What do you imagine their future relationship will be like?

8. Marianne's relationship with her grandmother does not, on the surface, appear to be a loving one. Is there love between them? What evidence do you find in the story to support your theory? Have you ever had a relationship like this one?

Q&A
with Julianne Donaldson

Q: What made you interested in writing a romance set in the Regency period?

A: When I was seventeen, I contracted pneumonia and spent a month in bed. A good friend saved me from boredom by giving me a stack of Georgette Heyer novels. I devoured each one, and then read them again and again. I have been in love with the Regency period ever since. I studied British literature in college, watched every movie produced that features the Regency time period, and dreamed of men dressed in breeches. When I decided to try my hand at writing a novel, my mind automatically went to the Regency period and refused to leave. It was like the hometown of my imagination.

Q: How did you go about conducting research for *Edenbrooke*? Was there travel involved?

A: Researching *Edenbrooke* was so much fun. I felt strongly that I needed to actually see the places I was writing about. So I dreamed big and called a friend and we went to England for a week. We spent a day in Bath, where I found the gravel path that Marianne walks on in the first scene and the Royal Crescent where she lives with her grandmother. My friend and I spent a day driving through the countryside in Kent, where a river called Eden actually does flow. (Although I didn't know that at the time when I imagined and named Edenbrooke; it was a cosmic coincidence, I suppose.) We also spent a day at Wilton House, which is near Salisbury. There I saw the bridge that inspired the twirling scene and the gardens that Marianne and Philip wandered through. I came home even more in love with England than I had been before.

Q: How do you get to know characters from a different time period?

A: I did not really set out to get to know my characters as much as I began listening in on their conversations. They talked to each other in my mind, which could be annoying when they interrupted real conversations I was having with real people. At first, my characters were imitations of other characters I had read and loved in other stories. But over time, they emerged as distinct individuals that poked at me if I wrote a scene wrong or put words in their mouth they didn't want to speak. When my imagination pulled me too far to the modern world, I would stop and think about what I knew about the time period and the world my characters lived in to get myself back in the right direction.

Q: How much did the books of Jane Austen and Georgette Heyer influence you?

A: Jane Austen and Georgette Heyer are undoubtedly the masters of Regency novels. I gobbled up their stories, savored them, studied them, and even wrote college papers on them. Along the way, of course their writing influenced my own. What we share in common is the subjects we write about. I love Austen's heroines and the dilemmas they face, the hard choices they make, and the growth they show in the space of their stories. I love Heyer's wit, her heroes, and the way she weaves in a good dose of intrigue. But as much as I love their works, I knew that I wanted my writing to be different from theirs. I wanted to keep the flavor of the Regency period but make my story accessible for a modern reader. So I intentionally made my language a little less formal and moved my plot along with greater speed.

Q: What were your biggest obstacles in writing this story?

A: The hardest part about writing this story was making it fresh while keeping it believably Regency. It was a very restrictive time to live in, especially for a young lady. I had to consider everything from language to geography to social customs to class distinctions to chaperones. There were many times I dreamed of writing a fantasy instead so I could shape an imagined world around my plot instead of trying to work my plot into the tight box of a Regency world.

Q: What do you think Jane Austen would say about the romance genre today?

A: I think she would be shocked at what can be written and published in a novel today, considering the innocent nature of her novels. I also think she would also be surprised that her writing sparked an entire genre of literature. And—this is strictly my own opinion, of course—I imagine she would wish for more elevating love stories and less of a focus on lust in today's romance novels.

Q: What is your favorite book, and why?

A: That is like asking me to pick a favorite among my children. There are so many books that I love that it's impossible to choose just one. But I do have a special shelf for my best-loved books, and featured on that shelf are books by Eva Ibbotson, Mary Stewart, Scott Westerfeld, Martine Leavitt, Nancy E. Turner, Megan Whalen Turner, and Kate Morton. I love compelling stories that are well-written and uplifting, have a moving portrayal of love, and end happily.

Q: What do you think is Marianne's favorite food? What is your favorite food?

A: I imagine Marianne would like fresh foods—anything she could pick off a bush or a tree while she is ambling through the countryside. I love anything made in a bakery.

Q: What is your favorite movie?

A: I'm a corset geek. I would have to list my top five favorites, because I can't pick just one: *Jane Eyre* (2006), *North and South*, *Emma* (the Romola Garai version), *Pride and Prejudice* (the A&E version, of course), and *Bleak House*.

Q: If *Edenbrooke* were made into a movie, who could you see playing Marianne and Philip?

A: There is a young British actress named Imogen Poots who I can totally see as Marianne. My favorite leading men right now are Jake Gyllenhaal and James McAvoy. I would pay good money to see either of them play dreamy Philip.

Q: Where is your favorite place to write?

A: Next to a window, preferably some place where no one will interrupt me. You can usually find me in my local library, but I would love to have a quiet writing room at home.

Q: Name one thing from your bucket list that you'd like to do or see or try.

A: I would love to learn how to play the cello.

Q: Can you give us a hint concerning what your next story is going to be about?

A: My next story, which is also set in the Regency period, is about a young lady who dreams of going to India. There is also a grand estate with too many secrets, a smuggler, a gentleman, and a bargain.